JIGSAW

Lilly Atlas

ISBN: 978-1-946068-28-6
ISBN-13: 1-946068-28-4

For my grandmother.
Not only did you give me my first romance novel so many years ago,
but you know a bird can't fly with one wing.
You'll always be missed.
All my love.

After being disappointed by her family one too many times, Izzy's convinced the only person she needs is herself. Seeking a life with fewer relationships, she leaves the bustle of the city and moves to small-town Tennessee. Her plans for quiet and solitude don't last long after she's adopted by both the men and women of the Hell's Handlers Motorcycle Club.

Once upon a time, Lincoln had a picture-perfect life. Sweet, loving wife, beautiful daughter, enviable career. But one fated night, it's all wiped out, leaving him scarred both mentally and physically. Now known as Jigsaw, he's a force to be reckoned with and a valuable asset to the Hell's Handlers MC. But he's also done. Done with love, done with dreams, done with women...unless it's to work off some tension.

Despite their resolve to avoid entanglements, chemistry blazes between Jig and Izzy that becomes harder to resist with each encounter. When the club's enemies set their sights on Izzy, the Handlers pull her even further into the fold. Everything Izzy believes about families is challenged as Jig and his club prove they can be counted on again and again.

Fighting side by side with a fearless woman, even one as smokin' as Izzy, isn't something Jig wants, but it might be exactly what he needs. If club business doesn't destroy them, is there a chance Jig and Izzy can let go of their pasts and find happiness?

PROLOGUE

Izzy May, 1995

"*Isabella* Monroe, do not make me ask you again! Bring me the suitcase from under your bed, and do it now!"

Izzy sighed and dropped her sketchpad on the deep purple comforter. Three was her mother's limit. Three times of asking and being ignored by her thirteen-year-old daughter, and then she'd storm in and let her Latina temper flare. And Izzy usually ended up grounded in that case.

Not that it mattered. Where did Izzy have to be? Who did she have to hang out with? All her non-school hours were spent hiding out in her room with her sketch pad and worn-down charcoal pencils, doodling as her mother called it.

With another sigh, Izzy flopped onto her paper-thin pillow and stared at the cracked white ceiling while she counted to five. Then she rolled over and dangled off the edge of the bed while searching for the giant suitcase her mom had stashed there a few months ago.

Their two-bedroom Bronx apartment didn't offer much in the way of storage space. Or living space for that matter. Her room was smaller than some rich lady's closet.

"Got it, Mom. I'm coming." Izzy towed the empty suitcase down the short hallway and into the master bedroom that was only about two square feet bigger than her own shoebox. "What

1

do you need it f—"

She stopped dead in her tracks and blinked her mother into focus as though the scene before her could change if her eyelids shut and opened again.

Izzy's heart sank to her toes. "He's leaving?" she asked, barely above a whisper.

"Don't you sound sad for that *pendejo, Isabella*. You do not know what he did, *mija*."

"What did he do, Mama?" Izzy asked because Catalina expected it. Izzy knew the routine by now. Her stepfather had committed some heinous offense in her mother's eyes, though Izzy never quite saw things from her mother's hysterical perspective. Catalina would rant and rave in a frenzied tantrum until she ran out of steam. Afterward, she'd sleep for two or three days straight.

Izzy asking for details usually got the ball rolling, and the faster Catalina got it out, the quicker the theatrical process would be over.

But the packing of the suitcases was a bad sign. This was the third time in Izzy's memory that the suitcase packing took place. And each time, it resulted in divorce. Three divorces in less than thirteen years, although really, Izzy didn't remember much before age five. Actually, her Mom packing a bag and running Izzy out of a house without her beloved teddy bear was her first foggy memory.

She'd never bothered to ask her mother if she had been married to Izzy's father. Part of Izzy was afraid to find out.

"What did he do? What did he do?" Catalina stopped haphazardly flinging socks and tighty-whities into the luggage and faced Izzy. Her dark, nearly black eyes, the eyes she'd passed on to Izzy, were wild, as was her ink-black hair, currently frizzing out of its messy bun in every which way. "He stuck his dick in that fucking teenager next door. That's what the *bastardo* did."

"Mama, Juliet isn't a teenager. She's twenty-two," she said, like that would somehow make a difference.

"And this makes it okay?" Her mother shrieked as she shook her head and stomped her foot like a petulant child. "We took vows, *Isabella!*"

Always with the vows.

Giant tears filled her mother's eyes then spilled over unchecked.

Here we go again.

Izzy bit her tongue to keep from blurting out that she was pretty confident there was no way in hell Juliet would have sex with a balding fifty-year-old toll-taker who was lumpier than a bowl of cold oatmeal. Juliet worked her ass off at a minimum wage job while taking night classes online and raising her two younger siblings. She had no time for a fling with a past-his-prime married man.

But those words would send Catalina into a further tizzy. So, another approach it was.

"Mama," she said softly. Izzy had learned over the years to approach with a soothing tone and delicate step when her mom had one of these irrational episodes. "Can I make you a cup of tea? Maybe, if you sit and relax for a while, you'll feel better, and you can talk it out with Len after he gets home. How does that sound?"

"Tea? My marriage is falling apart, and you want me to have tea? *Isabella*, don't act like a child. Hand me that suitcase and start filling it with everything in that drawer," Catalina said, pointing to the drawer where Len kept his shirts.

A lump formed in Izzy's throat. Len might be fifteen years older than her mother and not the most attractive of men, but he was kind and worked hard to provide for them. Best of all, he loved Izzy like she was his own flesh and blood, and she felt the same about him. So many nights she'd fallen asleep watching reruns of *Friends* with her head on his shoulder. He hated the show, though he pretended to love it and suffered through countless hours just for her. Her absolute favorite thing about

Len was his support of her art. He'd never called it doodling, never rolled his eyes like her mother did or told her that artists spent their whole lives begging for money. He praised her and bought her supplies with the few remaining dollars his meager paycheck afforded.

Len believed in her.

Izzy's chest started to ache, and her eyes stung. God, she was going to miss him.

Two hours later, all Len's belongings were stuffed into three bulging suitcases and waiting by the front door when he came home from work.

The oblivious smile that curved his mouth the moment he laid eyes on Izzy cracked her heart in two. Shame filled her, and she stared everywhere but at his happy-to-be-home-after-a-long-day grin. She could have told her mother no. Could have refused to help her fill those suitcases. Could have demanded Catalina stop giving into her raging insecurities and use her brain like a rational adult.

But Izzy hadn't. She'd kowtowed to her mother's wishes like she always did. Long ago, she'd learned standing up to her mother when Catalina was in one of those frantic fits was pointless. Her mom would scream. And not yell like a frustrated parent whose child did something wrong. No, this was an intense, lost all control, screeching like a banshee kind of screaming. Once, in a haze of mania, she'd even slapped Izzy across the face. Never again had Izzy backtalked in those tense moments.

Suddenly it was too much. The impending ugly words between her mom and Len, the sadness and pain on the horizon, the upcoming loneliness of the apartment once it was just her and her unstable mother. Izzy sprung from the couch and flew at Len. Her arms locked around his hefty waist, unable to meet in the back.

"I'm sorry," she sobbed into his soft stomach.

"Shh, Izzy-bella," he whispered into her hair. He sounded

resigned as if he knew this was coming and wasn't a bit surprised.

But he did sound sad.

"I love you," she said, the words muffled by his girth.

"Oh, honey, I love you, too. And I will miss you so much. But you're strong," he continued. "You're such a strong girl, and you're caring, and a beautifully talented artist. You have so much to look forward to in your future." He stroked a pudgy hand over her hair. "Make sure you turn that art into something someday, you hear me?"

She nodded against him as he held her tight. "Will you be okay?"

"Sure, Izzy-bella. I'll heal. Now you go on and get out of here for a while. No need to stick around for the rest of this."

One last time, she squeezed her arms around him as hard as she could. Then, without making eye-contact because she couldn't bear to see his pain, she kissed his cheek and ran out the front door, grabbing her backpack on the way.

She ran until her legs cramped and her lungs burned before finding a private park bench to collapse. Losing herself in her sketch pad, she drew her hopeless feelings until the sun vanished behind the high-rise apartment buildings.

Just as she was about to make her way back to what was bound to be a depressing apartment, laughter rang out.

"Look, it's Frizzy Izzy." Paula McLean, the most popular girl in the eighth grade, strolled down the sidewalk with her ever-present bitch-posse. Wearing designer jeans, a perfect, bouncy ponytail and more make-up on her face than Izzy had ever worn, Paula smirked. For some reason, Paula had taken an instant dislike to Izzy the moment they met in kindergarten and had made it her mission to keep Izzy's school-life miserable ever since.

The hair insults were the most frequent. Izzy had inherited her mother's ridiculously thick hair and had yet to learn to tame it.

"Hi, Paula. Have a good evening." She rose and started to scurry off, but one of Paula's little gremlins, Krista, yanked the sketch pad from under Izzy's arm.

"What do we have here?" she asked in the whiny tone she was known for. The sketchbook dangled from her acrylic-tipped fingers.

"Give it back!" Panic filled Izzy. No one was allowed so much as a peek in that particular book. No one, not even Len, and she'd talked to him about what she drew. But showing him, or anyone, was a different matter entirely. The drawings in that book were so personal she had a hard time looking at some of the sketches herself. It was where she poured her pain when life became too much and she needed an outlet.

Pages of agony, frustration, and teenage angst.

Krista flipped the book open to the first page. Without looking, Izzy knew precisely what the mean-girl stared at. A self-portrait Izzy had drawn after enduring a particularly rough day of bullying at school.

Izzy is chubby, and no guy will ever want her.

Izzy is so poor, she wears the same clothes three days a week.

All her mom's husbands leave because Izzy is so ugly.

And the insults had gone on and on. So, Izzy did what she did best and drew her pain away in a self-portrait where she wore her insides on the outside. Exactly how she'd felt that day. Exposed, vulnerable, ashamed.

Kind of like she did at that moment.

Krista lifted the next page and scrunched up her perfect nose. "Oh, my God." She giggled. "Look at this thing. It's gross. What the hell is wrong with you Izz—"

Without putting an ounce of thought into it, Isabella pulled her arm back and rammed her fist into Krista's nose. Crushing pain like she'd never experienced shot through her knuckles all the way up to her elbow. But it was a good pain. A satisfying pain. A powerful, life-changing pain. And the feeling only intensified when she looked up and saw blood gushing from

Krista's mangled purple nose. Eyes wide and horrified, Krista shrieked and started balling. "You crazy fucking bitch," she screamed in a nasal voice, then started spitting and gagging as her mouth filled with blood.

Paula and the other girl looked as horrified as Krista and started backing away. So much for the bonds of friendship.

That's right, bitches.

Izzy stared down at her aching hand as she flexed and extended her fingers. She glanced back up at the popular crew and smirked.

Never again.

Never again would she be bullied.

Never again would someone take something from her.

Never again would someone leave her alone and lonely.

Never again would she allow her heart to break.

She'd become strong both physically and mentally.

She'd harden her heart and learn to fight because it felt damn good to be the one on top. To be the one inflicting the pain instead of receiving it.

JIGSAW JUNE, 2012

Lincoln Miller couldn't keep the grin off his face as he navigated the packed street in front of his townhouse, searching for an empty parking spot. It seemed like he'd been a student his entire life and, well, he pretty much had. Twenty-six years old and he'd been enrolled in school in some form since he'd been four. Well beyond the majority of his years.

But it was finished. Over. Tomorrow he'd officially be dubbed Dr. Lincoln Miller. His internship would morph into an actual job title, pay would increase from crumbs to a healthy slice of the pie, and he'd finally be able to move his family off the busy street full of college partiers.

But the best part of the entire experience would be watching his wife's face as he received that Ph.D. diploma. As she did for his bachelor's degree, she'd beam with pride and love for him.

Heck, he should probably hand the certificate straight to her because without her support, encouragement and, above all, patience, he'd be nothing more than a brainy peach farmer following in his father's footsteps back in Georgia. Not that he harbored any ill will for the farming industry and his family's legacy; it just wasn't what he envisioned for himself.

At seventeen, he'd been so head over heels for his high school sweetheart, Callie, he hadn't wanted to leave her or Georgia. He'd convinced himself peach farming was the way to go despite dreams of an academic future. But when the letter arrived from the University of Alabama alerting Linc to his acceptance in the physics program, Callie encouraged him to attend in that soft and gentle way she'd had. Two years later, she'd transferred from Georgia Tech to Alabama herself, and they married at the young age of twenty.

Too young according to their families, but six years and one daughter later, they couldn't be happier or more smitten with each other.

They showed everyone that young love was real and could last.

He was still as devoted to that woman today as he was the day he married her. Probably more so. No other woman had even turned his head. Why would they? Callie appealed to him on every single level: physically, mentally, emotionally. Tender and small, he'd always felt like a man in her presence. Callie needed him to provide for her, protect her, care for her. Not in a money-grubbing way—certainly not with the pennies he made —but in a loving way a wife needs her husband. And he needed her particular brand of sweetness just as much. They were a perfect match.

Finally, he found a tight spot and maneuvered his ten-year-old Corolla between two parked cars with the skill of someone who parallel parked on the daily. Grabbing the bottle of wine and dozen roses he'd picked up on his way home from work, he started the trip along the cracked sidewalk to his humble home.

Jigsaw

Sure, he was the one who'd earned the Ph.D., but his wife went crazy for roses, and he pretty much used any excuse to buy her some. The clock read five after eight, which meant Mary, their two-year-old, would be well on her way to dreamland. They could crack open the wine and celebrate his accomplishment in his favorite way.

Naked.

Excitement surged, and his cock hardened just at the thought of what lie ahead of him. Callie was the sweetest woman he'd ever met. A true southern bell. Born well-to-do in the south, she'd been a debutant at fifteen, and he'd met her at her ball. One look at her shining blue eyes, platinum hair piled high on her head, and the sparkly pink dress that made her look like a feminine present, and he was gone, never to glance at another girl again.

Everything about their life together made him happy. They rarely argued, spent all their free time with each other, shared most interests, and made love a few times a week. Callie was a great cook, a wonderful mother, and a nurturing partner. In bed, she was pleasing and generous and looked like a dream when she came. What more could a man ask for?

With a smile on his face and a hard-on in his slacks, he jogged the three steps to his townhouse. For a split second, his brow furrowed. The porch light wasn't on. Callie always flicked the light on for him hours before the sun set. He'd teased her about it, but she said she hated the thought of him tripping on the steps because it was getting dark and he was tired.

Sweet woman.

His smile grew even more extensive. Maybe Callie had a surprise of her own planned. One that included some new lacy lingerie and her white-blond hair flowing around her shoulders just the way he loved it.

He stuck his key in the lock and frowned as it turned without resistance. Hmm… He was all for surprises, but he'd have to remind Cal to keep the door locked when she was alone. Putting her safety in jeopardy wasn't worth it no matter what she had planned. They didn't live in a sketchy neighborhood, but with so many college students enjoying their first taste of freedom, home invasions weren't unheard of.

"Hey, beautiful, I'm home!" he called into the dark house. Silence greeted him. Total silence. Not even the ambient hum of the refrigerator or churn of their decades-old HVAC trying desperately to combat the Alabama heat. "Cal?" he called out as he set the wine and flowers on a table full of picture frames in the foyer. "Where are you, sweetheart?"

He flicked the light switch next to the door, but nothing happened.

He pushed it up then down again.

Unease snaked down his spine, and the hairs on the back of his neck rose to attention.

This wasn't an ordinary power outage. Something was wrong.

He could feel it in his gut.

A thump from the kitchen had his heart stuttering.

Lincoln glanced around as best he could in the dark, searching for a weapon, but Callie kept the house so neat there wasn't anything to grab. Maybe the umbrella hanging on the hook on the wall. It was the only thing within reach beside the bottle of wine he'd brought home. He gripped the handle with a sweaty palm and started toward the kitchen.

The whirring in his head was so loud it drowned out his ability to listen for any unexpected sounds. He had no idea what he'd do if he encountered an intruder. Sure, he was tall at six-two, but he was a geeky science guy who hadn't seen the inside of a gym since his mandatory PE class in high school. Not exactly ninja material.

His gaze darted in every direction as he tiptoed his way down the hallway leading to the kitchen. He clutched the long umbrella in his hands like a lifeline. One of his loafers squeaked on the floor, and he cursed in his head. Should have left them at the door.

Step. Step.

Closer and closer to the kitchen.

He choked up on the umbrella, gripping it like a baseball bat.

With each stride, his eyes adjusted to the darkness until he was able to view the entrance to his kitchen on his left, just five feet away.

Step. Step.

Three feet to go.

Step. Step. Step.

He entered the dark and silent kitchen brandishing the umbrella like some sword-wielding pirate.

"Grab him! Watch it. He's got a weapon."

Linc spun left just as a massive fist flew into his stomach.

With his breath immediately forced from his lungs, he doubled over, choking and clutching his midsection. All his muscles seized while he tried to suck in air, and the useless weapon slipped from his limp fingers to the floor. He tried to get his bearings as he was wrenched upright by the collar of his Oxford shirt and yanked against the hard chest of a man. The next thing he knew, he was staring at a bearded brute in his kitchen while the other man banded his arm across his throat and pressed the blade of a knife into Linc's cheek.

Without thought, his hands rose in a position of surrender. Fear sludged through his veins, thick as oil. Was she here? Maybe she'd had time to take their daughter and flee out the back door. A tiny sprig of hope blossomed. "Wh-where's Callie?" he rasped out, still with difficulty breathing. First time taking a punch, and he had to admit they made it look much easier in the movies.

The bearded man grinned a gap-toothed smile and stepped sideways.

Lying face down on the kitchen floor, his wife was motionless. The smooth skin of her beautiful face was pale, too pale for the summer in Alabama. The gorgeous blue eyes that always danced with joy and love when he walked through the door stared still and cold. Beneath her, a dark puddle expanded across the beige linoleum.

Linc's knees buckled as bile rose, making him gag. His wife. His beautiful wife. What had these monsters done to her? "Jesus! What the fu—? Callie!" Linc cried as he tried to run to her.

It was a wasted effort. Whoever held him had an iron grip and strength Linc would never possess.

"What did you do to her? Oh, my god, Callie!" He struggled like a madman, screaming and sobbing, but nothing broke his captor's hold.

She hadn't reacted to his presence.

She hadn't even blinked.

There was no rise and fall to her chest.

She was dead.

"Nooo!" He screamed as his knees buckled, causing the arm across his chest to slip up into his windpipe.

"Get the fuck up, dipshit. I ain't carrying your weight," the man behind him growled in his ear.

They could let him fall. They could choke him out. It didn't matter. Nothing mattered anymore. His beautiful, sweet wife was dead. But what about...

His knees slammed straight. What about Mary? Part of him wanted to scream out. To ask about his daughter, but what if that only alerted these thugs to her presence in the house?

"So, Mr. Cannon, we have a little problem here."

What? Cannon? "I'm not—"

"Shut the fuck up!" the bearded man yelled. "Your job is to say yes or no when I ask you a question, got that Cannon?"

"But—"

The man holding him dug the point of the knife into his cheek so hard it broke the skin. Warmth trickled down his face, and Linc gasped in pain and shock.

"You stole from the big man, Cannon. That was your first mistake. Your second mistake was trying to blame it on someone else. How you managed to skim one hundred thousand dollars,

I'll never know, but I ain't paid to know shit like that. I'm paid to teach lessons."

One hundred thousand? They thought he stole one hundred thousand dollars from someone. What the hell was going on? He'd never taken anything from anyone in his entire life. It was so surreal his head spun, and the bearded man's words ran together. All he could think about was that his beloved wife was gone.

Forever.

A flood of tears coursed down his cheeks, mixing with the blood and soaking into the collar of his shirt. Despite the unfathomable pain of seeing Callie's lifeless body, he couldn't tear his gaze away.

"You listening to me, Cannon?" the bearded man asked. When Linc didn't respond, the bearded man rushed forward and landed another blow, this time to Linc's face.

Then another to his gut.

And one under the chin.

Thoughts of his daughter once again broke through his fog of shock and grief, fueling into a rage he'd never have thought himself capable.

He kicked and fought and struggled against the two men with every ounce of energy and strength he possessed. But there were two of them, and they subdued him with ease. Sweeping Linc under his legs, the bearded man took him to the floor then held him immobile.

His buddy again pressed the knife to Linc's cheek. "Just in case you didn't quite understand the message," he whispered before holding Linc's face against the floor and digging the knife deeper.

As one man punched him repeatedly, the other carved some sort of pattern into his face. His mind fully fractured, separating from his physical form until the pain didn't even register. Throughout the ordeal, he stared into his wife's unseeing eyes. He stretched an arm out as far as he possibly could, needing to feel her soft skin under his hand, but no matter how hard he tried, he couldn't quite reach her.

All that beauty wiped off the face of the earth because of mistaken identity.

Sirens wailed in the distance and the two men working him over froze.

"We gotta split," the knife-wielding asshole said.

"Yeah, let's move." The bearded man gave Linc one last kick to the ribs before bending down and whispering. "Don't worry about your daughter. She didn't hear any of this."

Mary.

They'd killed her, too. An animalistic sound of pain rose up in the kitchen. Linc barely realized he was the source of the agonized wail.

As the madman stood, maniacal laughter filled the kitchen, and the last of Linc's soul crumbled to dust.

They'd pay. Somehow, some way, he'd find these men and their boss and make them pay in the worst way possible.

Just as Callie died on that hard kitchen floor, so did Lincoln. The man who left the hospital three days later had bandages on his face, ice in his veins, and a heart as hard and black as a lump of coal.

CHAPTER ONE

A full five minutes early for his appointment, Jigsaw shouldered through the door into Inked, the one and only tattoo shop in Townsend, Tennessee. But even if it wasn't the lone ink provider, even if there was a tattoo shop on every corner, it'd be the only one to receive his business. Inked was the best, by far. Rip was a master with a tattoo machine and could bring anyone's vision to life.

Maverick and Rocket filed in after him, immediately taking seats on the ratty couch butted up against the display window. His brothers had tagged along despite knowing how much Jig hated an audience for this.

Every year on his wife and child's birthdays, which just happened to be only three days apart, Jig added to a tattoo on his thigh. Without fail, it put him in a shitty mood, and his brothers damn well knew it. But they couldn't just leave him the fuck alone. They had to stick their fucking noses in his shit and follow him, so he didn't "do something stupid."

Every damn year.

Assholes.

"Hey, Jig," Rip called out. "Lemme talk to you for a second." He stepped from behind the privacy curtain pulled around his customer. To say the shop was simple would be a ridiculous understatement. Inked was about as no-frills as it came, with two tattoo stations, a reception desk, a second-hand couch, and a few sketches on the wall. Rip didn't give a shit about the décor or ambiance. He gave damn good ink and had the reputation to prove it.

"What's up, Rip?" Jig asked after Rip waddled his large frame cross the shop.

"Hey, I'm running about forty-five minutes behind, man. I'm sorry." Rip gave Jig a sheepish half smile.

From the couch, Maverick laughed and rubbed his hands together. "Woohoo, does this mean Jig gets to have his face inked on you?"

Not one to find much shit funny, Jig snorted. Rip was a bit of a psycho when it came to lateness. Threatened to tattoo his face on a client if they were late to their appointment. He'd done it before, too, the bastard. That was the reason Jig never let himself be later than five minutes early. Last thing he needed was Rip's ugly mug on his ass cheek.

"I really am sorry, man," Rip said. He ran a hand through his receding gray hair and shifted uncomfortably, seemingly flustered, which wasn't him.

"Everything good?" Jig asked.

Rip lowered his voice. "Yeah, just had this broad come in crying a few minutes ago. Breast cancer survivor who recently had some reconstructive surgery. Wanted me to ink nipples on her. Someone recommended me specifically, and she's unwilling to go to anyone else."

"Well, fuck me, Rip," Mav said. "Why didn't you start with that? Now I feel like an ass for ragging on you."

With a shrug, Rip swiped the back of his hand across his forehead. "Shit, I'm sweating, guys. This is a lot of pressure."

This time, Jig let out a small laugh. "You did all our Hell's Handlers back pieces without blinking an eye, and you're afraid of some nipples?"

"It's a big deal," Rip grumbled.

Jig slapped him on the back. "Hey, man, no worries. I can reschedule." In reality, the change to his schedule pissed him off, but what the fuck could he do? He wasn't about to be the asshole who pulled Rip away from a cancer survivor. Jig might be an unfeeling bastard, but he wasn't a robot.

"Nah, not necessary," Rip said as he walked toward the desk. "I got someone else who can do it."

Jig froze and scanned the shop. It was then he realized there was a curtain pulled around the second chair as well. Muffled voices could be heard from behind the fabric wall but not well enough to make out what was being said. "You telling me you actually hired some help?"

For the past two years, Rip had been saying he needed to hire a second artist. Ever the control freak, no one actually thought he'd let another professional into his shop. He found fault with every other artist out there.

"Yeah, I did. They're just finishing up the aftercare convo. Then you can meet 'em."

"I don't know." Jig frowned. No one but Rip had gone near his skin with ink and needle.

"They're good, Jig. Wouldn'ta hired 'em otherwise. Trained 'em myself actually. About ten years ago, right before I moved to the area and opened up shop. Take a look at some of their work." He dug around behind his desk and pulled out a beat-up binder, laying it out on the counter.

Like a bunch of teenage chicks who didn't want to miss out on the gossip, Mav and Rocket hopped up to join him at the reception desk.

Mav, who had more inked skin than not, whistled. "Shit, Rip. These are fucking amazing. This guy might do better work than you."

It was meant as a joke, but Rip snorted and nodded. There was definite truth to Maverick's words. The lines were so precise, the images so vivid and perfect, it was hard to believe they were done by a human hand. One of the photos was a butterfly that looked like it was literally lifting off some chick's shoulder. Amazing.

"Give 'em a shot," Rip said. "Promise they'll do you right."

Jig sighed and rubbed a hand across his jaw. Time to trim his beard. He'd gotten lazy the past few weeks and had let the growth get a little out of control. He always kept some amount of facial hair because it covered the bottom third of his scar, but he tried to keep it neat. Most of the time. "All right, man. Let's do it."

Seemed like Rip was really trying to push the new guy. Probably wanted to build up his clientele. If the work in his portfolio was an accurate reflection of the guy's skill, he'd be a fool to turn down this artist. He could help a friend out and get some quality ink in the process.

"Great." Rip's yellow-toothed smile beamed. "Oh, here she comes now."

"Wait, what?"

She?

Maverick coughed in a weak attempt to cover his laughter, but it quickly turned to a gasp.

Oh, yeah," he said under his breath. "That one'll do you right, Jig."

"Holy fuck," Rocket whispered.

Rip wore a shit-eating grin, the fuckstick. He'd purposefully misled them into thinking it was a dude. Jig didn't want some bitch getting anywhere near him with a needle. He flipped his brothers off and spun to check out this lady tattoo artist for himself.

Ho-ly shiit.

About five-feet-eight inches—and that was without the four-inch stilettos—of pure sex and sin strutted her way straight toward him. Somehow, this woman had poured herself into the tightest black leather pants he'd ever seen. They molded around her long, shapely legs and, damn, if he didn't wish for her to turn around. He just bet she had a stellar ass that would only be enhanced by the grip of soft leather.

With each step, the side to side sway of her hips drew his eye like he was watching the pendulum of a clock swing back and forth. Forcing his gaze from her hips, he trailed it upward, not oblivious to the tight black tank top that cupped her breasts as snugly as the leather cupped her thighs.

"Hey, boys," she said, her voice on the lower side. Husky, he'd call it.

Mav whistled. "Damn, woman. And I say this in a totally non-creepy, non-flirting way because I have a woman that would shoot off my junk if I so much as hit on another chick, but you are some kinda fucking gorgeous."

Jig ground his teeth together as the new lady tattoo artist threw her head back and let out a throaty laugh. Fucking Maverick. Flirting and charming women was just part of his DNA. He truly meant it when he said he wasn't hitting on her. The man just couldn't let a beautiful woman walk away without her knowing she was gorgeous.

"Aren't you the charmer," she said, placing her hands on those fantastic hips.

Damn, her body was out of this world. Not skinny, not even too curvy, it was more...athletic. Sleek lines with swells of muscle in her arms and a flat stomach. The girl must spend some serious hours in the gym.

"Guys, this here is Isabella. I taught her everything she knew about ten years ago. She finally agreed to move here and work with me." Rip beamed with pride as he introduced his protégé.

"Please," she said, "call me Izzy. One of you boys looking for some ink?"

Fuck no.

Wasn't happening.

Rocket cleared his throat like he had a whole steak lodged in there. If the asshole wasn't careful, he'd have Jig's fist lodged down there instead.

A hand slapped down on his shoulder. "My man Jig here needs some ink."

Fuckin' Maverick.

"Don't want to mess up your schedule," Jig said. "I'll come back when Rip can fit me in."

Rip's face fell, making Jig feel like scum. Wasn't the shop owner's fault that Jig wanted nothing to do with most women. Unless he was fucking them. That was pretty much the only time he associated with them. Of course, his brothers' ol' ladies couldn't seem to leave his ass alone. Always trying to bring him food, fix him up, and acting like freaking mother hens around him.

Especially Mav's woman, Stephanie. He'd helped rescue her from a fucking psycho not long ago, so now he'd become her special project.

"Oh, I'll, uh, check my book." Rip waddled behind his desk and flipped through his old-school appointment book.

Izzy's dark, almost black eyes just stared at him, hands on her hips, earning her Jig's scowl. Who the hell did this bitch think she was?

Instead of caving under his murderous glare, one of her perfect black eyebrows arched high into her forehead. "You afraid your dick will invert if a woman puts some ink on you?"

She had a set of balls, he'd give her that much. "Nah, I—"

"I've inked hundreds, actually thousands of dudes." She gasped and covered her mouth with her unpolished fingertips. "Shit, I've even tatted some bikers."

Behind him, Mav and Rocket chuckled. Fuckers were enjoying this way too much.

Izzy leaned closer and dropped her volume. "Promise you, bubba, not one of those guys grew a pussy because I was the one holding the needle."

A strangled sound came from Rocket, and Maverick flat-out laughed. Rip joined in, and soon the three of them were cackling like a bunch of fucking hyenas.

Goddamnit. Not only had she interrupted him, sassed him, and tossed attitude at him, she'd thrown down a challenge. His damned male pride left him no choice.

Jigsaw

"Show me to your chair," he grumbled.

A massive grin of victory broke out across her gorgeous face. "Follow me, bubba," she said as she spun on one of those pencil-thin heels then sashayed to her station.

And fuck if he didn't feel a twitch of his dick and a twitch of his lips. Where his cock's interest came from, he had no idea. Miss Izzy couldn't be further from his usual type.

He liked 'em blonde, blue-eyed, small, sweet, and docile. Not tall, dark-haired, and mouthy. She'd even shaved the sides of her head, adding to her badass-bitch look.

But as he watched the very long tail of a tight braid swinging back and forth across the top of what was, without a doubt, a stellar ass, he couldn't deny his animal attraction to her.

Fuck. This was gonna be a shitty few hours.

CHAPTER TWO

Was this dude even capable of any facial expressions beyond scowls?

Didn't seem like it.

Izzy was a damn good tattoo artist, and fuck any man who didn't want to work with her because of what was—or wasn't—dangling between her legs. She'd show him. Happened every single time she worked with one of these macho sexist types. They sat their asses in her chair with low expectations, and she blew them away with her skill.

Every. Damn. Time.

This would be no different, of that she was sure. And she'd revel in his eventual praise while a small part of her would remain pissed she'd had to prove herself yet again. Someday it'd be nice to be taken at her word.

"All right, bubba, what are we doing today?" she asked, going for overly friendly to combat his stony expression. It might be a cold face, but it wasn't hard to look at and came attached to a scorching hot body. Dark hair, not as dark as her own, but pretty dark, navy blue eyes, and fairly scruffy beard that needed a date with some clippers. His whole appearance with dark wash jeans, ear gauges, a leather jacket, and sporty black sunglasses perched on his head was rough, a little scruffy, and a whole lotta sexy.

Just as she was about to turn toward her supplies, she noticed a pattern of white lines rising from the fur on his right cheek.

Scars.

She couldn't help but wonder the extent of it hidden beneath the hair growth.

This man had a past. A past that had been carved into his face in a shape that resembled a puzzle piece.

"Got a tat on my thigh I want to add to." No surprise that his flat eyes, and even duller expression, didn't change as he spoke.

Huh, interesting. Not a new project. She was always intrigued when clients added to previous ink. Usually meant something deeply personal. Remembering an event despite the passage of time. Keeping a memory alive. Often painful memories. What did this guy have churning around in his head that he'd expressed on his body? Whatever it was, she had a feeling those memories were responsible for the solemn personality he wore like a shield.

With a nod, Izzy said, "Okay. Gonna need you to drop your drawers. Want me to pull the curtain and give you a sheet to drape over yourself?"

The buzz of a tattoo machine kicked up over at Rip's station. She'd have taken the nipple job herself, but the woman's surgeon was actually the one to recommend Rip, and she'd been hellbent on working with him. Izzy had worked on a few breast cancer survivors in the past and loved seeing the elation on the women's—and one man's—faces when she made them feel whole again.

Without answering her question, the biker stood, loosened his belt, then lowered his zipper.

Guess he wasn't shy.

As he worked the denim over his trim hips, Izzy couldn't help but allow her gaze to shadow his movements. She was a female after all. Just because she had no desire to give a man any kind of significant role in her life, then or ever, didn't mean she couldn't appreciate the merchandise. Or sample a few of the products. Once in a while, a non-silicone-induced orgasm was a necessity. But that was as far as she ever allowed it. An orgasm or two then sayonara. Izzy survived damn well on her own and planned to keep it that way.

Thick, muscled thighs were revealed to her as the denim fell to the floor. Damn, this man was no stranger to a squat. Would it be weird if she asked him to turn around so she could see how his ass looked in the form-fitting royal blue boxer briefs?

Yeah, that would be weird. She'd have to content herself with pretending she wasn't sneaking glances at the monster he'd tucked into those boxers.

After an unreasonable amount of time spent watching him get off his jeans, she remembered she was at work and shifted her focus to his tattoo. She gasped at the gorgeous yet tragic image inked into his skin.

"Wow," she whispered on an exhale. "Rip did this?"

"Yes." If possible, he became even more guarded, as though he detested the fact she was getting a glimpse into his personal space. Dick ogling aside, she was a professional and would act like one. She had no interest in getting a reputation for prying into her client's private lives. So, while the urge to learn the story of the tat might eat a hole in her stomach, she resisted the impulse to ask.

"Have a seat," she said, gesturing toward the reclining chair. "What are you looking to add?"

"Flower petals. But I want them to look exactly like the rest of them, so if you can't make it look just like Rip's, then we're done here."

Under normal circumstances, she'd be offended by his antagonistic tone and words, but she was already lost in her craft, admiring Rip's incredible work. A dying tree took up the entire expanse of this man's broad and brawny thigh. The tree itself was massive and done with the darkest of browns, almost black. Each branch was leafless, twisted, and snarled as they decayed. The roots resembled those that had been carelessly ripped from the ground, red and dripping as though bleeding.

Twelve blood-red flower petals fell from the tree in pairs of two, a large and small petal grouped together. They were so well done she could easily imagine them moving, floating to the ground to escape the expiring tree. She didn't have a clue what it symbolized, but the pairs of petals had an almost parent-child feel to them. One large, one small, falling from the tree together as though unable to be separated.

Whatever happened in his life to inspire this memorial, it was dark and full of pain.

Emotion clogged Izzy's throat, and for one terrifying second, she worried she might tear up. Used to squashing any sentiment that didn't serve an express purpose at the moment, Izzy cleared her throat and pushed away her pity. He wouldn't want it anyway. These macho types of men never did.

"I assume you want another group of two?" she asked, still looking at his leg and giving herself an extra second to gather her composure.

A grunt was all she received in response.

"I can handle this, no problem. It will look just like Rip's petals. You have my word." As she spoke the last sentence, she gave him the respect of full eye-contact. It was important to her that he realize how seriously she took her craft and his memories.

Face neutral, he nodded.

"Anywhere specific you want them?"

"No. You pick where you think they should go. I trust you."

She froze, and her gaze flew back to his face, but he'd already blocked her out. Eyes closed, elbow bent and forearm thrown across his eyes, he appeared totally at ease with the fact that she was about to jab a needle into his skin.

"You got it, bubba."

"Jig," he said.

"Huh?"

"My name's Jigsaw, not fuckin' Bubba."

Her gaze flew to his scar again for a fraction of a second.

Jigsaw. Like a puzzle. Interesting.

"Right. Nice to meet you, Jig." When he didn't return the pleasantry, she got to it, preparing the ink then creating art on his body. After about three minutes, she slid into the zone and operated in complete silence. Some people liked to chatter away while she worked on them. Something to distract them from the pain. Jig seemed to appreciate the silence, which was fine by her. Quiet was her preference, actually. Small talk and bullshitting had never been her favorite part of the job. She was a loner. Preferred few people in her life and in her business. That was the main reason she left city life in favor of small-town living.

Jig's MC buddies hung around the entire time but kept off to the side. They seemed to recognize that he might not be thrilled to have them present and were trying to respect his space while supporting him at the same time.

Brothers, family, friends. Whatever it was called, it was kinda nice.

Izzy had been on her own for so long she couldn't remember what it felt like to have that unspoken backup of other people in her life. Last person who'd had her back, who'd cared about her above themselves, was Len. Or so it had seemed until her mother kicked him to the curb. Izzy hadn't seen or heard from him since that dreadful day. After Len vanished from their lives, her mom went on to marry twice more before committing suicide when Izzy was seventeen.

Fuck them. Fuck them all. There was only one person she could count on in life. One person who had her best interest at heart and would make sure she got exactly what she needed every time, and that was herself. Others might have played a part for a while in her past, but inevitably, they left. Because they didn't give enough of a shit to stay.

In the end, the only one anybody really had to count on was themself.

Shit, she was getting maudlin. Had to be Jig's depressing tree of mortality getting to her. Shaking off the heavy blanket of despair, Izzy lost herself in her task. Two hours later, she flicked off the tattoo machine, wiped off the final few drops of blood, and sat back to admire her work. Damn fine if she did say so herself.

"Damn, girl. You give good ink."

Izzy looked up into the flirty biker's smiling and open face, so opposite his brother's.

"Thanks," she said.

He clapped her on the shoulder. "Name's Maverick, and that's Rocket," he said pointing to the third in their group. "I ain't got much space left, but I just might have to find a spot for you to work on."

A grin spread across her face. Being appreciated for her talent was something that filled her with endless pride. "Anytime."

Jig lowered his arm and blinked a few times as if waking from a deep slumber. Raising his arms, he arched his back into a deep stretch that had his shirt lifting. A rack of impressive abs peeked out. Izzy curled her tongue inside her mouth. It was either that or let it come out to play and lick his stomach.

Might be bad for business.

Jig grunted and lowered his arms.

Had he seriously fallen asleep through that?

Mav laughed. "You taking a nap, brother?"

"Just in the zone," Jig said without inflection as he turned his attention to his thigh.

Izzy's lower lip tucked between her teeth. The moment of truth. For some reason, her heart picked up speed and a flutter of nerves jiggled through her stomach.

After about thirty seconds of inspecting her work, Jig lifted his gaze and gave her a single nod. "Wrap it up," he said, and her heart crashed to the floor. Asshole. Couldn't even toss her a quick "looks good" or "thanks."

A fucking nod.

Well, she sure as hell wasn't going to let him know his lack of appreciation affected her. "You bet," she said in what had to be an obviously false chipper tone.

Mav shot her a sympathetic smile as she dressed the tattoo and gave a quick recap of the aftercare. Without so much as a grunt, Jig left her chair, paid at the desk, and was out the door.

"Coming, Mav?" Rocket asked as he followed Jig.

"Yeah, be a minute. Just gonna make an appointment."

Rocket chuckled. "Jesus. You're a fuckin' addict."

Mav flipped him the bird then turned to Izzy.

"Rip can pencil you in at the desk," she said as she turned away to clean her station. It was time for the bikers to beat feet so she could take a few moments to compose herself in peace.

"Don't need an appointment, babe."

Izzy spun back, her brow scrunched. "Oh, but you said…"

"Yeah, know what I said." He stuck his hands in his pockets and rocked back on his heels. "Listen, Jig's a hard motherfucker. The shittiest of deals made him that way. I'm talking worst case scenario. You did right by him. Fuckin' beautiful work. He was more than happy with it, trust me. He's surly at best, but when he adds to the tat this time every year, it sets him off for a few days."

What happened to him? The words were right there, dangling off the edge of her tongue, but she sucked them back into her mouth. It wasn't any of her business. "Thanks for telling me. I guess I can get a little sensitive about my work." She shrugged.

"Well, that wasn't work. It was art, girl." Mav had a killer smile that must make panties disintegrate all over Tennessee.

Lucky woman, whoever she was, to be on the receiving end of all that sexy charm. Though, please, a man like him? Izzy gave him six months tops before he took off for greener pastures or bigger tits, rounder ass, thicker wallet, whatever tripped his trigger.

"Gotta run. Got me an insatiable woman to tend to." He winked. "I'll be back soon. Can't resist the needle, especially if there's a gorgeous woman on the other end. Have a good one, Izzy."

She gave him a genuine smile accompanied by an eye roll. He

was easy to like, and the flirting was obviously harmless and meaningless. When he spoke of his girlfriend, his eyes lit with a spark that was impossible to fake. Nice to see…while it lasted. "You, too, Mav. It was nice meeting you."

He nodded once then went the way of his friends. Soon, the roar of motorcycles drowned out the steady beat of music Rip pumped through the shop all day long.

"Looks like Jig was one satisfied customer," Rip said, walking his round frame toward her.

Izzy raised an eyebrow. "How the hell'd you get that impression? He took one look at it and ran for the door so fast he left skid marks on my chair."

Rip held up a crisp hundred-dollar bill. "Man left you a Benjamin as a tip."

Her jaw nearly dropped. Jesus, that was a fifty percent tip. She plucked the money from Rip's fingers. "Thanks," she said as her mind reeled.

What the hell did it mean?

Was it a compliment?

An apology?

An insult? He couldn't be bothered to speak to her like a human being, but he'd toss some cash at her to keep her from bitching?

With a chuckle, she tucked the money into her bra and finished clearing her station. What the hell did it matter? The man had played a two-hour role in her life. They'd probably have little or nothing to do with each other ever again. She'd give him about as much thought and consideration as he gave her tattoo.

Guess that meant she was done thinking about him.

Good riddance.

CHAPTER THREE

Three days after meeting Isabella, the sexy tattoo artist, Jig was officially sick of himself. He'd been wallowing around the clubhouse, living in the past, and chasing bad memories with bottle after bottle of whatever the hell he could snag from the bar.

Copper had let him slack off, but his time was running out. The club had too much shit going on, and the prez wasn't going to allow him to shirk his responsibilities for much longer. Especially since Jig was in charge of the whole operation. For the past three weeks, ever since the club discovered Lefty, a sex-trafficking local gang leader, was gunning for them, the Handlers had been beefing up security at the clubhouse.

Surrounded mostly by dense woods, they'd never had much need for security beyond an alarm system and a few well-placed cameras. But a few weeks ago, Maverick's woman was nearly kidnapped by some of Lefty's thugs. Before she escaped, she'd heard them talking about plans to set a bomb in the Handlers' clubhouse. Copper wasted no time getting Jig involved in a plan to protect the club and its extended family.

A metal security fence with wicked spikes at the top, additional cameras, lookout towers, and floodlights, were some of the new additions to the clubhouse and surrounding land. There were also a few surprises for any unsuspecting asshole who might somehow make it past all the keep-out measures.

Jigsaw

Booby traps so to speak.

Today the guys were working on the lookout towers. Jig had determined placement for two but wanted at least another three around what would soon be more of a compound than a clubhouse. As he strolled the back edge of the property along the line of the woods, he almost missed Copper sneaking up on him. For a giant man, Copper could move like a stalking panther.

"Done being a dick?" the prez asked as he sidled up to where Jig had been marking the ground with white paint.

"I'm done," he said, rising to his feet and accepting the hand Copper offered.

"Good. Quicker than last year. Last year it took a full week before someone was brave enough to talk to you."

Okay, so he became a bit of a fucktard twice a year, every year. First, on the anniversary of his family's death, then on their birthdays. "How the fuck do you expect me to act, Cop?" He dropped the can of spray paint and got up in his president's face. "Wanna put yourself in my shoes? Want to imagine it? Imagine if Shell—"

Copper had Jig shoved against a tree with a giant hand around his throat in under two seconds. Jig was no slouch when it came to fighting. He battled it out in a down and dirty underground fighting ring a few times a year, but he wasn't stupid enough to brawl against his president. Not because of Copper's size, Jig had a fair shot of taking him down, but because of respect. And even though his actions of the past few moments didn't express that respect, he had it in spades for his president.

"Don't you fucking say it, Jigsaw," Copper ground out, squeezing Jig's windpipe enough to make breathing difficult but not enough to choke him out.

Shit, it had been a dick move even for him. The big red-headed president was nuts about Shell, the daughter of the club's previous president. It was painfully obvious she felt the same about him, but Copper was stubborn in his belief that the sixteen years separating them made her off-limits. She'd left town a few years ago, probably sick of seeing Copper day in, day out. When she returned, close to a year ago, it was with an adorable red-haired kiddo in tow.

Jig had stayed away from the clubhouse for two whole weeks after Shell returned, unable to stand the sight of the child. Then, Mav showed up at his door and let him know what a shitheel he was being. So he sucked it up and pretended it didn't gut him every time he saw that sweet, smiling face. He still avoided her at all costs but tried to keep Shell from noticing.

It had to be a damn dropkick to the heart for Copper the first time he saw the little girl with hair just a few shades lighter than his own. In her heartbreak, or loneliness, or whatever she'd call it, Shell must have fucked the first man who came along and reminded her of Copper. And then she got knocked up for her troubles. As far as he knew, the topic was never discussed between Shell and Copper, but it bred some resentment on Copper's part. Not that Jig had any right to judge who and how people fucked. His own sexual preferences were the topic of discussion among his MC and their ol' ladies despite how discrete he tried to be.

"Fuck, Cop, I'm sorry. Shouldn't have thrown that at you." The grip around his throat lessened until it disappeared and Copper stepped back.

"My fault," Copper said. "Shouldn't have implied you need to handle your grief in any specific way. Shit, brother, not sure I'd ever be functional again if I were you. You're doing damn well, and if you need a few days each year to be a fucker, you go right ahead."

Jig chuckled. It didn't happen often, but once in a while, his brothers brought it out of him. "Nice job, Cop. Apologize and throw in an insult all in one shot."

Copper laughed, his white teeth gleaming between the red of his beard. "Don't want you to think I'm going soft on you, brother." He waved a hand around, growing serious. "How's this all going? We on schedule?"

With a nod, Jig pointed to the X he'd sprayed on the ground. "I've marked off three additional lookout spots. Add them to the two being constructed today, and I think I'm satisfied. Fence will be finished day after tomorrow, Mav installs the cameras this weekend, and we've got a few more irons in the fire we'll get moving on next week."

Scratching his beard, Copper sighed. "Good. I'll feel better when that fucking fence is up. We're stretching the guys real thin with watch schedules. At least when we're secure on all sides, we can let up a bit."

Jig grunted his agreement. "Any action from Lefty?"

"Been quiet over the last week or so," Cop said as he shook his head. "Has me on fuckin pins and needles. I'd almost rather he make a fuckin move. At least I'd know where the bastard is and what he's planning."

Jig got that. The calm before the storm was stressful as fuck. Had most of the club on edge. Between the long hours patrolling the grounds, the grueling work during the day, and not knowing what the hell Lefty was planning, the brothers were like a rubber band being stretched farther each day. Sooner or later, it was going to snap.

"Maybe we need to stop playing defense and make our own move." About two weeks ago, they'd caught one of Lefty's men. He was one of the guys who'd almost taken Stephanie. After giving Maverick a chance to play with him, Copper and Zach took over and got the information confirming Stephanie's story. Lefty had been planning an attack on the clubhouse. The only thing that had prevented it was Stephanie telling Copper what she'd heard. Since that day, the clubhouse had been guarded better than an army base. They weren't on lockdown, but security had increased tenfold, and the ol' ladies were accompanied everywhere they went, much to their chagrin.

Jig was getting tired of reacting to Lefty's moves. It was time to act.

"I hear ya, Jig. I agree with you, too. I just want this place safer before we move forward."

Well, he couldn't fault him for that. Copper would give his life without thought for any of the men. The brotherhood was the most important thing in their president's life. He was an excellent fucking leader. "I'm here, one hundred percent focused and present now. I won't let anything else distract me. Give us another week, Cop."

Copper stuck out his hand. "I can do that, brother."

Jig shook his president's hand and then got back to work, determined to finish ahead of schedule. Anything he could do to help lift the enormous weight of responsibility off Copper's shoulders.

And now that he knew the only thing standing between him and a little Gray Dragon's blood was completing the perimeter, he had even more motivation to hustle.

CHAPTER FOUR

"I officially suck," Izzy muttered to herself as she poured the horrible coffee down the drain. Up until she'd moved from New Orleans to Townsend, a grand total of twenty-six days ago, she'd had a handy-dandy Keurig in her apartment. When she'd purchased the small two-bedroom home she now resided in, she'd decided if she was big enough to own a home, she was big enough to brew her own espresso and lattes. So, she'd tossed the Keurig and purchased one of those fancy schmancy espresso machines, only to waste a half pound of expensive beans.

"How come I can't do this?" And now she was talking to herself. Or the devil-machine. She wasn't quite sure which was worse. Time to get the hell out of the house and interact with real people who weren't paying her to inject ink into their skin.

She stood, rolling her shoulders, and glanced down at her outfit. Camo print joggers and a fitted long-sleeved olive T-shirt. Not exactly a fashion plate, but passable. As she stuffed her feet into her favorite electric-purple Nikes, she stretched her arms over her head. Restless energy had been buzzing through her for the past few days. She had grown edgy, uncomfortable with the fact she'd settled into Townsend without a hitch.

The main reason she'd moved was to separate herself from people. That didn't mean she wanted to be a hermit, but she wanted to avoid emotional entanglements and keep people from getting too close. Letting people in only led to disappointment and heartache. Her life had been full of far too much of that, and she wanted it over. Problem was, she craved that human closeness even if she knew it wasn't good for her. Probably stemmed from her inner neglected child yearning for love and affection, or some nonsense like that. Time and time again, Izzy let people in, only to be hurt. The goal in moving to a small town with a slower pace of life was to inject some solitude in her life and avoid any more dings to her heart.

Clearly, she had mental problems if achieving her goal was making her twitchy. But it was. She needed action, tension, something to expend her energy on. Usually, there was only one thing that worked to relieve the tension. Okay, two things, but she didn't think she'd be getting laid any time soon. Yesterday she'd signed up at the local gym. It was time to start training again. The need to pound something would soon become unbearable. A heavy bag, speed bag, and a good sparring partner would take the edge off for a while, but soon she'd need more.

Today, a jog would have to suffice. She snatched her keys and phone off the kitchen island and started toward the door. At the very last second, she turned back and swiped the Post-it a client had left with her. All types of characters came in for tattoos, from impulsive college kids to grannies wanting to commemorate the birth of a grandchild to everything in between. But she definitely met her fair share of exciting players. Like the man who'd scribbled the phone number on the paper she now held.

Halfway through the brisk three-mile jog into town, the post-it was burning a hole through Izzy's pocket. It was time. She needed to fight more than she needed anything. She'd started with boxing and Brazilian Jujitsu shortly after Len left. It came naturally to her, and the discipline it taught kept the angry teenager she'd become out of some serious trouble. As she'd aged, she'd competed in MMA tournaments and did well. But there was always something missing. Then, at twenty-three, she tagged along with a friend to her first underground fighting ring.

It was rough, raw, no-holds-barred, dirty street fighting. She was fucking hooked from night one and anxious to get a chance in the ring. Not too many female fighters were willing to go unsanctioned, but there were some. Izzy didn't get the urge to fight all that often, just a handful of times a year, but her contact always came through for her when she needed it and found her a willing partner. On occasion, she'd even fought men, but it wasn't her preference. Kicking a dude's ass was a nerve-wracking experience. She never knew how a man was going to react to getting his ass handed to him by a woman. Last thing she needed was some sore-losing psycho showing up in her bedroom in the middle of the night bent on revenge.

A few days prior, she'd had an MMA fighter as a client. They'd been talking shop when he alluded to an underground ring. Her eyes must have betrayed her interest because next thing she knew, she had a number to text if she ever wanted a fight.

And she did. She wanted it bad.

Needed it.

She reached the center of town in about twenty minutes, jogging right up to the diner she had yet to check out. As long as they had coffee that was better than the swill she'd brewed, she was damn happy to fork over some cash.

A cheerful bell jangled as she pushed through the door.

"Table for one?" asked a tiny waitress as she paused in front of Izzy holding a tray with six heaping plates of food. The woman was small, but clearly had arms of steel.

"I can sit at the counter so I don't hog an entire booth," Izzy said, nodding her head toward one of the four empty stools at the long diner counter.

"Perfect, pick any seat, and I'll bring you a menu in two shakes," she said as she moved toward a table of burly guys who wore leather cuts much as Jig had in Rip's shop four days ago. Izzy was embarrassed to admit she'd had a few fantasies about the man since then. Good thing she didn't know any mind readers.

She chose a seat that had an empty stool on each side. Hopefully, they'd remain that way, and she could eat her meal in silence. So much for interacting with real people.

The cheerful blond waitress appeared in front of Izzy. "Okay, here's your menu." She had curly hair that just reached her shoulders, sparkly blue eyes, and a sunny personality. Usually, Izzy would hate her on sight, but it wouldn't kill Izzy to try to be a little more personable.

"Thanks," she said, taking the thick laminated menu.

"I'm Shell by the way. You want coffee?"

"Yes!" Izzy said, almost like she'd die if she didn't get some caffeination.

Shell laughed. "Got it, big mug."

Izzy smiled. "The bigger, the better."

Tapping her knuckles on the counter, Shell grinned. "Be right back with that. It'll give you a chance to check out the menu."

Two minutes later, a mug the size of a cereal bowl landed in front of her. "You're a goddess," Izzy said. "A coffee-bearing goddess."

Shell threw her head back and let out a loud laugh. "Oh man, today I've been called 'mommy,' 'hey you,' and 'damned woman.' I think goddess trumps them all. Could you say it again?"

Izzy laughed. Shell was hilarious. It wasn't often she made a connection with another female. Most found her intimidating. After all, she was tall, athletic, inked, and had been told she rocked a resting bitch face like no other. But Shell seemed unaffected by any of that. Maybe she was just a good actress, working it for tips, but Izzy had the impression she was just an all-around sweet person. "Damned woman?"

"Yep, twice." Shell pointed to the table of bikers. "Big red-headed one. I'm kinda the bane of his existence." She winked and set a bowl of sugar packets and a tiny pitcher of cream in front of Izzy.

"You say that like you enjoy it," Izzy said as she dumped half the small pitcher into her mug then tore open five packets of sugar in one move. Well, look at that. Back and forth conversation. Huh, maybe the move to Tennessee had been good for her. Perhaps she could loosen up and socialize while keeping herself and her emotions at a healthy distance.

"Gotta get my fun where I can." Shell snorted out a laugh. She pointed to Izzy's mug. "Oh, my God, you drink your coffee like I do! And you called me a goddess. I think I'm falling in love with you. Any chance you swing that way?"

It was Izzy's turn to snort, almost spilling the cream. Shit, had she read the situation completely wrong? Was Shell flirting with her? She'd hate to give the woman the false impression of interest. With a shrug, she said, "Sorry, Shell, I love dick too much to give it up."

Shell sighed. "Yeah, me, too."

Ahh, just being snarky. "And I don't think it's possible to get coffee light enough or sweet enough."

"Right?" Shell's smile was huge. "I'm surrounded by black coffee drinkers in my life. Nice to meet another who doctors the hell out of it. Decided on what you want to eat yet?"

"What do you recommend?"

"Cinnamon roll waffles. They're our best seller, hands down."

Izzy groaned. That sounded beyond amazing. "What do you recommend for someone who ate half a sleeve of Oreos last night and is doing penance today?"

"Well, if you were me, you'd still eat the waffles," Shell said with a grin.

Yeah, like the itty-bitty woman gorged out on fat and sugar-laden cinnamon waffles often.

"But you seem to be looking for something lighter so I'd go with the Mediterranean egg white omelet. Spinach, tomatoes, feta and a side of fresh fruit."

"Perfect." Izzy handed her menu back to Shell.

"It'll be up in a few. Enjoy your coffee." Shell moved on to a customer a few stools down as Izzy sipped her coffee.

Ahhh, sugar and caffeine, the perfect cavity-inducing, heart-pounding elixir. The next few minutes passed in peaceful silence. Well, not silence since there was a hum of chatter in the crowded diner, but Izzy didn't have to take part in it, and that was good enough for her.

But then, a body settled on the stool next to her. "You must be Izzy."

And there went the peaceful meal. Plastering on what she hoped looked like a genuine smile, Izzy faced the woman sitting on the stool. Geez, did the women around here come in anything but small and blond. "I am, and you are?"

She smiled, warm and welcoming. "Stephanie. Heard you're new here. Welcome to town. How are you settling in?"

Izzy pursed her lips and racked her brain. Was she supposed to know who this Stephanie was? "Sorry, I'm trying to place you but…"

"Oh, sorry." Steph rolled her eyes. "I belong to…" She turned and stared at the front door. "Just a second…" It opened, and Maverick strode in looking like he owned the place. His gaze caught Stephanie's, and he winked while moving his hand to his crotch.

Stephanie's face pinked, and she turned back around. "You know, I guess he's not here right now."

Izzy burst out laughing. She laughed so hard she could barely take a breath. "Oh, my God, that was funny," she said, slapping her palm on the countertop. "So you belong to Maverick?" she asked once she had control of herself.

Still bright pink, Stephanie nodded. "Guilty as charged. Anyway, he told me he met a new-to-here-but-not-new tattoo artist with long legs and an even longer braid." Stephanie pointed to Izzy's hair. "Had to be you."

Now it was Izzy's turn to feel heat in her face. "Sorry about the hot tattoo artist comment. I don't think he meant anything by it."

Stephanie waved her hand and rolled her eyes. "Please, I'm well aware of how that man operates, and he's well aware that he'll never be able to operate again if he crosses any lines. He's just a pathologic flirt. He's harmless."

Phew. A jealous woman was not something Izzy was equipped to deal with. "You'll have to come with him if he makes an appointment."

"I definitely will. I'd love to see you at work. It's such a badass job. And as you can see, my man is a fan of ink."

Shell returned then with Izzy's food. "Here you go. Need anything else? Ketchup, hot sauce?"

"Hot sauce please."

A bottle of Tabasco appeared. When Shell smiled at Stephanie, some of the light in her eyes was missing. Though both women seemed to know each other and seemed pleasant enough, Izzy sensed some tension. "The usual, Steph?" Shell asked, her voice flatter than it had been speaking with Izzy.

"Please. Thanks, Shell." Stephanie gave her a smile that looked a little sad, almost apologetic.

"Kay, be back in a few." Shell bustled off, busy with the morning rush.

Beside her, Steph sighed and picked at her napkin.

Stay out of it. Not your business.

But hadn't she been sick of talking to herself in her empty house? Maybe it was time to be friendlier and speak to others. Just because she wasn't about to form close attachments didn't mean she needed to become the town bitch.

"You good?" she asked Steph.

The other woman seemed to snap out of her funk. "Yeah, sorry. Just working through some stuff with some of the MC members. I, uh, did something that broke their trust. I'm getting back in, but it's not always easy."

Huh. It was admirable. Everyone fucked up on occasion, but in Izzy's experience, no one stuck around long enough to work it out, apologize, or fix what they'd broken. She wasn't much better. New Orleans had become more complicated than she'd bargained for, so she left. As she'd done with the previous two places she'd lived. Maybe she could learn a thing or two from Stephanie.

"You obviously care enough to try and fix it." Didn't matter what Stephanie did. She wasn't hiding the fact that she screwed up and wasn't making excuses for her behavior. She seemed genuinely willing to fix it. That was more than enough for Izzy to like her.

"Well, I love Maverick. And his club is his family. His world. Hell, they were well on their way to becoming my family before I mucked it all up. So, yeah, I'll do damn near anything to fix it."

Just then Maverick wrapped his arms around Stephanie from behind. "They're all coming around, baby," he whispered, but not low enough for Izzy to miss it. "You forget that you saved the ass of each and every man in the club. They all recognize that." He pressed his lips to the curve of Stephanie's neck, and she sighed in pleasure, melting against his chest.

There was a story there, too. This MC seemed to be full of them. A quick peek at the table of bikers showed Jigsaw still wasn't among the breakfast crew. Interesting. Was he still having a rough time due to whatever memories the tattoo evoked? Part of her wanted another look at him. He couldn't possibly be as sexy as her mind remembered, could he?

Nope. Not going there.

A strange pang hit dead center in Izzy's chest when she turned back to Maverick and Stephanie. She had to glance away. Love was written all over those two, and Izzy had no idea how to react to those feelings. She could honestly say she'd never spent any significant amount of time with people who loved each other, romantic or otherwise. Her mother loved only herself, and Izzy hadn't let herself get close enough to anyone to love them. By now, her ability to love had to be stunted for sure.

She chatted off and on with Stephanie and Shell as she

finished her meal then made her way back outside. She'd walk the distance back home since jogging on a full stomach was never a good idea.

Instead of curing the feeling of restlessness, her experience at the diner had intensified them. She wasn't used to putting herself out there, and it was starting to grate on her. Drawing the phone number out of her pocket, she opened a new text and entered the information she was instructed to relay.

Izzy Monroe.

5'8".

150 lbs.

10 wins 2 losses.

When she was just about home, her phone buzzed.

Friday night. 10pm. Will send directions Friday afternoon.

Immediately, some of the tension left her spine. She had five days to get ready for her next match, which should keep her mind and body occupied.

And away from thoughts of hot, brooding bikers with sad stories.

CHAPTER FIVE

Jig spit his mouthguard into his hand and sucked tremendous gulps of icy water straight from the gallon jug.

Damn, he was thirsty. The exertion, plastic mouthguard, and heavy breathing left him parched every time.

A hefty hand slapped him on the back, making the jug slip from his lips. Freezing water sloshed over his bare chest and ran in arctic-cold streams down his abs. If he hadn't been so overheated, the blast of frigid water would have made his balls shrivel, but since he'd just beat the ass of some punk from out of state, he needed the cooldown.

"Good fucking fight, brother," Zach said. "Somehow you managed to wipe the floor with him even though I haven't seen you in my gym in two weeks." He raised an eyebrow and tossed Jig a towel.

"Been working out at home," Jig said as he wiped perspiration off his face and neck.

Zach grunted. "Fuck that. You need to spar, not just lift and hit the bag. Don't want to say you got lucky tonight, but this guy wasn't the toughest fucker you've faced."

Was Zach for real? Jig just knocked some shitbag out in two rounds, and Zach was ragging on him? He opened his mouth to fire back at his brother when Zach's face broke out in a shit-eating grin.

"Messing with ya," Zach said.

Fucker.

Still cocky like he was the one who kicked ass, Zach said, "But seriously, you need to get back in the gym before the next fight. The next guy ain't a slouch. When is it? Six weeks from now?"

Jig nodded. "Yeah, and I will. Just been a rough few weeks." His heart gradually returned to a resting rate as the thrill of the fight seeped from his body. Already, just a few minutes out, the heavy weight of sorrow he'd been carrying around for the past few weeks had lightened. Always did when he pushed his body to extremes.

Nothing compared to the intense physical exertion of battling another human being when it came to ridding the body and mind of whatever toxicity had invaded them. Jig had tried to replicate the feeling in the gym, pushing himself to the limit for hours with weights, running, even flipping tires, but he could never shake the grip of despair unless he was fighting a down and dirty match.

Sometimes, as he dodged punches and used his intelligence to outwit his opponents, he was struck with the difference between the man who occupied the ring and the man he'd once been and always had planned to be.

If the Lincoln of just seven years ago had been told he would one day become an MMA-fighting, outlaw biker with more sins on his back than the devil himself, he'd have fallen to the ground with belly-heaving laughter. The man he'd been in those days felt guilty for killing a spider. Never would he have imagined laying his hands on another human being and enjoying the fuck out of it. Craving it, really. But life had changed him in the harshest of ways. Not just changed what he believed or how he acted, but fundamentally changed who he was at the core. At a cellular level, he wasn't the man he'd been.

Some days he felt at peace with the hardened, tough biker and fighter he'd developed into. No one fucked with him anymore. If they tried, they ended up bleeding and broken. Being on top of the food chain had its perks, and security was one of them. Of course, Lefty was stupid enough to threaten that security, but Jig had no doubt his MC would take care of the Gray Dragons gang in time.

Once in a while, though, something would trip a memory, and he'd be ravaged by thoughts of Callie and how she'd hate the man he'd transformed into. Maybe hate was a strong word, but she'd sure as hell fear him. She'd loathed motorcycles, shaking her pretty blond head every time one zipped by them on the highway. Would she have changed her mind if she'd had the chance to experience the wind in her hair and the freedom the open road provided? Would she have gone off the deep end and morphed into a completely different version of herself had she been the one to come home to a scene straight out of a slasher film?

He'd never know.

Life sure was one confounding bitch.

"Hey, Jig, you with us, brother?"

Jig blinked the world back into focus. Shit, he'd really wandered. Zach was looking at him like he was two seconds away from dragging his ass to the looney bin, as were Maverick and Stephanie who must have joined them during his quick vacation from reality.

"You take a hard hit to the cranium or something?" Zach asked.

Jig shook his head. "Nah, I'm good. Just thinking about some shit for a minute. How'd you like your first walk on the dark side, Steph?" Up until she'd met Mav, she'd been quite the line-toeing FBI agent who would've only been at an underground fight if she was the one busting it up. But she had some martial arts experience, so she'd been interested in checking it out.

Surprise registered on her face before it lit up with happiness, making him feel like an ass. He didn't associate much with the ol' ladies unless he was forced to or they sought him out. Steph was constantly trying to engage him, so she looked thrilled that he'd initiated the conversation. Anything to keep his brothers from prying into his dark and twisted mind.

He bet Izzy wouldn't shy away from something like this. She seemed like the type of woman who could handle just about anything.

Not that he was thinking about her...again.

"This place is out of control," Steph said, a flush of excitement deepening her blue eyes. Her face was glowing as well; from excitement, adrenaline, or the heat of the fucking warehouse, he had no idea.

"Yeah, it takes a minute to get used to it." The locations of the fights varied constantly. It was rare to use a spot twice in a row. Less risk of the cops sniffing it out. Old warehouses were most common, sometimes up to ninety minutes away from Townsend. During the summer months, they'd occasionally be held on an abandoned farm or large clearing in the woods, but it was getting too fucking cold for outdoor games.

"I didn't expect it to be so..." She let her gaze wander around to where men drank, smoked, and generally acted like animals. There was a fair number of women present, all much less dressed than Stephanie, assets on display. "Grrr."

"Gets pretty intense," Zach responded. "Toni refuses to come to 'barbarian night.'" He crooked his fingers in air quotes. Zach's woman had never been a fan of the fights. Most of the women associated with the club tended to skip it. They typically had a wine-soaked girls' night instead or some shit. Jig avoided that scene like he avoided overused snatch.

"I like it," she said matter-of-fact, like she was deciding whether or not she liked a new blender. Looks-wise, Steph was his typical type to a T. Small, blond, blue-eyed, delicate looking. But she was tough as shit, sassy, and a ball-buster. That's where the appeal ended for him. Who the hell wanted a back-talking woman full of snark?

Not him.

Dressed in black pants that hugged her legs and a skin-tight Hell's Handlers T-shirt under a leather jacket, Steph nuzzled her nose into the crook of Maverick's neck. She was always wearing Handlers' shit. Mav seemed to have some fetish for the club's name scrawled across her tits.

Speaking of, the man in question leaned in and whispered something in Stephanie's ear that had her turning bright pink. Those two had been known to get it on in public a time or two so Jig wouldn't be surprised if they found a dark corner to go at it in a few minutes. Maybe another round of watching two near naked sweaty men wailing on each other would get her motor revving enough to throw caution to the wind.

"Can you two keep your pants on long enough to make it through the next match? I got some serious money riding on this one." Zach grinned and rubbed his palms together.

"Oh, fuck, is this the one?" Mav looked like a kid about to dive into a giant bowl of ice cream. "Been waiting for it." All three of them peeked at Jig then seemed to purposely avoid his gaze.

Jig frowned and shrugged into his own Handlers' tee. "Who's fighting?"

"Oh, just you wait, my brother," Mav said. Even Stephanie had a mischievous gleam in her eye. What the fuck was going on?

"All right, all right. We have a very special matchup for you next," the announcer boomed through the microphone. Jig followed the sound to the elevated ring and waited for the reveal. "Not too often do we get two bitches fighting, but what man doesn't love a little girl on girl action? Huh?"

This was the first time in five years Jig had seen a match between two females at one of these events. Underground fighting wasn't for the faint of heart. No biting, no eye-gouging, and no weapons were pretty much the only rules. Otherwise, it was anything goes. There were nights when bloodied men were carried out to cars limp and barely breathing. Jig had sent one or two of them that route himself.

He'd always had a thing for girly girls. Soft, gentle woman

who needed protection. A hardened fighter wouldn't trip his trigger. Maybe he'd just bail on the rest of the evening.

"First up, we've got Kristen, The Razor, Hudson." The crowd of drunk and horny men screamed and shouted as a beast of a woman jogged into view. She wore a hooded jacket, as was custom, and bent forward to slip through the ropes. When she arrived next to the emcee, she tugged the hoodie off. A buzz cut, a scorpion neck tattoo, and a six-pack that rivaled his own greeted the crowd. Her face was a mask of jaded concentration. The woman looked like she ate nails for breakfast, lunch, and dinner.

Jig would rather get stung by the scorpion on her neck than let her within ten feet of his dick. She'd probably rip the thing off and toss it across the room.

"Yikes," Steph whispered. "That is one scary lady."

"Don't worry, our girl'll be fine," Mav whispered back.

Our girl? Who the fuck were they talking about? Did they know the opponent? Jig wracked his brain but couldn't think of a single female he knew crazy enough to step into an underground fighting ring.

"And coming in on my left we have, Isabella, The Empress, Monroe."

"Here she comes, here she comes." Stephanie bounced up and down, dislodging Maverick's arm from her shoulders. "I'm so excited. I'm so nervous."

Who the fuck…?

Jig stared at the ring as the second woman, also in a hooded jacket, jogged out. As with the first woman, she removed her jacket when she reached the MC. Jig sucked in a breath—

Holy. Mother. Of. Fucks.

Izzy. The badass tattoo artist whose ink he swore he could feel deep in the meat of his thigh stood in the ring looking like a warrior ready for battle. Insane of course, but true.

Izzy was about to let someone attack her?

Every protective instinct he'd buried deep flared to life. Every lesson he'd learned from his Southern gentleman father as a young man about chivalry, shielding women, taking on a traditionally male role, came rushing back to him. Even though he'd met some tough as hell women who could more than take care of themselves since he'd joined the MC, he forgot all about them.

With tunnel vision, he took a step forward only to meet the surprisingly powerful slap of Mav's hand on his chest.

"What the fuck do you think you're doing?" Mav asked, his smirk so big it almost reached his ears. The asshole was loving every second of this.

"Nothing. I'm just getting a better view."

Both Zach and Mav laughed like his face and his ass had switched positions. "Told you he had a hard-on for her," Mav said to Zach, who was also enjoying this too fucking much.

"Guys," Stephanie said, slapping Mav's arm. "Leave Jig alone." She beamed at him, and he resisted the urge to roll his eyes. If Stephanie planned on playing matchmaker, she'd be sorely disappointed when her plan fell on its face. His reaction had been a combination of shock at seeing Izzy and a momentary lapse of judgment.

"Betting is closed," the announcer said. "Ladies, to your corners." Izzy strode to the front left corner of the ring with all the confidence of a queen. Hips swinging, flat stomach rippling as she walked, she looked fucking hot. Her hair was pulled back into a tight braid as it had been the last time he'd seen her, but tonight she'd coiled the long tail into a bun at the base of her scalp. Smart. Hair pulling was allowed, and that long braid would have been the perfect handle for her opponent.

She wore a mask of intense concentration, seemingly oblivious to the crowd. Did she know he was there? Had she seen his fight? He almost laughed out loud. Like she was supposed to give some kind of fuck that he was there. Like he was supposed to give a fuck whether she gave a fuck.

He was losing his mind. Maybe he *had* taken a hard hit to the head.

Izzy's opponent had a coach of some kind with her, but Izzy was alone. She shouldn't be alone. Even Jig had Zach in his corner. She'd need someone to hand her water, wipe away any blood—*Jesus, she might bleed*—and give her pointers. Someone to catch something she might miss about her opponent. Occasionally being so close to the action, fighters missed little details about their opponents a third party would notice.

Jig sure as hell wasn't volunteering for the job, but...

"How the fuck did you know she was gonna be here, Z? How do you even know her?" Jig asked.

"She's been training at the gym for hours every night over the past week. She's damn good, brother. Overheard her muttering to herself about a match and put two and two together."

"She by herself?"

Zach nodded. "Always."

"So why don't you go up there and be her fucking trainer?" He hadn't meant it to sound quite as hostile as it did but, come on, no one fought completely solo. Who the fuck would drag her out if something happened?

Running a hand through his perfectly styled blond hair, Zach pursed his lips. "Hmm, not a bad idea. Sure you don't want the job?"

"Yes, I'm fucking sure." Shit, all the tension-relieving benefits of his own fight were flying out the goddamned window as restless agitation crept back in.

"All right then. Super Zach to save the day." Zach shrugged out of his cut and handed it to Jig. "Keep it safe for me, brother." Then he clapped his hands together three times. "Gonna go win me some more cash." Bounding up to the ring, he let out a whistle and a holler that broke through Izzy's focus. She turned her head in the direction of the noise, and her gaze met Jig's.

A quick flare of the eyes and parting of the lips was her only acknowledgment of his presence but showed she hadn't known he was there. Ignoring the hot punch of desire that struck low in his gut as he imagined those lips parting for his cock, he dipped his chin once.

She blinked then lifted her own chin back at him. Zach ducked through the ropes and slung an arm across her shoulders, bringing his head close to hers. They whispered back and forth, and, if Jig wasn't mistaken, relief spread across Izzy's face.

He sure as fuck couldn't leave now. Crossing his arms, he stared at the ring and tried to block out the nagging question boring a hole into his brain.

Why the fuck did he care what the hell happened to Isabella Monroe?

CHAPTER SIX

Thank God for Zach.

Izzy's nerves were stretched so tight the air wafting by irritated her skin. She might not let people into her life easily, but she'd always had a trainer with her at an event like this. The moment she walked into the old warehouse and saw the hundreds of half-wasted men being rowdy and battle-drunk, she had realized her mistake. If she conked out during the match, there'd be no one to make sure she made it out in one piece. Nor would there be anyone to critique her form, catch any subtleties she might miss in her opponent, give her pointers, or slap her ass and tell her job well done if she won.

Then Zach, who owned the gym, appeared out of nowhere like a giant, tatted biker angel of mercy. Just as Zach wormed his big body through the ropes, she caught sight of Jig standing with Maverick and Stephanie, the same scowl he'd had in the shop plastered on his face. His dark hair was matted to his forehead, his shirt was soaked through with sweat, and a puff of purple was growing under his eye. Sometime between when she met him and now, he'd tamed his beard as well.

Was he a fighter? Had he fought tonight?

She'd been hiding out in the makeshift locker room, wanting complete solitude before she was called up. Missing his fight was a damn shame. Watching him unleash all that power bubbling just beneath the surface would have been an experience. She bet he looked beautiful in action. Most people would probably think she was crazy, but she found the dance of fighters attractive. Sexy at times. And she just had a feeling Jig's fight would have gotten her blood singing and her pussy wet.

He nodded at her, and contrary to how it made her feel in the shop, this time the chin dip warmed her heart. He'd sent Zach over. Somehow, she just knew it.

So she gave a nod of appreciation back and forced herself not to feel disappointed that he hadn't joined her himself.

"Damn, woman, you look ready to rock this bitch into next week," Zach said as he slung an arm around her shoulders. "Don't look too shabby in this tight-ass getup either."

She snorted out a laugh. The shorts she wore were barely bigger than some of her boy-short underwear, but she couldn't stand loose fabric when she fought. At some point, she'd become immune to prancing around in the ring in a sports bra and itty-bitty spandex shorts.

Zach put his head close to hers. "You good? Nerves under control?"

After flicking a quick glance at her opponent, Izzy nodded. "Think so. She's a beast."

He cupped the balls of her shoulders in his large hands and squeezed. Though he was hot, she felt nothing for the man as far as attraction, but it was nice to have the support. Her wayward brain couldn't help but wonder how her body would respond if it were Jig's hands on her.

"But she's on the bulkier side. Big shoulders, thick legs. I bet she's slow as shit," Zach replied.

"You think?" On the other side of the ring, her opponent stretched her arms high and bounced on the balls of her feet. Zach might be right. Due to the bulk of her deltoids, she didn't have quite the range of motion Izzy did.

"See?" He bumped her hip with his.

"Yeah." The buzz of excitement that had been absent from the night started to flow through her. She needed this bad. The release, the physical exertion, even the pain.

Maybe she needed to work on getting laid instead of beating her frustrations out of her system.

"How're you on the ground?" he asked. She'd mostly been working on her strikes at his gym. She'd have to find a sparring partner soon, but she was still confident in her groundwork. "Pretty damn good," she said.

"There you go, girl. Seeing some fire in your eyes now." He turned her to face the announcer and rubbed the muscles in her shoulders. "Go win me some cash. My woman's got a birthday coming up."

Izzy laughed. "And here I thought you were just interested in the sport."

Zach snorted. "Think green thoughts, babe."

Waving them to the center, the announcer spoke into the mic. "Okay, ladies, no biting, no eye gouging, no weapons. Anything else is fair game. Fight's over if one of you two fine things taps out or goes limp. Understand?" Both women jerked their chins in understanding.

Izzy inhaled a deep breath, pursed her lips, and blew it out to the count of six as she slowly rose to the balls of her feet. She liked to be ready to spring straight into action when the fight began.

"Feel free to throw in a tit grab or two. Give the crowd a thrill," the emcee said into the mic as he wagged his eyebrows. The man wore a button-up shirt that screamed seventies porn star, complete with gold chains and bushy mustache.

Izzy rolled her eyes. Over the years, she'd come to expect asinine comments at these games. Didn't mean they weren't annoying as shit. The crowd of mostly men laughed and screamed catcalls, though she swore she heard one voice above them all shout, "Shut the fuck up. Let 'em fight." If she didn't know better, she'd have sworn it was Jig. But the man was way too stoic for an outburst.

The announcer called for the fight to begin, and Izzy blocked out everything but the woman out for her blood. They danced in a circle once, twice, sizing each other up and seeking the perfect in. Never one to wait for someone else to make a move, Izzy lunged forward and caught her opponent with a jab to the midsection followed by a rib-crushing cross, then a quick hook to the side of her head.

"That's fuckin' right!" Zach screamed out. "Stay light on your feet, girl."

Right. She ducked a lightning fast hook that flew at her head and aimed another well-placed strike at The Razor's ribs. Her opponent grunted and stumbled back a step.

Not getting away from me, bitch.

Izzy came at her with another wicked combination. This time, The Razor crouched low and came in hard for the takedown. Izzy saw it coming a mile away and lifted her knee as The Razor opened her arms and tried to grab hold of Izzy's waist. Quick as the crack of a whip, Izzy's knee slammed into The Razor's chin, sending her head snapping back.

"Fuck yeah," Zach yelled. "Take that bitch down, girl. Get her on the ground."

Razor didn't lose her footing as Izzy hoped she would, but sprang up and down, shaking off the jarring knee to the face. She caught Izzy with a solid jab to the side.

"Ooof." That shit hurt.

Izzy couldn't help but smile as she breathed and absorbed the pain. It fueled her, chased away her demons, gave her something to work with. She was fucked in the head. A psychiatrist would have a field day picking around in her brain to find out why she enjoyed the pain of taking a punch.

Razor's left hand came around the back of Izzy's neck, grabbing and holding her close. Izzy returned the move, clasping her fingers across the back of Razor's neck. Locked in the clinch, she knew what was in store for her, a hard knee to the gut. But Izzy's reflexes were fast as fuck, and this was her absolute favorite takedown. She turned her head to the left, looking away from Razor at the same time she slammed her right forearm up under Razor's arm, breaking her hold. Then she rolled her right shoulder inward and knocked Razor's arm clear off.

The action spun Razor straight into Izzy's arms, and she grabbed her opponent around the waist, used her legs and hips to lift the larger woman, and thrust forward, taking her to the ground.

The high of adrenaline and triumph coursed through Izzy. Fuck, yes, she loved this shit.

Sparing a fraction of a second, she glanced up and right into Jig's captivated eyes.

The man was impressed with her.

She was impressed with herself. Time to put this match to bed.

WEDGED BETWEEN JIG and Maverick, Stephanie jumped up and down, slapping their arms and screaming, "Oh, my God! Get her! Get her!"

Jig laughed as Steph grabbed both men's arms and dug her fingernails in. "Jesus, woman, leave me a little skin, would ya?"

Stephanie patted his abused arm, but never tore her gaze from the ring. "Sorry. So sorry, but would you look at her? She is such a badass. We are totally going to be friends."

What? Women were weird.

Steph faced him, smile toothy and wide. "And were you actually laughing at me? Like a sound that expresses enjoyment of life? I knew you had it in you."

The squeal that came from her had him wincing. Shit, at that decibel, dogs from the neighboring town would come running. He rolled his eyes and playfully pushed her chin away so she was facing the ring once again. Out of the corner of his eye, he caught Mav's slack-jawed expression.

Jesus, he knew how to have fun. He could enjoy life. It shouldn't be such a headline-making event.

Jig tuned out Stephanie's excited ramblings and focused on

the ring. He hadn't known what to expect from Izzy, but it wasn't the skilled fighter taking names in the ring. She was fierce, full of concentration, intelligent strikes and maneuvers, and like Stephanie said, she was just plain badass.

She was also hot as fuck. So hot he had to adjust his stance as the fit of his shorts grew uncomfortably tight. A problem most men in the room probably had, if their dicks weren't too drunk to work. But unlike most men in the room, it wasn't the vision of the two women shedding the rest of their clothes and switching from fighting to fucking; it was straight-up Izzy herself.

In every calculated movement she made, her strength was evident, with muscles flowing and bunching under her tattooed skin. And even though she was engaged in a physical battle, there was still an overtly feminine quality to her. Something he couldn't describe. The experience was nothing like watching two men fight.

Izzy was all woman.

On the ground, she grappled with her opponent for about a minute, and Jig's respect grew tenfold. Damn, she was impressive. He could probably learn a thing or two from her. As the bell dinged, indicating the end of the first round, he had to hold himself back from rushing to her. She didn't so much as glance in his direction, but guzzled water and listened intently to everything Zach told her.

Once or twice Zach demonstrated something, showing her an effective maneuver to use against her opponent. Despite being the smaller woman, she had this in the bag. Jig could feel it in his bones.

"Enjoying the fight?" Mav asked with a smirk, his eyes drifting down to Jig's crotch before returning to his face.

"Shut the fuck up. Maybe you should be paying more attention to your woman and less to my dick."

"Huh?" Mav spun, just realizing Stephanie had wandered toward the bar. "Goddamnit!" Mav growled as he stormed off after her. "Woman! What the fuck did I tell you about leaving my side?"

With a chuckle, Jig focused back on the ring. The second round began much as the first, but within thirty seconds, Izzy had used one of the techniques Zach recommended and had her opponent back on the ground. Without hesitating a second, Izzy flipped her body until her legs were across The Razor's chest. She jerked Razor's arm into a painful armbar, arching her hips to increase the angle and give Razor the feeling that her arm would snap in two.

The Razor withstood the position for about ten seconds then slapped her palm against the mat. The crowd erupted in unruly cheers and more than a few sexual slurs. Jig wanted to lay out every one of the motherfuckers who shouted something about Izzy's tits or, even worse, her pussy.

Rising in the middle of the ring, Izzy extended an arm to help her defeated opponent up then gave Razor a back-slapping hug before the announcer grabbed her wrist and lifted her arm high. Zach whooped and hollered, running to the center of the ring. Arms coming around Izzy's waist, much in the same way Razor failed to achieve earlier, Zach lifted Izzy off her feet and paraded her around the ring for a victory lap.

Jig couldn't help but smile at the elation on her face.

After a few moments of celebrating in the ring, Zach guided her straight to where Jig waited. Izzy was grinning from ear to ear, and a spark of electricity crackled all around her, almost sexual in nature. Jig got that. He loved nothing more than a hard fuck after a victorious fight.

Was she the same? Would she go out and find some asshole to fuck a few orgasms out of her? Shit, the thought of it made him want to climb back in that ring with whomever she chose for the job. Maybe she'd just go home and take care of it herself, plunging a thick vibrator in and out of her pussy and buzzing it across her clit until she was as sweaty as she was now.

Jesus, what the hell was wrong with him?

"Damn, Jig, our girl was on fire!" Zach licked his finger and touched it to Izzy' shoulder, making a sizzling sound.

Before Jig had the chance to respond, or even think of what to say, Stephanie bounded over and flung her arms around Izzy. "You are seriously the most badass woman I've ever met."

"Whoa," Izzy said with a laugh as she caught Stephanie. "Had a few drinks, have you?"

Mav snorted. "A few turned into many about twenty minutes ago." He pulled his ol' lady off Izzy and wrapped his arms around her waist from behind. As Steph fussed at him for making fun of her, he nipped at her neck and she giggled.

There was a time when Jig hadn't been able to tolerate being in the same room as happy couples, but he'd long since hardened his heart and shoved his emotions into a two-foot-thick vault. Now he reacted no differently than he did watching two people shake hands.

"Oh, I just had an amazing idea!" Stephanie shouted right next to Mav's ear, making him flinch and draw back.

"Shit, babe, wasn't planning on hearing aids for another forty years or so."

Giggling, she rubbed Mav's arm. "Sorry. Izzy, what are you doing now?"

"Oh, uh…" She shrugged. "I was just going to go home and crash."

So, the vibrator it was. Jig had no business thinking this way, but a tiny bit of relief hit him knowing she wouldn't be searching for a flesh and blood cock that night.

"No, no, no! That's so boring. Come to the clubhouse. We're having a party. You should come. Shouldn't she come, Mav?"

Jig hadn't known Stephanie all that long, so it was safe to say he didn't know if this bubbly thing was her drunk-norm, but it sure as hell was entertaining.

However…Izzy at the clubhouse?

He needed to get wasted and find someone to fuck, and the last thing he wanted was the strange attraction he had for Izzy scratching at his back all night.

"She should definitely come." Mav might have been speaking to Steph, but his snarky gaze was all for Jig. "What do you think, Jig? You want Izzy to *come*?" When he stressed the word "come," Jig's dick twitched.

Asshole.

He cleared his throat and met Izzy's gaze. She was amped, pumped from her fight. As ready to fuck as he was. But it would never happen. Izzy was the exact opposite of the women he sought out.

"Sure, she can do whatever she wants." He didn't miss the quick flash of disappointment that crossed her face at his statement. "I'm heading out. See you guys later."

Without another word and ignoring Stephanie's muttered "dickhead," he weaved his way through the crowd.

His night was fucked. He shouldn't even go to the party, but he had no choice. The perimeter they'd been working on non-stop was finally complete. His brothers needed to blow off some steam. It was pretty much mandatory fun.

How the hell was he supposed to find someone to fuck when he had some weird attraction to the kickass woman he'd just left behind?

And God fucking help any of his brothers who came on to her.

CHAPTER SEVEN

What was she doing here?

Izzy had moved from New Orleans to Tennessee because she wanted fewer entanglements. Fewer people with the chance to screw her over. She'd had a roommate walk out three months before the lease ended, leaving Izzy in a lurch. Three months! Izzy was stuck paying double rent. It was the last straw in a long string of letdowns. She'd known taking on a roommate was a mistake, but had fallen in love with the expensive two-bedroom apartment in the French Quarter of New Orleans. And she'd paid the price…literally.

She was sick and tired of people being unreliable. Such a shame because, at her core, she wanted social connections. Enjoyed interacting with others, playing, having fun, but the pain of desertion and neglect far outweighed the pleasure of other's company. Never once had someone been willing to put her above themselves. So she'd closed herself off emotionally, and when Rip offered her the job, for the tenth time in three years, she'd jumped at the chance to separate herself physically.

Small town. Peaceful life. Easy to fade into the background and avoid people beyond working hours.

And here she was, four weeks after moving to Tennessee, letting people into her life. Giving them the opportunity to hurt her. No. Not this time. This time she'd keep the walls around her heart and mind. She could have a few drinks, blow off steam, chat with the girls, maybe even find someone to supplement her vibrator when the urge for some human flesh grew too strong.

The image of one particular scowling biker popped up in her mind, but she shoved it away. He was not for her in any way. No matter how he made her lady bits stand up and pant.

Didn't really matter who she chose. No one would be allowed close enough to actually have an impact on her life or any power over her.

And that's why she allowed herself to walk into a clubhouse full of bikers.

Oh, and whores. Yikes, the whores.

A lady—woman—wobbled by on what had to be six-inch heels, wearing an outfit she could have purchased in the children's section. Izzy could rock sexy clothes with the best of them and was firmly a "to each his or her own" believer, but come on, something should be left to the imagination.

"Izzy!" Stephanie screeched, waving from a cluster of women huddled at the bar. At least this group had clothing on. "Get your champion ass over here, girl." Five sets of eyes landed on her, a million questions in their gazes.

Again, what was she doing here?

Had nothing to do with the sexy, brooding man who made certain neglected parts of her body tingle.

Nothing.

With a deep breath, Izzy wove her way through the throng of bikers to the group. Thankfully, she recognized Shell from the diner as well as Stephanie. "Hey, Izzy," Shell said. "Nice to see you again." Her sunny smile matched her curly golden hair.

"Thanks, Shell. Good to see you, too." Polite, formal.

"Heard you kicked some serious ass tonight," Shell went on.

"Oh, my God, she so did!" Stephanie said, her eyes growing wide. "Let me introduce you. This is Toni," Steph said of the brunette on her left. "Toni owns the diner and is Zach's woman. Zach coached Izzy through her fight tonight, T."

Toni held her hand out. "Nice to meet you. Zach told me you

were amazing tonight. Glad he could help."

"You own the diner? Guess that means I have you to blame for the tight fit of my jeans?" Izzy relaxed a bit when Toni threw back her head and laughed. So far, the women were awesome.

"I'd say sorry, but I wouldn't mean it. The more you gals eat, the less I have to work out." Toni rubbed her hands together and evil-laughed.

A groan left Izzy as she thought about the cinnamon roll waffles she'd finally succumbed to two days ago. "That's just mean. And so smart. Hey, thanks for loaning your man out tonight. He knows his stuff."

Shell snorted, and the others snickered.

Izzy looked at their laughing faces. "What'd I miss?"

With a roll of her eyes, Toni said, "Zach's the club's enforcer on top of owning the gym. He has a bit of experience in fighting, I guess you could say."

"Got it." Enforcer. Interesting. He came across as too…fun to be the enforcer. Somehow, she'd imagined an enforcer would wear a perpetual scowl and glare at everyone like he hated them. Hmm, Jig seemed to fit that bill.

Stephanie linked her arm through Izzy's and turned to the other women. "This is Jasmine. She just moved here from Arizona. She's managing Toni's diner. You met Shell, and this is Mama V. She's Viper's ol' lady," Steph gestured to a graying woman with long wavy hair.

Izzy held up a hand. "Hey, everyone."

A colossus of a man behind the bar wandered over their way. "This has to be the woman Mav was talking about. I was told to look out for a hot as fuck chick with a long braid, wicked nice tits, an ass you could bounce a quarter off, and who could kick my ass in under two minutes."

"Oh, Maverick." Stephanie dropped her forehead to her palm and shook her blond head back and forth while the others rolled their eyes. This was an intriguing group. In the past, if one of her friends' boyfriends called her hot or commented on the state of her ass, they'd be jumping across the circle to claw her eyes out. These women seemed confident and secure in the knowledge that their men loved them even if they were surrounded by willing women.

Izzy smiled at the attractive bartender. She couldn't stop her lips from curling in delight. Some of the party vibes in the air were rubbing off on her. Plus, what woman didn't love compliments about their body? "Well, considering I did kick some serious ass tonight, and I am the proud owner of this..." She twisted her right hip forward and slapped her own ass while winking. "Looks like you found the right person."

"Whooo!" All the women chorused while hooting and clapping.

"Shit, Izzy, you're gonna fit in here just fine," Toni said.

"Jesus," the bartender muttered. "I'm LJ, and I've been instructed to keep your glass full of whatever you want all night. On the house. President's orders. Apparently, Zach bet on you for him, and you won him a decent chunk of change."

Well, far be it for her to buck the president's order. "Thank you. Bourbon, please. The good stuff."

LJ sent her a panty-scorching grin. "Nice choice." He grabbed a bottle off the shelf and poured her a double. "Holler if you need anything, babe," he said before moving down the bar.

"So when did you move here, Izzy?" Toni asked.

The bourbon slid its way to her stomach in a perfect combination of burn and soothe. She took a quick second sip then addressed Toni's question. Gave her something to do besides scan the room for Jig. Before she arrived, she made herself a promise she would not seek him out. "About four weeks ago. Moved from New Orleans. Just looking for a slower paced life."

Toni laughed. "So you came to a Handlers' party?"

"Seriously," said the woman named Jazz. She had chin-length, shiny black hair with pink streaks hiding throughout the bottom layer. She seemed a little quieter, more reserved than the others.

Maybe for the fact she was new in town as well. What did these ladies do, adopt all the newcomers?

Izzy pointed at Stephanie and mock scowled. "Yeah, I tried to go home, but Steph wasn't having it."

Steph just shrugged. Whatever tension she'd sensed between Shell and Stephanie seemed to be gone tonight, or at least put on hold. Or at least drowned out by the free-flowing alcohol.

"Is it true you're the new tattoo artist Rip hired?" Toni asked.

"That's me," Izzy said. "He trained me years and years ago and has been trying to get me to move here ever since. I finally had enough of city life and took him up on the offer."

"I've wanted a tattoo for a while, and I know exactly what I want," Shell said. "Maybe I'll book an appointment with you."

Izzy swallowed another healthy sip of her drink. Already, the smooth bourbon was loosening her muscles, putting her at ease around all her new-found friends...errr, acquaintances, she meant. Friends had the power to hurt you, acquaintances did not. "Why haven't you done it yet?"

Shell's face pinked, and Toni burst out laughing. "Because she happened to mention it in front of Copper, and he flipped his shit. Told her there was no way in hell Rip was touching any part of her body."

Staring down at her beer bottle like she could somehow disappear down the neck, Shell waved her hand. "You guys know him. He's just overprotective about stuff."

Izzy's forehead scrunched. "Wait, are you two—" A sharp elbow to her side had her huffing out a breath. "Shit, Steph, you hit harder than The Razor did."

"Damn straight." Steph chuckled then gave a quick shake of her head.

Message received. Talk of Copper and Shell was off limits. Toni changed the subject, bringing up some changes they were implementing at the diner now that Jazz was on staff and taking over many of the managerial duties.

Izzy followed the conversation until heat bloomed across the back of her neck. All the little hairs rose to attention and a shiver so in contrast to the warmth coursed through her. For about thirty seconds, she ignored it, until the sensation grew too intense to dismiss. As subtly as she could manage, she peeked to her right and locked gazes. He sat across the room, alone at a table, nursing a drink and staring at her with laser focus.

She felt the weight of that stare in her bones. In her nipples. In her long-neglected pussy. Damn, the man was potent. He had this whole pissed off, don't-fuck-with-me, I-hate-the-world vibe, and for some insane reason, her body wanted all that angry passion directed her way.

Typically, she went after easygoing guys, guys she could boss around, pushovers. In bed, Izzy had no problem directing the show. She'd tell them what she wanted, get hers, and send them on their way. A dominant man wouldn't put up with that. A dominant man might try to get under her skin or into her life. No chance of that with a man who took a back seat to her control.

But, for some reason, ever since she'd met Jig, she had this fantasy of him on top of her, holding her hands down, teasing her and denying her the one thing she wanted until she was begging for it.

Crazy. Because if there was one thing Izzy didn't do when it came to men, it was begging. She gave the orders, and if they couldn't be filled, then bye-bye, buddy. Plenty of others out there, and there was always her vast collection of self-love toys to get the job done.

"Damn, girl, that man is looking at you like you're the last steak on earth and he's starving," Toni said in a low voice that startled Izzy.

"What? Jig? No," she chuckled a shaky laugh. "I'm pretty sure he can't stand me. He just glares and tries to turn me to dust with his eyes."

Steph snorted. "He's not trying to kill you, Izzy. He's eye-fucking you."

It was Izzy's turn to snort. "No way." Shit, did someone turn up the heat? She fanned herself.

"Oh, my God, you're getting all flushed. You want his cock!" Steph rubbed her hands together in glee.

"Okay, if you're all gonna start talking about my boys' body parts, I'm out of here," Mama V said with a wave.

"Hmm," Toni said after she drained her glass. "This is the first time I've seen him stray from his type. Know what I mean, Shell?"

Shell nodded. "I know. I think it's great. You should totally go for it, Izzy. I think you'd be good for him."

Okay, someone needed to pull the emergency brake on this freaking runaway train. "Go for what? There's nothing to go for. He has a type?" Whoops, that sounded way too interested.

All four of the girls laughed.

"I've been here six weeks, and even I have his type pegged," Jazz said as she adjusted her slinky black top. "Tiny, blond, blue eyes, delicate, non-assertive, timid…am I right?"

Izzy's jaw dropped, and she almost spilled her drink as she lifted her hand. "What? Seriously? And you guys think he's interested in me?" She barked out a laugh. "Uhh, hello?" Izzy grabbed the end of her braid. "Black hair, tall, dark eyes, snarky as shit, and not a delicate bone in my body. You girls are nuts."

"Hey," Toni said with a shrug. "I just call it like I see it."

"Well, let's be real here," Steph said then turned to the bar. "Another Mic Ultra, LJ," she called out. Two seconds later, LJ handed her a bottle, mumbling something about her fake beer. "Are those girls really his type, or is he just trying to replace—?" Her mouth flapped open and shut as though she hadn't meant to say so much. "Never mind, I'll shut up now."

Izzy wagged her finger back and forth. "No, no, no, you can't do that. Replace what? Or who?"

A heavy sigh came from Shell. "All right, I've been part of the club since long before Jig came around. Most of what I know about him is rumors and gossip. But I know he was married and had a kid and a job working for NASA. I don't know the details, but his family was killed. Rumor has it, he went a little crazy after that before he connected with the club." A sad smile crossed her face. "His wife was a short, tiny, gentle, blond woman, or so I've heard. Rumor also has it his, uh, tastes run toward the darker, rougher side, and a lot of the guys think he's working his way through all the delicate blond women in America to punish himself or his wife for dying. I don't know. What I do know is that the women never come back for a second round."

Flicking a discrete glance in his direction, Izzy asked, "Think he hurts them? Or just kicks them out?"

"No, I don't think he hurts them," Toni piped in. "He steers clear of friendships with us for the most part, but he's quietly protective, even more than most of these guys. I think, well, I'm guessing he scares them away with his intensity."

Intensity, huh? She must be crazy because hearing that Jig was scaring women away with his rough, angry rage-fucking had her pussy clenching with need.

So much for tonight's fight settling her.

CHAPTER EIGHT

Her presence was like a tight-fitting shoe, slowly rubbing the skin off the back of his heel one painful step at a time. Whenever he looked up, there she was, laughing, smiling, fucking flirting with LJ.

The women sure seemed to love her, dragging her straight into the fold. Who the fuck knew what they were talking about? More than a few times, their gazes drifted in his direction. Was he the hot topic of conversation?

Jesus, why the fuck did he care? Izzy was not his type. He liked his women reserved, almost shy. There was something about seeing the wide-eyed shock on their faces when he shoved them against a wall, pulled their head back by their hair, or slapped his palm across their ass. He wasn't a jerk, wasn't trying to hurt or scare the women he fucked, but there was a small part of him that got a thrill from seeing a spark of uncertainty in their eyes.

Shit, he probably needed years of therapy. He knew he was fucked up, so that had to count for something, right?

"Good fight?" Rocket asked as he took an empty seat at Jig's table. Rocket wasn't much of a talker, which had always been a positive in Jig's view. Unless the man was blitzed, then his tongue loosened. Like tonight, apparently.

"Not bad. Won before the second round was over." Jig sipped his drink and tried to keep his focus on Rocket instead of stealing glances at the warrior woman fucking with his head.

"Good deal. What the fuck you doing sitting over here like some loser at a high school dance drooling over the prom queen?"

An innocent enough question, but Rocket had no idea how it sliced into Jig's gut. His wife had been prom queen. And he'd been prom king. Lifetimes ago, it had been the most perfect night of his life. He'd taken her virginity, given her his, and thought she'd be the only woman he'd ever sleep with. She'd be fucking disgusted if she had any idea how many women he'd fucked and didn't give a single shit about. The him of years ago would be just as disgusted, but now, dead inside, he didn't give a shit.

"Fuck off, Rocket."

"That's all you got? Thought you were supposed to be the smart one."

"What's up with you? You've been in a shit mood for weeks. Ever since you pulled that chick from the motel and brought her to the hospital." A few weeks ago, Rocket had rescued a woman Lefty kidnapped and planned to sell to the highest bidder. She'd been in piss-poor shape when Rocket found her, and something had been off with him ever since.

"I'm fine. Worry about your own shit, Jigsaw. Like why you can't seem to get off your ass and go after that sexy as fuck woman who has your dick all twisted up."

Jig drained his glass and grunted. Fuck, he needed a few more drinks to properly dull his mind. "If I wanted her, I'd go after her. Not interested."

"Here"—Rocket slid his nearly full glass across the table —"I'm done for the night. Don't want her, huh? So you good with all the puppy-dog looks LJ's sending her way?"

Fuck. So, it hadn't been his imagination. LJ had a hard-on for the sexy tattoo artist. "LJ's a fuckin' child. He doesn't stand a chance."

Rocket's lips quirked. "He may be young, but gossip around

the club is he's swinging ten inches at the ladies."

"How the fuck do you know that? He's a prospect. Honeys are off limits to him." Handlers' Honeys were the girls who hung around the club, offering their vast services to the members. Club whores for lack of a more accurate description. Only full patched members were allowed a crack at them.

"Didn't hear it from a Honey. He can go after whoever he wants as long as it's not a Honey." Rocket lifted a hand. "All chicks talk."

After running a hand through his hair, Jig downed Rocket's drink in three gulps. "You wanna tell me why we're sitting here talking about a prospect's dick?"

With a shrug, Rocket smirked. "Because I figure you'd rather talk about that than why you're only interested in punishment-fucking women who resemble your dead wife."

Despite the pulsing music and partying crowd, the silence that descended between the two men seemed to overtake the room. Jig sent his brother a cold, deadly stare. Rocket had some balls on him, that was for sure. No one, not even Copper, ever broached the subject of Jig's family. It was off limits, untouchable unless someone wanted a trip to the local ER.

But Rocket, the fucker, didn't know the definition of fear. Nothing intimidated him, and he said whatever the fuck he wanted. Apparently, tonight he wanted to rake Jig over burning hot coals.

"Leave it, brother," Jig said, his voice like ice.

Another shrug was the only reaction he got in return. "Tired of everybody pussy-footing around the subject. You ain't the only one with shit in your past. You ain't even the only one with seriously fucked-up shit in your past. But you are the only one letting that woman slip through your fingers." He pointed to Izzy who was now dancing with the rest of the women.

The minute his eyes landed on her, his cock sprang to life. She moved gracefully, sensually, pure sex in tight denim. As she moved, she raised her arms and tipped her head back, lost in the beat and perhaps a little drunk. The ends of her braid swished back and forth across the top of her very tight ass.

Jig was struck with a visual of Izzy, bent over the arm of his couch, her hair wound multiple times around his fist, a low moan leaving her lips as he tugged, and a very visible Jig-sized hand print across that bitable ass.

He almost laughed out loud. As if Izzy would tolerate that kind of fucking. She was way too brassy for what he required. Probably needed the upper hand during sex. Hmm, maybe he needed to use her personality to his advantage. A few times of hanging out with her and her ball-busting ways and his dick was bound to lose interest.

"Good pep talk, brother," Jig said as he rose to his feet.

Rocket watched him through narrowed eyes. "What are you up to?"

"Nothing for you to get your panties in a twist about. Besides, you seem to know everything. I'm sure you'll figure it out." Jig rapped his knuckles against the table. "Later."

Just as he started toward Izzy, LJ moved in behind her and placed his large hands on her hips. She peeked up and over her shoulder, smiling as she realized it was him.

A hot flash of jealousy stabbed at his gut.

"Hey, Jig," Rocket called after him.

"What?" he barked.

"Church tomorrow morning at nine." Any traces of fun, teasing, or levity were gone from Rocket's expression.

"Shit." The air in Jig's lungs felt like it was being sucked out. "He get another girl?" Fucking Lefty. The prick had been warned the Handlers would rain hell down on him if he continued trafficking women.

"Think it's worse than that, man. Got some chatter from the streets about a place he's housing them."

Them? Jig's stomach rolled. Could Lefty have a stash of women they weren't aware of? The thought was sickening. "I'll be there."

Rocket nodded. "Good luck, brother. Better hurry before she's swooning over those ten inches."

Flipping his brother the bird, Jig made his way toward Izzy and LJ. "Fuck off, prospect," he said when he was a foot behind them.

They stopped dancing and turned. LJ's hands fell from her waist and were replaced by her own hands and a pissed-off look. Yes, this was precisely what he needed. The woman to give him sass and attitude. Nothing would kill his dick's interest faster.

"She ain't a Honey, Jig. Not off limits to me." LJ clearly had a thing for her. How could he not? A light sheen of sweat dotted her forehead, and her chest rose and fell in a gentle pant. Minor exertion from dancing.

"Ain't cockblocking you, brother. Just need to talk to her for a second." That little half-truth would stay between Jig and the alcohol he'd consumed.

LJ rolled his shoulders and glanced at the ceiling before returning his gaze to Jig's. "Five minutes," he said, then pressed a kiss to Izzy's cheek. "I'll be back, darlin'," he said. "Don't let this moody asshole push you around."

Izzy snorted out a laugh. "He could try." When she raised an eyebrow at Jig, he felt a fist squeeze around his cock. What the fuck?

"Hey, prospect," Jig called as LJ strode away. "I'll take all the fucking time I want. Remember your place. Don't see a patch on your back yet." In reality, LJ was one of, if not the best, prospect they had. He was set to patch in soon, and short of betraying the club, nothing would keep that patch off his back. Still, it was fun to remind him he wasn't quite there yet.

"Did you have to do that?" Izzy asked. "Wouldn't it just be easier to whip it out and compare lengths?" Her tone was harsh, but a teasing sparkle lit her eyes.

Of course, her question reminded him of Rocket's comment on LJ's dick size. Jig was no slouch but, come on, ten inches? That was the stuff porn stars were made of.

Jigsaw

"Would have, fighter-girl, but I didn't want to shock all you lovely ladies in here. It's not something everyone's used to seeing."

"Ha! I'm sure it's nothing I haven't seen before, stud. You should see some of the cocks I've put my mark on." She winked and folded her arms across her body in a defiant stance. "Ink-wise, of course." There it was. Ball-busting. And he hated it. Perfect.

"One time—" she continued, apparently not letting it go.

"Want to train tomorrow?" he said just to end her cock tirade.

"Huh? What?"

Finally, he'd stolen the advantage. "Train. At the gym. Tomorrow. MMA."

"I get what you meant, bubba. Just didn't expect the offer from you."

He shrugged. "Zach's been on my case about sparring more. Told me you needed to as well. Figure I'll be at the gym, you'll be at the gym, we might as well work together."

She wasn't very good at hiding surprise and was standing still in the middle of the dancing crowd. "Oh, um, sure. Okay. That sounds good. I get off work at eight and usually head straight there. Zach's kindly kept the place open late a night or two for me."

"Good. See you a little after eight, then." Jig nodded and started to back away. "Want me to send your little boy-toy back over. That puppy is dying for a good belly rub."

Izzy threw her head back and let out a throaty laugh that had his dick thickening once again. "Please," she said with a wave of her hand. "The boy's cute and a fun dance partner, but I'm not looking for a child," she said. Then she winked and played with the tail end of her braid. The combination of the buzzed sides, tight braid, and smooth exposed neck made his mouth water. "I'd eat that boy alive."

Perfect comment. Jig had no desire to be consumed by a man-eater. If anyone was going to do the eating, it was him.

"See you tomorrow night," he said, giving her a two-fingered salute.

CHAPTER NINE

Jig leaned back in his chair and propped his right ankle on his left knee as he waited for Copper to speak. A black cloud had followed the prez into the chapel, and every man in the room was eerily quiet. Whatever news Copper had, it wasn't going to be good. Calling church for nine am after an epic party when ninety percent of the guys were hungover and over-fucked? That never happened.

Until it did.

Copper tracked to the head of the table and planted his giant hands flat on the smooth surface, allowing his head to drop between his shoulders. "Sorry about the early hour," he said without looking up. "Guess you all figured out I wouldn't have called you here this early if it wasn't serious." He raised his head and studied his men, mouth flat, eyes troubled.

Dread slithered through Jig's gut. Images of his wife, broken and bleeding on their kitchen floor came at him in a barrage of misery. She hadn't been raped, but the violence against women in their little slice of the world was bringing back all kinds of horrific memories.

As it often did when shit was about to go down, the scar on his face burned as though a fresh slice. It had become a sort of barometer for bad news. Resisting the urge to rub away the phantom pain, Jig bit the inside of his lower lip, transferring the discomfort elsewhere.

"We had prospects rotating through a watch of the clubhouse's perimeter all night. About halfway through the party, Rocket went outside the gate and did a wider border search. Caught two of Lefty's guys in the woods. He took one down and dragged him back. We got him down in The Box. The other ran off, probably straight to his boss."

"Fuck," Jig spit out. That must have been right before Rocket spoke with him last night. No wonder his brother seemed off.

"Yeah, fuck's a good word for it," Rocket said, all business. "The one that got away had a sniper rifle, and the guy I tagged had a hand grenade. I think we'da spotted him before he got too close, but he still could have done some damage. Tossed a grenade in one of the towers or taken out a section of fencing."

"So Lefty isn't rolling over," Mav said. He had a particular hatred for Lefty since he'd sent some of his goons after Stephanie a few weeks ago.

"No," Copper said. "He's actively looking to take us down."

Zach slapped his hand on the table. "Doesn't make any fucking sense. He doesn't have the manpower to take us out. Is he just stupid?"

"I think his ego's just bigger than his brain." Copper leaned back in his chair. His green eyes were flat with dark smudges circling under them. He probably hadn't gotten a lick of sleep the night before. Like the heavy weight of running the club was pressing down too hard on his massive shoulders. He might be a big man, but everyone had their limit, and the club had been under immense strain for the past few months. Copper took every damn thing that happened to his club personally and made it his mission to remedy it.

"I want the women covered," he said. "At all times. I don't think we need to be on lockdown just yet, but I want your ol' ladies guarded. Screw, you get with Zach and work on schedules and assignments for protection as well as getting more eyes on Lefty."

"You got it, prez," Screw said. He sat a little taller in his chair.

Jigsaw

It was reassuring to see the kid taking his first official duty as a patched brother so seriously.

"No parties for a while. Don't want the Honeys around here either. If you think any of the regulars need to be shadowed, let Screw know. We're not taking any chances with lives here. Lastly, I think we should close the bar to the public as well." He turned to Jig. "How're we with cash?"

For the past three years, Jig had been serving as treasurer. He had a way with numbers, and the club had been thriving since he'd taken over the books. "We're good, Cop. More than good, actually. Loan business is bringing in a ton of green these days. Closing the bar for a stretch shouldn't impact our bottom line. Fuck, we give out so much free booze, that bar is not our moneymaker."

A huge sigh heaved Copper's chest, and he tugged at his red beard before saying, "We need to end this shit before someone we love is hurt...again. And before Lefty gets his hand on any more women. I want to know his schedule, who he associates with. I want his life turned inside and out. We won't be leaving any loose ends. I'd like to avoid a bloody war if possible. We're gonna start small, fuck up his drug deals, try to turn guys against him. That doesn't work, we'll step it up, but let's see if we can do this without too much bloodshed."

The men murmured their agreement. Part of Jig wanted to argue. Lefty needed to be stopped and stopped permanently, as in six-feet-under, but he got it. War meant loss of life on both sides. Jailing of club members, women left without their men, and maybe even harmed themselves.

War would be a last resort.

Copper rose from his chair. "Zach, you're with me in The Box. Fifteen minutes."

The Box was a basement room, probably originally meant as a storm shelter of some kind. Basically, a boxy room the Handlers used for...sensitive matters. Like extracting information from enemies hellbent on destroying the MC. Jig didn't envy the man waiting on Copper and Zach's company.

"Looking forward to it, Cop." Zach may be a fun brother with pretty-boy good looks who was head over heels in love with his woman, but he could be the meanest sonofabitch when crossed. And Copper? Well, within Copper lay a beast no one wanted to let out. Ninety-five percent of the time he kept his wild temper under control but, fuck, that five percent stuck with a man after he'd seen it in action.

"All right, we're done here. I want all you fuckers safe. Got me?"

"Got it," chorused the group.

Jig left the chapel and headed for his office, a small room next to Copper's office where he managed the club's finances and ran the loan shark business. Since his focus had been on assisting with the clubhouse security the past few weeks, he'd lagged on the bookkeeping. It took him all fucking day, but he updated, balanced, and organized everything he'd been putting off. Really, he didn't mind. Numbers made sense. Numbers were logical. A puzzle he could easily solve. And it kept him distracted from any messy emotions or thoughts of sexy tattoo artists.

By the time he finished, it was almost seven, an hour until he was set to meet up with Izzy.

With no reason to head to his house and no reason to hang around, he made his way toward his bike. The air was no longer chilly, but downright cold. Time to put away the bike and roll the truck out of the garage. Always a sad time of year.

As he was walking out the door, rapid footsteps came flying up behind him. "Uncle Jig! Uncle Jig!" Beth, Shel's three-and-a-half-year-old daughter, flung herself at him with a high-pitched, "Catch me!"

Automatically his arms reached out and captured the energetic bundle, but not before his heart clenched with the force of a vise, as it did every time he laid eyes on the adorable strawberry-headed kid.

"Sorry, Jig," Shell said as she rushed toward them. "Beth, get down. Don't bother Uncle Jig. He doesn't really like you hanging around. Oh, I mean, sorry that was rude." For a second, her eyes grew glassy then she cleared her throat and all seemed normal. "I'm just frazzled. We're late getting to Mama V's and I have to work."

Jig blinked and stared at Shell. "No, it's okay. I'm, uh, glad she didn't fall. Glad I was there." His heart pounded so loud he could barely hear his own thoughts. Though the little kid couldn't weigh more than twenty-five pounds, the weight of her in his arms felt astronomical. Sweat broke out along his hairline. If he didn't get her out of his arms, he was going to have a panic attack and probably traumatize Beth for life.

"Oh, you don't mind?" Shell stopped trying to pry the boa constrictor grip Beth had from around Jig's neck.

Beth fit in his arms just as he remembered a three-year-old fitting. And it hurt so bad he couldn't draw in a full breath. Beth beamed at him, and somehow he found the strength not to lose his shit. It wasn't fair to take out his issues in front of the kid. She had no idea what monsters lurked in Jig's past.

"Mind keeping a hold of her for a minute while I find my keys?"

"You got a brother going with you?" Jig asked, focusing on Shell rather than the wiggling bundle in his arms. Hell would freeze over before Copper let Shell drive anywhere alone.

"I'm going ten minutes away, Jig. Nothing to worry about." She probably had no idea of the increased danger. Copper should have told her. Even though it wasn't true and might never be true, most of the guys considered Shell Copper's woman. They steered clear of her and differed to him when it came to her safety. What was he thinking not setting her up with a shadow?

"You can't go without a guard, Shell. Shit, uh, stuff's changed." He flicked a glance at an oblivious Beth who was tracing the scar on his face with her delicate little fingers. Every touch was a combination of innocent child softness and the tearing pain of the knife slicing into his face.

"You got a boo-boo," she said.

"Jig, I'm running late. If I wait for someone to come with me, I won't have time to drop Beth at Mama's V's." Shell worked two jobs. In the mornings, she waited tables at the diner Toni owned, and cleaned offices in the evening. Mama V watched her daughter most evenings and refused to take a single dime from Shell, which bugged the independent woman to no end.

"Copper," Jig bellowed, making Beth giggle.

"You loud," she said. "Want a princess Band-Aid for your boo-boo?" she asked unaware of the adult tension and discussion.

"No, squirt, I don't need a Band-Aid." He managed to keep any tremor out of his voice. Shell would pick up on it for sure and then feel terrible for pawning Beth off on him even for a moment. "You save it for next time you fall down."

"What the fuck you shouting for, Jigsaw?" Copper ambled out of his office, his entire demeanor changing when his gaze landed on Shell and Beth.

"Uncle Copper!" Beth dove from Jig's arms and beelined toward the prez. The instant she was gone, Jig was able to breathe fully once again.

"Hey, princess," Copper said as he scooped her up. He and Zach had spent hours with their captive in the box, but none of those horrors showed on his face when he held Beth.

The false grin wasn't fooling Shell, though. Concern marred her face, but she'd been part of this club her whole life and would have known not to push for answers, especially not in front of Beth.

"Put someone on your woman," Jig said, ignoring Copper's scowl.

"Fu—udge," Copper said. The club sure sucked at curbing their language around Beth.

Shell rolled her eyes. "I'm good, Copper. Just dropping her at

Mama V's then heading to work."

"Not by yourself, you're not. LJ's in my office. He'll be done in five, then he'll tail you."

Shell's blond curls bounced as she shook her head. "I won't have time to drop Beth off."

"I got her," Copper said. "I'll take her to Mama's. My truck is out back, and you know I have a seat for her." Beth rubbed her small hands on his beard like she was trying to lather it up with soap.

Shell's lower lip curled in. Jig could see the argument forming, but she kept it inside. She was independent, but knew her limits. Or rather knew Copper's limits. "All right," she finally said. "Thank you."

Copper nodded and disappeared into his office with Beth.

Shell followed, grumbling about bossy bikers and pigheaded men.

Jig smirked, imagining Izzy in Shell's situation. She'd have probably told Copper to shove his head up his ass and left on her own.

Why that thought made him smile, he had no idea.

Maybe it was just the image of her pert ass twitching as she angrily marched out the door. Well, shit. Now he had to go roll around with her at the gym.

Sporting a rock-hard boner.

CHAPTER TEN

Jab. Cross. Uppercut. Hook. Cross. Jab. Hook.

Jab. Cross. Uppercut. Hook. Cross. Jab. Hook.

"Come on, champ, thirty seconds left. Don't puss out on me now."

Izzy growled and picked up her speed as she pounded out the combination.

Puss out.

Please.

Why did men always think her vagina was going to make her turn tail and puss out?

Just as she was about to give him the tongue lashing of a lifetime, Jig winked. Actually winked. The bastard was playing with her. He knew just what to say to get under her skin and motivate her to push harder. She just didn't realize he could be playful.

Every muscle in her body burned with the delicious ache of exertion and power. For the past two hours, she'd been pushing herself to the max. Each time her gloved fist connected with Jig's punch mitt, beads of sweat jumped from her body, sometimes landing on his straining biceps, his rounded shoulders, or the smooth expanse of his chiseled chest.

Ninety-five percent of her focus was concentrated on precisely landing each punch and speeding through the combination, but that rogue five percent couldn't keep from imagining other ways their sweat could mingle. Maybe with direct skin on skin contact. Or perhaps she could drag her tongue over the damn ridge of the Adam's apple that teased her every single time he swallowed.

"Pick it up, woman." Jig barked out the order, snapping her back in the game.

Jab. Cross. Uppercut. Hook. Cross. Jab. Hook.

Jab. Cross. Uppercut. Hook. Cross. Jab. Hook.

Just as her muscles reached the point of exhaustion, Jig called out, "Time," and she slackened her arms, letting them flop to her sides.

He pulled off his punch mitts and tossed them on the floor against the wall mirror.

"Shit, woman, you've got some power," he said as he grabbed her shoulders and massaged the aching muscles. "You got any fights on the horizon?"

For a second, Izzy froze. Jig's large, warm hands were on her. For the first time. Electricity seemed to travel from his fingers throughout her entire body, waking the muscles that had just been fatigued. She shook her head as she yanked one of the gloves off with her teeth. "Nothing anytime soon. Not too many women looking for an underground fight. I've fought a few men, but I'm very selective and won't get in the ring with a dude if I haven't seen him in action before." Using her now free hand, she wiggled the other boxing glove off and tossed them on top of Jig's mitts.

Jig frowned. "You shouldn't be fighting men. Don't be stupid."

Over the past two weeks, she'd met with Jig and Zach five nights a week at the gym. Zach kept the place open well past closing just for them. Most of the time, it seemed they were making progress toward some kind of mutual respect, if not tentative friendship. When they were working balls-out, Jig forgot to be a standoffish, macho asshole. Hell, he even complimented her on occasion, like telling her she was a powerhouse.

But then reality would set back in, and he'd say something dickish like the garbage he'd just spewed. Two steps forward, one step back. Still, progress overall.

"You don't think it's possible for a woman to fight a man? Well, bubba, it's possible. I've done it. And I've won. All four times." Let him chew on that for a while.

After releasing her shoulders, he bent and scooped up her water bottle. "I'm not saying you can't beat a man, just that you shouldn't," Jig said as he underhanded the bottle in her direction.

She caught it with one hand and took a long drink of the cool liquid. "Why the hell not?" she asked once her mouth wasn't full of the thirst-quenching water.

"I already told you. It's stupid."

"Oh, it's stupid." She rolled her eyes and jammed her free hand on her hip, not blind to the way his gaze tracked the motion. The guy may not be thrilled with her, but he sure had an appreciation for her ass. Those haunted eyes of his drifted to her booty every chance they got. So sue her if she made sure to wear the shorts that gave her a little extra oomph. A girl needed an ego boost every now and again, and nothing did it quite like knowing you had power over a man. "Now I totally get it. Thanks for that eloquent explanation. Aren't you supposed to be some kind of genius or something?"

One side of his mouth quirked. "You asking around about me?"

Seriously? He was going to go and get all cocky? "Sorry to disappoint you, bubba, but no. People just talk. And don't try to change the subject. I wanna hear why you think a woman shouldn't fight a man."

He ran a hand through his damp hair and pulled at the strands like she was frustrating the hell out of him. Oh, yeah? Too bad. He was the frustrating one. "Of course, you're gonna win against a man in the ring. They'll hold back. The instinct to avoid hurting a woman is strong."

Throwing her hands up in the air, Izzy walked in a circle then stopped right in front of him. "Seriously?" she asked, getting right up in his face. "Maybe you should give that bullshit speech to all the women in shelters, running from abusive assholes."

"That's not what I me—"

"Okay, okay, fighters to your corners," Zach said as he strode out of the locker room. "You two about done with the foreplay here? I got a woman waiting at home naked, if I know her." He winked. "And trust me, I know her."

"Yeah, just gotta grab my shit," Jig said. With a narrowed-eyed nod for Izzy, he stalked off to the locker room.

"Ugh," Izzy said as she gathered her things and shoved them in her duffle. "That man is infuriating."

Crossing his arms, Zach propped his bulging shoulder against the mirror. "That man is changing. And I think we all have you to thank for it."

Bent over, Izzy peered up at him. "What do you mean? I haven't done anything. Unless you count pushing his buttons and arguing with ninety percent of what comes out of his mouth."

Before he spoke, Zach shot a quick glance toward the locker room. "Listen, babe, Jig's been through shit you can't even imagine. The kind of shit that would send most people to a padded room. And I say that only knowing the surface details." Zach shook his head, and Izzy couldn't help wondering what skeletons hid in Jig's closet.

"Not sure I want the full story. It's nightmare shit. Known him almost five years, and he's always been a loner. Trust him with my life. Hell, I trust him with Toni's life, which is saying something. I know he's a brother through and through, but he's always been one step removed from all of us. Hardly smiles, laughs maybe twice a year, doesn't argue, doesn't come here and work out with anyone else. He fights and he works. Wanna know why?"

Izzy straightened and slung her duffle over her shoulder. "Why?"

Zach pushed off the wall and closed the distance between them. "Because he doesn't give a shit about anything beyond his role in the club and surviving the fucking demons in his mind."

"He trains with me. And he argues with me. All the time."

"Exactly." Zach bopped her on the nose like she was a child who just learned her ABCs. "You have to care to argue. You have to give a shit to be willing to help someone train."

"You're trying to tell me he cares about me?" Nausea churned through her gut. Caring wasn't in the cards. Caring meant feelings. And feelings led to commitments, promises, and eventual soul-crushing disappointment.

"Not claiming to read the man's mind. Just telling you, he's changing. Acting differently than he was two weeks ago. That's all."

Jig emerged from the locker room and walked straight toward the exit without so much as a glance in their direction. "Night, brother," he called over his shoulder. Then he paused at the door and turned, snaring Izzy in his gaze. "Tomorrow?"

She swallowed. Getting close enough to let anyone in wasn't part of her plan. Still, hearing that she might be helping a man who'd suffered warmed her heart. How many times over the years had she wished someone would put her first, help her through her trials, and support her? She could do those things for him and keep her ten-inch steel walls intact. "Same bat time, same bat place," she said.

Jig rolled his eyes, and a ghost of a smile appeared. "Dork," he said before pushing through the door.

Zach's shoulder bumped hers. "See? That's not Jig. At least not the Jig I've known for years. Smiling? Fucking teasing?" He started toward his office. "Keep casting whatever spell your ass is casting, Iz. And get the hell out of my gym so I can close up and go fuck my woman."

Izzy laughed. "I'm going. Tell Toni I said hi. But make sure your clothes are on when you do. I do not want my name crossing your lips while you're nekked."

The final thing she saw as Zach disappeared into his office was his middle finger wiggling in her direction. Chuckling, Izzy gathered the last of her equipment and headed for the parking lot.

As she stepped outside, the chilled air blew across her perspiration-soaked skin. "Shee-it," she muttered as she dug through her bag for a sweatshirt while still booking it toward her car. Zach's truck was the only other vehicle parked on the opposite side of the lot. He liked to give his patrons the close spots, so he always parked the farthest from the door.

"Gotcha," she said as she pulled the soft fleece from her bag. Just as she freed the hoodie, strong hands gripped her upper arms and slammed her face-first against the side of her ten-year-old Accord.

"What the fuck?" She struggled in vain against two bulky men trapping her against her car. Her fight or flight response kicked in immediately, jacking up her heartrate, tunneling her vision, and causing a tremor to run through her. But there were no thoughts of flight. She'd fight her way out or die trying.

"Turn her around," a third man said, and she was wrenched away from the car only to have her spine crunch against the metal two seconds later.

"Who the fuck are you? What do you want?" she asked as she used her training to control her breathing. Accustomed to quick thinking when under attack, Izzy did a millisecond survey of the situation, and it wasn't good.

Three men on one woman? Sure, she was a badass in the ring and had whooped a few men in her day, but three on one was never good odds. Her arms were completely immobilized by the large thugs on either side of her, and her body was pinned to the car. Still...

She inhaled a slow, deep breath, then struck out on the exhale, slamming her right foot into the knee of one of her attackers.

"Fuck!" he screamed, catching himself just before the joint that gave out took him to the ground.

"You two assholes can't get one woman under control." The man in front of her drew his arm back and rammed it into Izzy's stomach. She knew how to absorb a punch, but honestly hadn't seen it coming, distracted by the men restraining her. The metal of her car crushed her spine again as her stomach and diaphragm spasmed in misery.

"Ooof." All the air rushed from her in a painful expulsion as her upper body folded forward. The grips on her arms didn't lessen even a fraction, and her shoulders pulled in an agonizing stretch as her body tried to curl in on itself but was held captive by two jerkoffs.

Trying to inhale, all Izzy could manage was a high-pitched wheeze. There went the idea of screaming for Zach, which had been plan B if taking the goons out didn't work. Perhaps it should have been plan A before she got socked in the stomach.

There wasn't time to feel fear, only anger and frustration at being helpless. While she struggled to right herself, a long-fingered hand wrapped around her throat and pushed her upper-body back against the car.

The men on her sides hooked their feet around hers, spreading her legs and holding her completely immobile. Now the fear slithered in. Three men, spread legs, unable to move… not a good position for a woman to be in. The only consolation she had was that someone would have to let go of her to remove her clothing. And that's when she'd strike.

Even though it was a wasted effort, she thrashed against their hold. Maybe she'd be smarter to conserve her energy, but she didn't want these pieces of shit to think she was weak for one second.

The hand on her throat tightened, and she stared into the eyes of a guy who couldn't have been more than twenty years old. As he continued to increase the constricting pressure, he said, "This would go a lot easier and faster if you'd stop thrashing around."

"Fuck…you," she whispered, because it was the loudest sound she could manage.

He smirked and squeezed tighter, completely cutting off her ability to speak. And breathe. If she hadn't trained for years, hadn't had her neck in a choke hold countless times, she'd have fallen into a complete panic. Instead, she embraced the feeling and concentrated on looking for an opportunity.

"Now, we have about thirty seconds before you pass out, so listen closely. I need you to deliver a message to your friends for me. Tell them no amount of fencing and little boys on watch will keep their clubhouse safe. Our business is booming, and Lefty won't let anything fuck with that. If he has to kill every one of those motherfucking bikers, he will, and there ain't a thing they can do to stop him."

Darkness closed in on her vision, tunneling it down to a pinpoint as she wrenched her neck and tried to break free.

"See how easy it is to catch someone off guard?" he whispered against her ear right before releasing her neck.

Izzy sagged and immediately sucked in giant lungsful of air. Her vision returned and the buzzing in her ear died out. She was so focused on oxygen and not passing out, she missed the continued attack. Another fist plowed into her stomach. This time, the men liberated her arms, but she was weak from lack of breath and the second punch.

She collapsed to the ground just as a booted foot connected with her side. Once, twice, she absorbed the punishment as best she could, curling up to protect her vital organs.

Shouting could be heard in the distance, but it was mostly drowned out by the buzzing in her ears.

"Fuck! Move out," the leader said as he delivered one last kick, this time to her low back. Suddenly they were gone, and Izzy's body went limp against the asphalt.

"What the ever-loving fuck?" From her position on the ground, Izzy caught sight of Zach's running shoes speeding in her direction. As best she could, she rolled to her back and, within seconds, he stood above her, a wooden bat in his hands.

Opening her mouth, she tried to speak, but all that came out was a frog-like croak that began a round of painful coughing. She tried to sit, but her stomach muscles wouldn't obey.

"Holy fuck, babe." Zach dropped to his knees beside her and put a hand on her shoulder. "Don't move."

She ignored the order and, once she was sitting, rested against the wheel well of her car and shook her head. "I'm okay," she rasped. Her throat felt like it'd been raked over a cheese grater.

"Your neck's a mess. I'm calling an ambulance."

"No," she tried to yell, then winced.

"Sorry, babe. It's the hospital for you." He yanked out his phone, called nine-one-one, and two minutes later was tucking the cell back in his pocket. "What the fuck happened? I heard a bang, so I grabbed Louie and ran out."

She nodded. "Three guys." Even to herself, it sounded like she'd swallowed a bucket full of rocks. Hopefully, there wasn't any permeant damage to her vocal cords. "Tried to fight them, but..." She shrugged. "Three."

Zach let out a mirthless laugh. "You may be a badass, but even you aren't superwoman."

Izzy allowed her eyes to close as she huffed out a laugh. "They gave me a message. Never said it was for the Handlers, but..."

Zach tensed. "What did they say?"

"In a nutshell, clubhouse isn't safe. Their business is booming. It's easy to get to you guys. And you can't stop them."

"Godfuckingdamnit," Zach spat out as he stood and paced in front of her car. He ran a hand down his face, scratching the five-o'clock shadow. "Jig's gonna have my ass. Shoulda walked you to your car. Hell, that stupid fucker shoulda walked you out. Can't believe we didn't put a guard on you. Shit, I can already tell Louie is pissed he didn't get a piece of them."

That was the second time he'd mentioned someone named Louie. As far as she knew, she and Jig were the last in the gym.

Jigsaw

"Who's Louie?" she asked.

Zach lifted the bat, and an evil grin crossed his face.

"Your bat's name is Louie?"

"Fuck, yeah, and he's a vengeful motherfucker."

Oookay. Totally normal.

"I'm the club's enforcer, Izzy. Bat's cleaner and leaves far less DNA than my fists or bullets. You okay if I make a few calls, babe?" he asked.

In a sick way, it made perfect sense. Keeping her eyes closed, she nodded and waved him away. "Go for it," she whispered.

"Shit, Iz, I'm sorry our club business touched you," Zach said before he stormed off a few feet, barking orders into his phone.

A few minutes later, the shrill sound of a siren signaled the ambulance's arrival. Two paramedics climbed out the back and rushed toward her.

"They'll have you feeling better in no time, girl. And I called Jig. He freaked the fuck out and will probably get to the ER before you do."

Huh? "What? Why did you call him?"

Zach just grunted and rolled his eyes.

Why on earth would Jig show up at the hospital? They weren't in a relationship. Hell, they weren't even really friends. Just two people who trained together a few nights a week.

Izzy sagged against the car as she answered the rapid-fire questions from the paramedics. Zach stayed by her side the entire time, snapping at the EMTs if he felt they weren't gentle enough. It was strange and kind of nice to have someone to lean on during a difficult time.

And Jig was coming to the hospital. She almost laughed. She'd believe that when she saw it. There was no reason for him to come, and in her experience, people didn't stick their neck out for others, even those they claimed to love.

CHAPTER ELEVEN

Jig stared at the harsh ruby-red lights of the emergency room sign as a familiar feeling of dread coursed through him. Nothing scared him anymore. Not a single blip of fear in over six years. But Zach's call sent terror through every cell in his body.

A woman had been hurt. A woman he knew. A woman he... liked.

Not again. This could not be happening again.

He hadn't even been able to admit to himself that he felt something for her. With her sass, her ball-busting, and her strength, she was the complete opposite of every woman he'd ever gone for, but somehow she snuck in. Now she was lying in a hospital bed because he'd treated her as an outsider. He'd made sure Copper protected Shell, but never even considered protecting Izzy. The years after his wife's death were spent honing his skills so he could protect himself, his brothers, and anyone else in his world. But he hadn't protected Izzy like he hadn't protected his wife and child.

Sickness rolled in Jig's gut, but he couldn't force his ass to move from the cab of his pickup. The scar on his face prickled more than ever before, and he was dying to rub it, but denied himself the simple comfort.

Why the fuck hadn't he waited to follow her out? Why hadn't he had a tail on her? In his defense, he hadn't thought she was close enough to the club to blip on Lefty's radar. Or maybe he was just fighting the notion. Either way, it was a neglectful oversight that cost her.

A knock at his window had him jumping out of his skin. Christ, he needed to get his shit together and remain alert before someone else got hurt. Copper stood on the other side of his closed door.

Jig opened the door, and Copper immediately said, "She's okay, man. You hear me? She's gonna be fine. Nothing life-threatening. She didn't even want to come here. Only reason Zach could get her ass into that ambulance was she wasn't at the top of her game. Otherwise, she'd have kicked his nuts into next week. She still might once she's feeling better."

Blowing out a breath, Jig nodded.

"Hey," Copper said, all business. "You're good. Just old shit rising to the surface."

Right. Of course. So he got a stiffie every time the woman was within fifty meters? And so her brand of spit and snark was more likable than not? He could admit all that. He could even form some kind of friendship with her. That's all it had to be. Nothing deeper. His dick would survive hanging around her and not inside her. Plenty of women more his flavor were waiting in the wings.

"Thanks, Cop. I'm good." Jig slid from the truck and fell in step with his prez, the two hurrying toward the ER entrance in silence.

Silence until Copper said. "You got something going with her?"

"Not fuckin' her, Cop. Helping her train, end of story."

"Hmm." He stroked his beard. "I like her. She's no drama, no BS, does fantastic fucking ink—"

"She worked on you?" She inked Copper? That was new to him.

"Uh huh."

The twist in his gut had to be nerves over her wellbeing. There was no other reason. Especially not jealousy over her performing a professional service on a man who had no interest in her because he was secretly not-so-secretly in love with someone else. "What'd you have done?"

"Ain't your fucking business." Copper shot him a dark look. "As I was saying, she's tough, definitely not a piece of fluff to hang off a man's arm. Not a woman to hang around the club and take it from any brother. Good stock."

Jig half-coughed, half-laughed as he tried to imagine Izzy as one of the Honeys. "Good stock? You running a breeding program now?"

"Just trying to tell you if you ever get your head out of your ass and decide to let a woman at more than your cock, she'd be a good one."

Jig's jaw tightened with the force of his bite. "All due respect, Prez," Jig said as Copper snorted because they both knew "all due respect" was code for "fuck off." "Don't think you're the best one to be playing doc-fucking-Phil, do you?"

Copper's features hardened as they reached the sliding double door entrance, and the conversation was dropped. Prez could go fuck himself if he thought he had relationship advice to give. With the way things were going in his life, his dick was going to shrivel up and die before it ever got sucked again. He hadn't touched a woman since Shell returned to town almost a year ago.

"This way," Copper said, turning left down a busy hallway. Doctors, nurses, and aides bustled around, weaving in and around the visitors and dragging equipment along. It wasn't long before Copper stopped outside a curtained-off area. "I'll give you a few. Gotta talk to her about the attack, though."

Jig nodded as he gripped the curtain. "Sure. Whenever you want."

With a smirk, Copper moseyed on down the hallway. Jig knew what that smirk was. It was an "I told you so" smirk. Jig hadn't even stepped in the room yet, and he was acting as gatekeeper. Screw that, he'd do the same for any women hurt because of their association with the club. Hell, he carried Mav's woman out of a basement of horrors just a few months ago. Just because he wasn't the friendliest and didn't want to hang out with them all day long didn't mean he wouldn't give his life for any one of his brothers or their women.

With a grunt, he pulled the curtain back and stepped into the small triage room. Her eyes closed, Izzy was reclining with the head of the bed elevated slightly. Next to her, Zach was sprawled out in a high-back chair with his giant feet propped on her bed.

"You raised in a barn, asshole?" Jig asked as he shoved Zach's feet to the floor. His brother jumped then grinned.

"Told you," he said to Izzy. "Teasing." Patting her on the shoulder, he rose. "Gonna grab a cup of coffee and give Toni a call. I had to tell the prospect to sit on her so she wouldn't come here. Need to make sure the poor schmuck's still got both balls."

"Zach," Izzy said in an exasperated tone as though she'd been saying the same thing a hundred times. "Go home to her. I'll get a ride or call an Uber." Something was wrong with her voice. It was raspy, gravelly, and she scrunched up her nose as if talking hurt.

"I'll take her home." Jig stood at the foot of her bed and crossed his arms over his chest. An Uber? That wasn't happening. "Go be with Toni, Z."

"You sure?" Zach asked, looking between Jig and Izzy.

"Yes! Go!" they both answered at the same time. Izzy chuckled, and Jig cleared his throat to disguise his own amusement.

Once Zach was gone and the privacy curtain was back in place, Jig studied Izzy. Her neck was dotted with at least eight purple circles. Someone had squeezed her so hard they damaged her voice. His fists curled and his body tensed. Give him five minutes alone with the men who dared to touch her. He'd snap their fucking necks with a giant smile on his face.

"It's not as bad as it looks." Izzy winced. "Or sounds." Some hair had slipped loose from her always-perfect braid, giving her a mussed, almost post-fucked look. Perfect time for his dick to join the party, when a woman was bruised and in pain.

He was turning into a creeper.

"It looks bad," he said. "Sounds worse."

"You calling me ugly?" she asked with her usual snark, but some of the effect was lost due to the ruined voice.

"Tell me," he ordered.

For a moment, she looked like she was going to throw her usual sass, but she sighed and let her head fall back on the pillow. "Bruising, tweaked muscles, all surface stuff. No permanent damage. Voice should bounce back in a few days. I'll scare small children for a bit, but that's the worst of it."

It was bullshit, and they both knew it. She'd be sore as fuck once whatever meds they'd given her wore off. But it was clear she didn't like to show weakness, so he let her think she was pulling one over on him.

"Never should have let you leave without a shadow. This is on me." Thankfully, she'd closed her eyes so he didn't have to see any disgust or hatred directed his way.

One eye popped open, and she gestured toward the chair before closing it again. "Guessing you're planning to stick around for a while. Have a seat. And don't be stupid."

He chuckled as she threw his words from the gym back at him. "We got shit going on with the club. Got constant eyes on all the women attached to us. I'm sorry we didn't take care of you."

Her pretty face twisted into a scowl that was sexier than it should have been. "First of all, bubba," she croaked, "I take care of myself. Me. *Numero uno*. Got it?" When he nodded, she went on, "And I've been to one party at the club. How the hell were you guys supposed to know they'd come after me? You can't watch every woman who's ever been to the clubhouse. I hear there have been millions."

She was right, but he'd carry the guilt a little longer. They'd spent a lot of time together over the past two weeks, and the reality of it was she was more to him than a sparring partner.

Or even a piece of ass.

Her eyes narrowed. "I'm serious, Jig. Don't take this on."

They held each other's gazes for a few seconds, the air between them crackling and popping. How she could be bruised and in a hospital gown yet still look sexier than any other woman, he'd never know. But Izzy did. It was just her. The confidence she wore. The comfort in her own body. And what a body it was.

"All right," he said. A small lie wouldn't hurt. "No guilt. They gonna let you go tonight?"

"Think so. Just waiting on someone to read the X-ray of my ribs. I don't think they're broken, and if they're not, I'm free to go."

Free to go, but not alone. No way, no how. He didn't make the same mistake twice. He'd work her into the protection rotation for the upcoming days. Jig nodded just as the curtain opened and Copper stalked in like he owned the place. Pretty much how he moved through life. "Hey, killer," he said. "How you feeling?"

Izzy smiled. "Not too terrible. They gave me the good stuff."

Resting his hand on the footboard, Copper loomed over the bed. "Think you can go over what happened with me? We need to nail these guys as soon as possible to keep the rest of the club safe."

Izzy had no loyalty to the club. She wasn't an ol' lady, wasn't a Honey, wasn't even someone who frequented the parties. Jig wouldn't blame her if she told them to fuck off and leave her the hell out of their problems. But Izzy was a fighter, so he shouldn't have expected her to back down.

"I was leaving the gym when two guys grabbed me," she said with a small scoff. "Coulda taken either of those losers one on one, but then there was a third, so I didn't stand a chance."

As she filled them in, Jig focused on the words and their impact on his club instead of on what happened to Izzy. He had to or he'd go tearing out of the hospital on a rage-filled murder mission. Listening to her talk about Lefty's men putting their hands on her was almost more than he could handle. He might be able to keep his ass in the chair, but it didn't stop him from wanting to permanently end anyone associated with Lefty.

"You recognize any of them? Seen them anywhere before? Any distinguishing marks?" Jig fired one question after another until Izzy held up her hand.

"Geez, Jig. You sound like a cop." She sighed. "Oh, uh, no and no. Didn't get that great a look at the two guys holding my arms. The guy who choked me was young. Twenty? Maybe not even that old. Not very bulky. Muddy colored hair. He had quite a few tats as well. Two I recognized as prison tats."

At both Jig and Copper's raised eyebrows, Izzy laughed. "What? I stay current on trends. You wouldn't believe how many requests we get in the shop asking for prison tats. Little posers wanting to look tough for the big boys. Rip's policy is that we send 'em packing. Anyway, his other ink was shitty. Definitely not from Rip or myself. Probably not from a shop anywhere. More like my-brother's-best-friend-inked-me-in-his-garage kinda thing. Pure garbage."

Jig couldn't help but laugh. Here she was all beat-up, telling an outlaw MC president about the gang leader who sent men to give her a message, and she was more worried about the shitty artistry than her own welfare.

"What?" she asked, scrunching her forehead.

"Nothing, sweetheart, go on."

Sweetheart? Where the hell had that come from?

Izzy's eyes widened, and she cleared her throat as best she could, though it sounded weak. "Uh, where was I? Oh right, they wanted me to tell you the clubhouse wasn't safe despite the extra security, their business is booming, and they can get to anyone easily." She pointed to her neck. "Exhibit A."

"Fuck." Copper looked at Jig with an unspoken question in his eye and Jig nodded. They were on the same wavelength.

Jigsaw

Business was booming. Somehow, flying under the Handlers' radar, Lefty was still trafficking women. And now they'd put their hands on Izzy. Wrapped them around her neck and squeezed hard enough to bruise. Rage bubbled in him like a pot about to boil over. Slaughtering them would be a pleasure.

"What's that look?" Izzy asked. "You just talked to each other with your eyes."

"Nothing, killer," Copper said, and Jig stifled a laugh. He'd spent enough time with Izzy over the past two weeks to know she wasn't gonna let that fly.

Her eyes narrowed in what he was coming to call her oh-hell-no look. The one that said she wasn't buying what Copper was selling.

"What's their business? Drugs? Guns?"

Copper studied her for a moment, looked to Jig, then back to Izzy. "Women."

Her forehead scrunched. "Women? They're pimps?"

The prez shook his head, that red beard moving back and forth. "Maybe I should have said girls. Young, unwilling girls."

"Holy shit," she breathed. "Sex trafficking?" At Jig's nod, she said, "Well what are we going to do about it?"

"*We* aren't going to do shit about it," Jig said. She was out of her ever-loving mind and probably needed an MRI of her head if she thought her involvement with this wasn't over. "The club will handle it."

Those eyes narrowed again, dangerously this time.

Copper cleared his throat. "We're gonna put a man on you, Izzy." As her mouth opened, he held up his hand. "It's as much for our benefit as your protection. I know you can handle yourself, but Lefty apparently does too, which is why he sent three guys to take you out. I want those men." His voice dropped to a deadly timber. "If I can catch them by tailing you, that's what I'm going to do."

With a heavy sigh, Izzy stared up at the IV pole next to her bed. They'd given her some pain medication through an IV.

"Fine," she said.

Copper nodded and patted her foot. "Thanks, Izzy. You didn't have to tell me shit. Appreciate it. I'll see you around."

He disappeared behind the curtain, leaving Jig alone with Izzy. They stared at each other in silence for a few moments before he finally shifted his gaze away. He hadn't been in a hospital since his face had been carved up and associated them with pain, grief, and deep depression. Yet, here he was, sitting by Izzy's side. He hadn't had a chance to sit by his wife's side because she never had the chance to heal from her injuries.

Shit. He had to get his mind out of the past if he was going to survive the night. "Anything I can get for you?" he asked.

When he saw that squinty look, he knew what she was going to say before she even opened her mouth. "Yes. Hell, yes. You can get me the fuck out of here."

CHAPTER TWELVE

By the time Izzy let herself into the small house she'd closed on exactly six weeks and two days prior, it was almost two in the morning. The place wasn't anything to boast about, but it was hers. With Townsend's lower cost of living and the generous salary Rip was paying her, she'd have no problem making the mortgage payments. With tips and the occasional prize money, she'd have a surplus for the first time in her life.

No more roommates, no more relying on others to make ends meet. No more let downs. Just herself and her own hard work.

"If you want a drink or something, help yourself," she said to Jig, who'd insisted on following her into the house. Some poor kid in a truck was gifted the very mind-numbing task of sitting outside her house all night in the cold while she slept. For about ten minutes, she'd put up a good fight, but was exhausted and the pain medication took away her ability to come up with logical arguments, so she'd agreed to the MC's offer of protection. It was either that or she feared Jig would have bribed the doctor to keep her in the hospital overnight.

"I'm good, Iz," he said. "Just want to make sure you get settled, then I'll bug out and let you sleep."

Sleep. Oh man, that sounded too good to be true. "You sure I can't invite that poor kid in and let him crash on my couch?" she asked for the third time.

Jig's expression hardened. "I'm very sure. I find out that little shit's been in here, and he'll never get a patch. You hear me?"

As she walked through her den toward her couch, she raised her hands to shoulder level. "All right, all right. Don't shoot. I just feel bad for the guy." She grabbed the armrest and lowered herself to the couch, biting her lip to keep the cry of pain at bay. Jig did not need to know she'd lied when she told the male nurse her pain was four out of ten. Really, it probably floated at the seven, eight level, but the man would have insisted she stay the night if she hadn't fudged the numbers a bit.

Following behind her, Jig frowned as he watched her sit and thankfully didn't comment on the awkward way she lowered herself to the couch. Bending wasn't exactly comfortable. "Where do you want your meds?" He held up a brown paper bag full of all sorts of goodies.

Her head flopped back on the cushion. "Kitchen table," she said, pointing to the kitchen entrance off the den.

Thirty seconds later, Jig returned with a glass full of more ice than water. "Here," he said, holding it out to her. "Figure the ice will feel good on your throat."

She eyed him before taking the glass and a greedy gulp. Okay, he was right. The icy water felt terrific sliding through her abused throat. After lowering the glass, she met his assessing gaze. "What? I'm good now. You don't have to stick around." She wasn't used to men in her personal space, and his presence was making her twitchy. There had to be some ulterior motive. People didn't just hang around waiting to be needed by someone they barely knew.

He dropped into a chair across the coffee table and smirked. "Nice view."

"Thanks." The view through a row of six long rectangular windows were what had sold her on the house. Neighbors were spread out, and she had a fantastic shot of the mountains straight out her front yard. "So, you going?"

With a shake of his head and a huff, he said, "Just want to make sure you're good. See if there's anything you need."

Jigsaw

If her throat wasn't so sore, she'd have growled. "Look, Jig. I thought you were over the guilt thing. I'm good. I'm a fighter. This sure as hell isn't the first time I've been bruised to shit. Right now? There are only three things I need, a drink"—she held up the water—"much harder than this, an orgasm, and about a year of sleep. So, yes, you can help by grabbing the bourbon off my counter and then leaving so my vibrator and I can get down to business."

Fuck the pills, a stiff drink and a good orgasm were better pain relievers any day of the week. For about ten seconds, Izzy thought Jig was going to feed her some line about mixing pain pills and alcohol, but he eventually rose and disappeared into her kitchen. She should have known better. Outlaw bikers weren't exactly big on sticking to the rules. They were supposed to be good at the orgasm thing though she'd never ask him for one. She'd make due on her own.

He returned with two glasses, doubles of bourbon.

Stepping up to her, he handed one over. Without hesitation, she swallowed the entire thing in two gulps. Felt like fire on her throat, but within a few minutes, she wouldn't care. Jig chuckled as she plunked the glass down on her end table. He still stood between her coffee table and her knees, watching her with that brooding gaze she couldn't quite decipher. A constant mix of pain, rage, sadness, and sometimes heat. With his rock-hard abs, bad boy scar, chiseled jaw, and biker cut, it was a dangerous combination. The kind of mix that made a woman want to figure him out and heal him with both her heart and what was between her legs.

Good thing Izzy had already learned to steer clear of entanglements.

"Want another?" he asked, holding the open bottle over her empty glass.

She raised an eyebrow. "A bird can't fly with one wing."

His little chuckle was music to her ears. It didn't happen often, which was what made it so special. The day the man let it all go and belly laughed, she'd be able to die a happy woman.

And, well, fuck if that didn't sound like she was getting sucked into his web.

"Have at it." Jig refilled her glass, but this time she took a sip and didn't slam the entire thing.

"Thanks." She rested her head back and closed her eyes. "Seriously. For all the help, but I'm good now. Go home and get some sleep. As soon as I get the energy to move, I'm gonna give myself that orgasm then sleep until Christmas." And if she visualized his head between her legs or his large body hovering over hers while she pleasured herself, that would just be her little secret.

The next thing she knew, he'd wedged one thigh between her knees, then the other. Her eyes flew open just as he widened his stance, spreading her legs. His gaze had darkened, and his jaw ticked. Predatory. That's how he looked.

She swallowed, hard, and didn't feel an ounce of discomfort. "Wh-what are you doing?"

"Giving you what you need." He shrugged out of his cut and chucked it on the couch next to her. When it landed with a soft *whump*, Izzy couldn't keep her hands from reaching for the buttery leather. She traced a finger over the rim of the upper rocker. Hell's Handlers. That's what he was. That's who he was. A biker, an outlaw, a man with a past who suffered. A man she should not want to fix. A man she would not let past her defenses.

She tilted her head. "You gonna make me come?" It was almost a challenge, but not in the way he probably interpreted it. More a challenge for herself—take what he offered and let it be what it was. Orgasms. Fucking. Nothing more.

He slowly dropped to his knees between her spread legs, placing the heel of his hand on her mound with just enough pressure to make her clit go crazy with need. "I'm gonna eat this pussy you've been teasing me with for weeks. And, fuck yeah, I'm gonna make you come. And you're gonna have to work harder not to scream than you've ever worked at anything in your life. Because you will want to scream. You'll need to scream, but I won't have you damaging your voice further."

Ho-ly shit, that was some confidence right there. It'd been a while since a man had spoken to her like that. Years, really. She tended to be the aggressor and go for men who allowed her the upper hand, even needed it. More comfortable for her to walk away when it was over.

If she'd been in her right mind, she'd have shown him the door, but with pain meds, bourbon, full body soreness, and a desperate need for release, she was weaker than usual. Or at least that's what she told herself. No matter, she still had her defenses, and snark was the best one. "Well then," she said, spreading her legs farther apart. "By all means, get to work."

He caught her legs around the outside of her thighs and pushed them closer together. When her knees were nearly touching, he said, "Lift that gorgeous ass for me."

She hesitated for a second, then lifted her hips. "Don't need the compliments, Jig. Just the orgasm."

He smirked like he saw right through her. "Call it like I see it, sweetheart," he said as he peeled the skin-tight leggings down her hips and straight off her body. Everywhere his fingertips trailed, little sparks of electricity kicked up, making her wetter and needier by the second.

Shit. This was a bad idea. Compliments and pet names. She closed her eyes. All she'd need was eye contact, and her walls would crumble.

Buck up, girl. You're stronger than a man and some sweet talking.

Once her pants were off, Jig palmed her inner thighs and pressed outward, spreading her wide once again. Legs splayed, clad only in her stringy thong, she waited for his next move. When nothing happened for at least thirty seconds, she risked opening her eyes. Jig's gaze was fixed on her pussy, and it clenched hard with need at the look of hunger on his face. "Jig," she said. "I'm turning gray here. Get to it."

He snorted and lifted his gaze. "Nothing there to turn gray, babe," he said, his breath on the hairless skin of her mound.

She couldn't help the wicked smile. "Like the way it feels when I'm walking around bare." His eyes darkened. Hmm, this could be fun. Always up for a good power play, Izzy said, "I like the way my panties feel, silky ones, rubbing all over my pussy with nothing in the way. Lacy ones too, with a bit of texture."

His nostrils flared, and he grabbed her ass, yanking her hips to the edge of the couch. She yelped, but not in pain—no, she wasn't feeling any of that at the moment. "How about when they're wet," he asked as he ran his finger under the string of her thong. "Because you're fucking soaked now, sweetheart." He tugged on the cotton, pulling the string forward and up against her clit with just enough pressure to be maddening.

Izzy gasped and, needing more, tilted her hips, trying to grind herself against the panties, but it was pointless. Jig kept the pressure light enough to be pleasurable but also had her craving a firmer touch. She wasn't a shrinking violet, didn't like slow and easy fucking. She loved it fast, rough, and wild. "Jesus, Jig," she said on a low moan. "Just eat me already."

"Yes ma'am," he growled as his fingers curled around the string. One of his knuckles bumped her clit, and her hips jerked in response.

He yanked, tearing the flimsy fabric straight from her body.

And then he dove in. Dove. The. Fuck. In.

Izzy cried out, her upper body coming off the couch as sharp, almost painful pleasure assaulted her. There was no build up, no soft tonguing or sweet licks. Only a vacuum strong suction over her clit. Had she not been so primed and ready for him, it would have been too much too fast, but as it was, her body was screaming for it.

"Jig, fuck." She panted and squirmed against his mouth, but he gave her no respite. Instead, he tongued her clit, pressing it to his upper lip. Her head fell back as the room spun.

He abandoned her clit, moving down and sucking her pussy

lips into his mouth before ramming his tongue into her and fucking her with it for all he was worth.

Izzy had never been eaten quite like this before. There was an intensity to it that was almost violent in nature. He didn't give her a second to breathe, a second for her mind to catch up with her spiraling body. His hands were still on her ass, massaging the cheeks.

Grinding her pelvis against his face, she moaned as he licked his way back up to her clit. Instead of closing his lips around it again, he fluttered his tongue over it in a move she hadn't experienced before. "Jesus," she gasped out, her hands diving into his hair. If Izzy found something she liked or wanted, she made it happen for herself, and she wanted this. Gripping the short strands of his hair, she held his face against her as she thrust her pussy against his face.

"Fuck," he murmured against her. "Sweetest fuckin' pussy ever." Or at least that's what she thought he said. The rushing of blood in her ears roared so loud she could barely make out his words.

In the next second, he tore his mouth from her, and she screamed, "No!" as the loss of pleasure made her gut clench. He sunk his teeth into her upper thigh, and her pussy flooded. This was precisely what she needed. The fierce act not only brought her physical pleasure, but it was calming the restlessness inside her. The need for exertion, combat, something to still the demons in her mind.

Chuckling, Jig kept his mouth suctioned on her thigh and sunk two fingers deep into her pussy. His touch was rough, demanding, as he fucked her with his fingers. She was beginning to realize this was just how he was. Raw, harsh, unbridled. And God help her, she wanted it all. This was what she'd been searching for, at least physically.

She'd been with her share of men, and all had left something to be desired. Some elusive, unattainable unicorn floating out there that left her just slightly unsatisfied every time. That wasn't going to happen this time.

God, that mouth on her leg was going to leave a mark.

His fingers continued to ramp her closer and closer to coming, moving fast and furious inside her. She canted her hips and rode his hand hard. For one second, her mind went crazy, and she imagined herself thrown over the arm of the couch with Jig ramming from behind. Not her typical style, but something told her Jig would make the loss of control worth her while.

"You ready to come for me?" he asked, lifting his head.

"Yes, yes." So, so ready. She was minutes away from begging, and she hadn't begged for anything in her entire adult life. But a monster of a climax hovered just out of reach, and she'd do damn near anything to reach it.

Izzy risked glancing down and met his smug gaze. He winked, and she almost came on the spot. Playful Jig was something else.

"Here we go, baby," he said before lowering his head.

Baby. Damn him and those endearments.

She had enough brainpower to call him on it and almost did, but then he sucked her clit into his mouth again as he fucked her harder with his fingers. Her pussy was going to be sore tomorrow from his brutal fingering, but damn she'd happily add it to her list of aches.

"Oh, my God," she cried out as he gently grazed her clit with his teeth. His left hand landed on her lower stomach, holding firm pressure, as his fingers curled inside her. The intensity kicked so high she lost her grip on reality and splintered into a million pleasurable pieces.

"Don't fucking scream," he said just as her mouth fell open. She whipped her fist up to her mouth and bit into the fleshy pad beneath her thumb. Any pain, any discomfort, any stress completely bled from her being. There was no space for anything but satisfaction.

Boneless, Izzy sagged into the couch cushions. Jig lifted off his knees and sat on the coffee table, clearly turned on. The bulge in his jeans beckoned to her, and for one weak instant, she almost caved and begged him to stay the rest of the night.

At the last second, she remembered that feeling she worked so hard to avoid. Abandonment, neglect, disappointment… loneliness. And while, sure, she got lonely from time to time on her own, at least she was in control of it. Not a man, not a friend, not a relationship.

So, instead of begging for his cock, she gave him a contented smile and said, "Now that's what they should be handing out prescriptions for."

Jig blinked and, for the barest of seconds, had a soft expression. Then the shields were back in place, and he snorted. "Maybe they should." Rising to his feet, he grabbed his cut and shrugged back into it. His body was a work of art, and even under the T-shirt, his strength was apparent.

And enticing.

She couldn't tear her eyes off him as he strode to her door. His hand reached for the knob, and he turned. "Get some sleep, sweetheart," he said.

And he was gone.

Blowing out a breath, Izzy stared at her ceiling. It was then she realized she was naked from the waist down, legs splayed open, wet pussy on full display. She hadn't shifted a millimeter since she came.

For the first time since she moved in, the emptiness of the house was noticeable. Jig melted her mind and made her think about things she'd promised herself she'd steer clear of.

"Shit," she said to the vacant home.

Of course, no one answered her. Because she was alone.

Just like she wanted.

CHAPTER THIRTEEN

"Okay," Zach said in a hushed tone. "Here's what we know as of now." Jig and the other four men leaned in, their breakfasts forgotten. "They've got a stash of girls somewhere. I had a contact I trust feeding me info from the cops, and they haven't had any missing persons reports filed in a hundred-mile radius for women under twenty-five in the past four months. The last one was one of the girls we know Lefty snatched." He cleared his throat. "And eventually killed."

Jig lifted his coffee mug to his lips. By the time he'd left Izzy's place, it was well after three am. Two back-to-back rounds of jacking himself off to the memory of her taste and the way she greedily shoved her pussy against his face, and he'd finally crashed somewhere around four-thirty, still not completely satisfied. At nine, the jarring ringtone of his phone pulled his dream-dick out of dream-Izzy with Copper's invitation, or more like mandate, to meet for breakfast at ten thirty.

So, there he was, overtired and under-caffeinated, trying to stay with the conversation. He gulped the scalding liquid and sighed in pleasure. At least he could remedy the problem of under-caffeination.

"So he's getting them somewhere else," Zach said, also sucking down the java.

Jig set his mug next to his uneaten omelet. "Or he's strategically choosing women who don't have anyone to report them missing."

The rest of the men stared at him. In telltale thinking mode, Copper rubbed his beard with his thumb and forefinger. "You think Lefty's savvy enough to put that kinda operation in play?" he asked.

Jig shrugged. He scooped up a hunk of the cheesy omelet and plopped it on the corner of a slice of wheat toast. "He's been smart enough to keep the operation up and running while flying under our radar. We thought Chloe was the only woman he had. And when he handed her over, we assumed that was it for his stock of women." With a wide mouth, he bit halfway through the toast. Damn, no one did breakfast like Ernesto, the diner's chef.

At the mention of Chloe's name, Rocket's hand tightened around his fork to the point of punishing. Good thing it wasn't a plastic utensil, or it'd be in pieces. Rocket had been the one to pull Chloe from Lefty's clutches not long ago. Something went down that night, but Rocket's lips were sealed as to what happened. But that was a problem for a later date.

"Well, fuck," Zach said. He shoved his plate away and leaned back against the booth's vinyl cushioning. "We gotta find those fucking girls. Cop, I know you wanted to keep this as clean as possible, but I'm starting to think the only way out of this thing is to get our hands a little dirty."

"I ain't worried about getting our hands dirty, Z." Copper's voice had risen almost to a yell. Behind the diner counter, Shell's head whipped in their direction. The frown on her face said she'd heard. She grabbed the coffee pot and started in their direction.

Jig pressed his lips together and gave her a quick shake of his head. Her steps faltered. She looked between him and Copper, then nodded and made her way to another of her tables.

"Shit, prez, keep your panties on. I only meant shit might have to get a little bloody."

Copper blew out a breath and slammed his heavy fist down

on the table, making all the platters and silverware jump then clatter back down. For a second, the diner went totally silent as every eye in the place landed on the table full of bikers.

Not exactly ideal.

"You good, prez?" Jig asked in a low voice.

"Fuck, yeah, sorry. This shit's like having my skin peeled off with a rusty knife." Copper bowed his head for a beat then lifted it. His eyes were sharper, deadlier. "We've fucked up six of Lefty's drug transfers over the past week. Fucked them out of about thirty K."

Jig cleared his throat. Taking their money was great, but it wasn't enough. They'd attacked a Handlers' woman at a business owned by a Handler. Stealing money was child's play. Jig wanted blood. "Been thinking about something, boss. We keep grabbing their drug money, they're gonna need to make up for the losses somewhere. Might up their trafficking game to recoup their cash. That could be good, or it could be a total fucking nightmare for the girls."

Mav dropped his fork midbite. Jig knew the feeling; his appetite fled as well. "Goddamnit, Jig," Mav said. "Why you always gotta be the voice of mother fucking reason?"

Rocket snorted. "Let him finish, Mav."

Before he went on, Jig lifted his mug. Damn, empty. It'd have to wait until he'd said his piece. He couldn't call Shell or Toni over and risk them catching wind of the conversation. "If they're feeling the pressure to up their game, they might get sloppy, grab a girl with family. Someone from town. If we get eyes on them, we might catch something."

Back to stroking his beard, Copper nodded. "Makes sense. And the flip side?"

"They just turn up the heat on the girls they already got. Out of the fire, into the frying pan kinda shit. They've already shown they're willing to touch a woman associated with us. They're ballsy and willing to make bold moves." It was times like this that Jig was damn glad not to be driving the ship. Copper listened to the advice of his executive board, considered everyone's opinion and judgment, but in the end, the final decision fell to him. His shoulders might be broad as fuck, but they could still crumble.

"Okay, Rocket, you're in charge of the watch on Lefty. I want eyes on him and his crew twenty-four seven. We can't just take the fucker out because there's a stash of girls out there, and we gotta find them first. Finding them is number two priority after protecting the clubhouse and family. Use whatever resources you need to make that happen. I know we're stretched thin as fuck right now, but it needs to happen."

"On it, boss," said Rocket. He slipped out of the booth. "Gonna head out and get working."

"Thanks, brother," Copper said, grabbing the hand Rocket extended. With his left, he snagged Rocket's forearm, and they held for a second. Brothers working hard to protect their family.

"I want to continue hijacking their drug deals until they wise up and get more discrete, but start taking his guys out of commission, too. The guy we had in The Box was clueless about the human trafficking side of business, and I assume most of these lower level dealers will be as well, but it can't hurt to put a little pressure on them and see if they know anything. No deaths yet, just break some fucking kneecaps." He looked at Zach on his left. "You good with that?"

"Fuckin' great with that. Louie was robbed of action last night. He's itching for a little revenge." Zach rubbed his hands together then dug back into his food. Mav did as well. Jig's stomach growled. Seemed like a little talk of offense had everyone's appetite flaring to life again.

Mav paused in the shoveling of cinnamon roll waffles into his trap. He raised an eyebrow and smirked.

And, here it comes.

"Speaking of last night, heard you took the sexy fighter chick home and disappeared into her house for about an hour. Anything you wanna tell us, brother?" Mav stuffed the overflowing fork into his mouth. The man ate those waffles at least four times a week, yet remained lean as a whip.

"What is this, fucking study hall?" Jig said as he stared into his coffee cup. Last thing he needed was his asshole brothers finding out he ate the fuck out of Izzy last night. And, Christ, she was sweeter than those damn waffles...

"Oh, ho, ho." Zach laughed, and even Copper grinned like a red-bearded loon.

The jangle of bells rang out, indicating someone had entered the diner. At that moment, Jig would have sworn he was fucking Spiderman because his sixth sense went wild.

"And speak of the she-devil," Mav said, his evil grin so big it nearly split his cheeks.

Jig couldn't help it; it was as though he'd been invaded by a body controlling alien. Glancing over his shoulder, he watched the woman in question step into the diner. He was struck with an instant hard-on. Let's face it, he'd never entirely lost it, even after two colossal self-induced orgasms, but the sight of her had his balls aching with renewed need for release. But not from his fucking hand. No, he wanted that sassy, snarky mouth all over his dick.

For the first time, he was getting a glimpse of her with her hair down—literally—and it stirred his blood in a way he hadn't felt in ages. Black as night, thick, glossy, and long, long, long, it tumbled midway down her back. She looked hot with it in the braid, fierce, warrior-like, but now she revealed a feminine softness he'd yet to witness.

And if he thought he'd wanted her before, he'd been sadly mistaken. Now, he fucking wanted her.

As though she sensed attention on her, she turned and met his gaze. Her eyes flared then narrowed in his favorite pissed-off look. She hadn't known he'd be there. Probably wouldn't have come if she had. Damn, the woman was prickly. He winked then felt a tapping on his shoulder.

"Here, brother," Mav said.

He twisted forward, back to his table and the laughing eyes of his brothers. "What?"

Mav held a napkin out. "Gotta wipe up that drool. Slobber does not impress the ladies."

"Funny." He grabbed the napkin, balled it up, and shot it into Mav's face, then took another quick peek over his shoulder. Izzy had turned away and was walking to meet her girls at the counter—walking stiffly as though in pain.

Well, Jesus, of course, she was in pain. What the fuck was the woman thinking, coming out just hours after she'd been attacked? Jig started to rise from the table but caught Shell's eye. Much as he'd done to her, she gave him a quick head shake followed by a wink, and he sat back down. Those women were thick as thieves and a damn nuisance.

The rest of the guys laughed, and conversation moved from business to general bullshit.

And all the while, Jig sat there with a pipe in his pants, fully aware of the woman who caused it just twenty feet away.

COME HAVE BREAKFAST, they said. *The boys are busy with business*, they said. *It'll be fun*, they said.

Dirty, rotten, lying bitches.

Izzy tore her gaze away from the man who made her come like a supernova less than eight hours ago. As she gingerly made her way to the counter where Shell and Toni promised to have breakfast with her, she bristled with frustration.

Granted, they had no idea that just a few hours ago Jig had buried his face between her legs. Maybe she should cut them some slack. Hopefully, they'd attribute her foul mood to the pain and stress of being attacked the previous night and not the frustration of wanting a man with her body but not wanting that same man with her brain.

Almost to the counter, she ran a hand through her hair. Shit! The only reason she'd left it down was that she'd assumed the guys would be at the clubhouse talking business and not in

Toni's diner. Well, that, and it hurt like a mofo to raise her arms and braid it. She'd given up after about ten seconds of trying.

The braid was kind of her shield. With the shaved bottom layer of hair, it made her look fierce, intimidating. And she needed that right now to ward off the very sexy man who muddled her mind. Especially since she was running on four hours sleep, Percocet, and not one cup of coffee.

"Hey, sweetie," Shell said as Izzy made it to the counter. Her new friend's face was full of concern. "How are you?"

"Coffee. Must have coffee."

"Yeah." Shell smiled and grabbed the pot. "I can see that. You want me to just stick a straw in this thing?" Her eyes twinkled, and it actually made Izzy smile.

She appreciated the fact that while Shell seemed concerned for her wellbeing, she wasn't in freak-out mode, trying to do everything for Izzy. It was important she be able to take care of herself, bruises and all. "Not a bad idea, sister."

"Hey, Shell—" Toni burst through the metallic door leading to the kitchen. "Oh, Izzy! Shit, girl, how you feeling? Zach stole my phone and fucked me into a coma last night so I wouldn't bother you, but I've been super worried."

That had Izzy laughing a genuine laugh that felt good emotionally but terrible physically. "Ow, girl, don't make me laugh." Leave it to this group of women to get her out of the funk she'd been in since she woke up. "And if he gave it to you that good, getting my ass beat might just have been worth it."

With a snort, Toni took the stool next to her. "Please, he does not need an excuse to curl my toes." Then she sobered. "Seriously, though, you okay?"

With a nod, Izzy wrapped her hands around the warm coffee mug and inhaled the heaven-sent aroma. "I'm all right. Sore as fuck, but it's all just bruising. And this raspy voice. No permanent damage done."

"All right then," Shell said. "I'm gonna go ahead and guess you don't want us to harp on it, so we'll just trust you know you can ask us for help with anything anytime. Now that we know you're okay, we'll drop it, yes?"

Fuck yes. These women rocked. "That's perfect."

"'Kay, let me have Ernesto make you a cinnamon roll waffle. I'll be right back," Shell said as she dropped the bowl of cream and sugar packets in front of Izzy.

"No, I'll have—"

"Nu-uh." Toni shook her head and pointed a slightly scary finger in Izzy's face. "No egg white nonsense today. Fat, sugar, and calories for you, missy. And I better not hear you went to the gym. In fact, I told Zach not to let you in the door."

What the hell? "I was just gonna go later for a little while. Do a slow jog for a few miles. It's getting too cold to run outside."

Jazz emerged from the kitchen, and Toni waved her over to the group before she spoke to Izzy. "Sorry, girl, not happening. You hear me? I'll tell Jig on you. Let him spank your ass."

"What?" Her sex clenched at Toni's words. She'd never had a flicker of interest in a man's palm cracking across her ass, but the thought of Jig's large hand landing there with force had her blood heating. Shit, maybe the pharmacist mixed some mind-altering drugs in with the Percocet. "Jesus, Toni. That is not something that will happen. Ever. Ever, ever."

"Wow," Jazz said as she slid onto the stool on the other side of Izzy. "Someone's protesting a little much, isn't she?" With a wink, she reached over the counter and grabbed herself a coffee mug. As Shell came back out, Jazz held up her cup. She smiled as the dark liquid flowed into it. "Is it bad that this is my third cup of the day already?"

"Nope," Izzy said. "It's not bad. What's bad is you bitches thinking something is going on with Jig and me."

"Well," Toni said. "The man has looked over here about every thirty seconds since you walked in the place. If nothing's going on, what's that all about? Hmm?" Her smug eyebrow raise had Izzy laughing.

"It's probably about him having to cart my busted ass home

last night. Hello? You're with one of those guys. I can't imagine you missed how overprotective they are."

"Only of people they care about," Shell fired back. "Ha! Gotcha there."

Blowing a raspberry, Izzy rolled her eyes. "Just go check on my waffle, wench."

They all laughed together, and Izzy realized she was feeling pretty damn good. She liked these women, really liked them. It would be hard to keep them at arm's length, but something she'd have to work on. Because clearly, they were pulling her into the fold. That was okay. She could keep herself hard so when it eventually petered out, she wouldn't end up filleted once again.

"There a reason you all invited me here? A reason beyond torturing me?"

"Yes!" Shell bounced on the balls of her feet, her blond curls springing around her radiant face. "Copper's fortieth birthday is in three months, and I want it to be epic, so I want to start planning now."

"Oh, yes!" Toni said, slapping her palms on the countertop. "Let's do it."

With a frown, Izzy said. "What did you need me for?"

"I'll refrain from smacking the injured woman, but are you stupid? You're one of us now. So you get to help." Shell smiled.

"You could just get a bunch of skanky strippers and call it a day," Jazz said on a giggle.

"I don't think so." Shell swatted her with her order pad. Then she shrugged. "They'll probably do that after, but we're throwing a party we can all attend first."

Izzy studied the other woman, so excited over planning a party for a man who wasn't hers and who'd never be hers if chatter was true.

"What?" Shell asked. "You're looking at me funny."

Busted. "Oh, sorry, just thinking." She sipped her coffee and shifted her focus to a table of teenagers across the diner.

"I don't think so. You got something to say, say it."

After swallowing the liquid fuel, Izzy said. "Fair enough. I just, I guess I'm wondering why you're doing this. For Copper, I mean."

Toni's eyes widened, and she busied herself straightening a stack of napkins while Jazz pretended to find something fascinating in her coffee mug.

"Ah." Shell heaved a heavy sigh. "Our past is complicated." Her small laugh was humorless. "More complicated than even Copper knows. But he's important to me. Has been for most of my life. And the club is my family. They're in my blood. So, I may be a fool, but I'm a fool with my eyes open. I won't let myself get hurt."

Toni reached out and squeezed Shell's hand. If Shell thought that explanation would make sense to Izzy, she was dead wrong. Never having a family she could count on, Izzy had no idea what that kind of blind loyalty felt like. Envy, ugly and dark, twisted deep in her soul, but she shoved it away. Part of her wanted to warn Shell how foolish her thinking was. How she was most certainly setting herself up to be hurt, disappointed, crushed. But she didn't do it. Shell's faith in her family kept her moving forward despite difficult circumstances. Who was Izzy to steal that away from her?

She'd learn in time that people couldn't be depended upon.

After Shell returned with their plates, the four women got down to business, planning an epic blowout for Copper. Jig and his brothers stayed for a while, never interrupting their girl time. As he was leaving, his gaze met Izzy's again, and she nearly combusted from the heat wafting her way. He didn't come over to speak with her, only turned her to dust with the lusty stare.

Shit, she was in trouble. It was only a matter of time before she was alone with him again and she feared there wasn't a firehose with enough pressure to douse the flame he ignited in her.

At some point, she was bound to make a monstrous mistake.

The only comfort was that it would be one helluva pleasurable mistake.

CHAPTER FOURTEEN

Jig exited his office and turned straight into Copper's. The door was open, so he rapped on the frame. "Hey, boss."

"What's up, Jig?" Copper snubbed out his cigarette and folded his forearms on the desk. "Come on in."

"Just need you for a minute," Jig said as he entered the room, holding out a thick envelope full of cash. "Another ten thousand, straight off one of Lefty's guys. These idiots need a better system. No one should be walking around with this much coin."

Stretching his long arms over his head, Copper said, "Don't question it. It's easy money for us. They get any intel off the guy?"

"Nope, kid was fifteen. Fucking wet himself and practically threw the money at Screw. He blabbed every single thing he knew, which was jack." Screw was spending quite a bit of time with Zach. As enforcer, Zach needed guys he could trust as backup and extra muscle. Screw was motivated, a tad bloodthirsty, and a fast learner. Perfect for the role.

Copper chuckled then shook his head. "Fifteen fucking years old. Christ." He held out his hand for the money, and Jig tossed him the envelope. "It'll be in the safe."

"Got it."

"Shut that door behind you. I'm expecting a call from Rusty." Rusty, Copper's brother, was in a federal prison out west. He'd been there for the past four and a half years. Aggravated assault.

Guy was beaten so badly he'd be spending the rest of his life breathing through a tube. And Rusty was given a dime behind bars.

Despite the conviction, Copper was adamant about his brother's innocence. Jig wasn't stupid enough to contradict his prez over such a personal matter, but he'd never been Rusty's biggest fan. Something about the guy was off. Like burning animal carcasses in the woods off.

"Give him hell for me," Jig said, and Copper grinned. Prez lived for the weekly phone calls from his brother.

"Will do."

After quietly closing Copper's door behind him, Jig made his way to the bar. It was around six in the evening and bizarrely calm in the clubhouse. Between Copper's edict of no Honeys, the closed bar, and all manpower on Lefty-watch, the place had been a ghost town over the past week. Jig couldn't quite get used to it.

Shaking off the odd feeling, he made his way behind the bar, poured some whiskey, and downed it. As the liquid warmed its way to his bloodstream, the door swung open and Izzy stepped in, glancing around the empty room. It was the first time he'd seen her since the diner, and her customary tight braid and makeup were back in place. She was also moving with a fluidity that showed what a fast healer she was. The bruises on her neck had faded considerably, though even the pale sight of them made him want to tear Lefty apart.

He cleared his throat, and she jumped, snapping her head in his direction.

"Oh, hey," she said, voice almost at full capacity, just an octave lower than usual, huskier. Sexier. Heels on, she walked toward him, those hips swaying in that unconscious sensual way she had. Strong, sure, and confident, yet now he knew some softness lie beneath her armor. He'd glimpsed it in her un-made-up face at the diner.

"What's up, Izzy? What are you doing here?" He poured himself another drink. It was the least he'd need to survive this encounter without tossing her on the bar, messing up that flawless hair, and fucking her hard. Good thing Copper was still in the building and could emerge from his office at any moment, or Jig might not have the willpower to keep himself in check.

Izzy reached the bar and held up a manila envelope. "Have something to give to Steph. She was supposed to meet me here, but just texted to say she's running about twenty minutes late, so she told me to come in, hang with the guys, and have a drink." She made a dramatic point of looking around. "No guys."

"Nope, just guy. Bourbon?" he asked. What she'd had the two times he'd seen her drink.

"Yeah, thanks," she said as she slid onto a stool and dropped her packet on the bar top. Her face took on a teasing glint. "Hmm, kinda like this. You fixing me drinks. A girl could get used to this kind of service."

With a snort, Jig slid her tumbler across the bar. "Don't get used to it. I graduated from bartender as soon as I was done prospecting. With how much liquor our guys can put away, it fucking sucks to work the bar at our parties."

She let out a soft hum. "I imagine it does."

"How you feeling?" Jig shoved the bottles aside but didn't return them to the shelf. Chances were, they'd be back for more. "You're moving better."

"Not bad. Much better, actually. A little stiff and achy when I first get going in the morning and by the end of the day, but that's the worst of it right now." She gave him a smile that had his jeans shrinking.

Jig held up his glass. "To kicking ass," he said.

Izzy's eyes sparkled. "I'll gladly drink to that," she replied as she clicked her glass against his.

They both drained their drinks in seconds, then Jig grabbed the bottle of bourbon and raised an eyebrow.

"Remember what I told you about that bird?" She'd pulled the tail of her braid over her shoulder and was twirling it around her fingers. It was cute, and there was an innocence about it he knew she didn't possess. But it made her look younger, with a hint of vulnerability.

He chuckled and poured her a healthy drink. "Yep. Can't fly with only one wing."

"Exactly. So, Jig," she said, gaze on the tip of her braid as she fingered it. "I'm not sure I ever properly thanked you for meeting me at the hospital and taking me home." Unspoken was the thanks for the orgasm, but it was there in the slight flush that rose on her cheeks.

Izzy was blushing. Jig wouldn't have believed it if he hadn't seen it with his own eyes, but there it was. An adorable pink flush she'd probably unman him over if he called attention to it.

"Ain't a thing, sweetheart."

"No, it was a thing." She lifted her gaze to his face. "Everyone in your club has been so incredibly kind. The girls have been bringing me food and forcing me to rest. Copper's checked in a few times. Even guys watching my house are quick to jump in and help. LJ even carried in my UPS packages the other day."

Jig frowned. Those assholes were supposed to be guarding her, not strolling through her house and getting all chummy. Fucking LJ, still slobbering after her. He'd be having a chat with LJ later. "Seriously, Izzy. It's no big deal." He'd practically had to cuff himself to his office chair to keep from checking in on her all week. Toni and Shell had a blast filling him in on every detail. It was enough to satisfy his curiosity about her wellbeing.

That left him with no reason to visit but to fuck her. And he'd promised himself that wouldn't happen, so somehow, he'd found the strength to stay away.

And now here she was, looking like a delicious treat made just for him.

"Well, thanks all the same. You've got a great family." There was something almost sad about the way she said *family*.

The word sent a sharp, stabbing pang straight to his heart. He'd *had* a great family once upon a time, and while she was talking about his MC family, and they were great, the word family made him recall what he'd lost. The girls must have filled her in on some information about his past. While he supposed it was natural for her to be as curious about him as he was of her, being the subject of her chats with the ol' ladies didn't sit well. The past wasn't something he discussed, and hopefully she wouldn't ask.

Because there was no way in hell he'd be sharing it with her. Time to divert the conversation from himself. "What about you?" He filled their glasses for the third time.

Her nose scrunched. "What about me?"

"You got a family?"

The light drained from her eyes, so thoroughly he almost took the question back. But now he had to know because there was a story there.

"Nah, it's just me."

"It's never just you. There's gotta be someone somewhere."

And there was the look. Narrowed eyes, compressed lips. Her feathers were ruffled. His cock twitched. He needed to cut the poor thing a break. With all the hand-to-dick action he'd been giving himself over the past week, he was about five strokes away from rubbing the skin off.

"Well, bubba"—she seemed to call him that when she was in her prickly mode—"I've never met my dad. My mom married and divorced five different men before offing herself when I was seventeen. She had no siblings, her parents are dead, and thankfully she never procreated beyond me, so I guess, sure, I've got someone. I've got a sperm donor floating out there in the wind, no doubt dying to learn of the long-lost daughter he fathered thirty years ago. That what you were looking for?" She sucked back what was left in her glass.

Well, fuck. That explained the *fuck off* scrawled across her forehead and her fierce independence. Jig might mimic a stone half the time, but he wasn't completely devoid of emotion. He slid his hand over hers and smiled at the widening of her eyes. "Hey, sorry I asked. Your shit is your shit, and I shouldn't have pushed."

Izzy heaved a sigh. "No, I'm the one who's sorry. Kinda a touchy subject, if you hadn't noticed." She flipped her hand over and curled it around his.

"What happened with your mom?"

With a huff, she tapped the top of her glass, but he didn't bother reaching for the bottle. Three drinks in ten minutes were plenty. "Mental illness. She had severe bipolar disorder and was with a long line of loser men who never cared to get her help. She had these erratic moods and intense swings from high to low. Her boyfriends and husbands just called her crazy. By the time I was old enough to understand she had an illness that could be treated, she was too far gone and refused any help. Couldn't get her hospitalized involuntarily if she wasn't a danger to herself or others. The one time she proved to be that danger, she got the job done." She shrugged. "Sucks, but that's life."

Such a hard exterior. Such a lonely life. Jig tried that, going it completely alone, and it nearly ended in disaster. Copper saved his ass, and his brothers brought him back from the dead. No way Izzy's insides were as matter of fact and unaffected as she portrayed on the outside. He was starting to understand what made her tick. She burned hot, felt too much, but had years of practice suppressing it. Unable to deal with the tumultuous emotions, she handled them differently, fighting them out in the ring. Something Jig fully comprehended.

For the first time since his wife had died, he felt an urge, a need, to soothe a woman. If he didn't think she'd kick him in the nuts, he'd draw her into his arms and remind her she wasn't alone anymore. She had him. She had his club brothers and the women that loved them.

Jig cleared his throat and shoved down those primal urges. His own head was a mess; he was in no position to meet anyone else's emotional needs. Nor did he want to. "You said you were seventeen when she died. What happened to you?"

Jigsaw

Izzy watched him, her gaze assessing, as if trying to decide if she trusted him enough to share a vulnerable piece of herself. He had no idea why it mattered to him, but it did. He wanted her to trust him, to open up and share a little fragment of her inner workings. Because it was obvious she didn't do this often. Didn't form relationships, platonic or otherwise, didn't let others have any piece of herself deeper than surface knowledge.

And that meant anyone she handed the information to was important, trusted, and significant. It wasn't smart. In fact, it was downright stupid and a mistake, but he felt something for her. Something more than just his cock's response to her body. And while he'd never act on it, never take it to a deeper level, he was selfish enough to want her to feel the same.

He waited her out, not speaking nor pressuring while she glanced away, breathed, then came back to him. Something unspoken passed between them at that moment. An understanding and acceptance. Whether it was the peace and quiet of the clubhouse, loneliness, or, hell, maybe the alcohol, they saw each other. Two people too damaged by life to have successful relationships or tap into their emotions in a healthy way. Maybe something could be formed from that. A friendship of sorts. No promises, no guarantees, no potential for more agony. Just a...bond of pain.

"I was still underage, so I would have ended up in foster care somewhere. But I fled before social services could get their hooks in me. For about a year, I lived on the streets in New Orleans. Rip found me outside his shop one day, sketching in this ratty old book I had. He took pity on me and hired me to keep the place clean. Eventually, I apprenticed with him."

Her gaze bore into his as if to say, "Go ahead, pity me. I dare you." But he never would. Many of his brothers had shit backgrounds, some so horrifying the stories made your ears bleed. Hell, his own story made grown men cry. Survive, overcome, move on. That's what people did with shitty circumstances.

It was clear how Izzy had made it through life. Living through darkness made her strong as fuck. Made her capable of taking care of herself and surviving the harsh realities of the world. Hell, if his wife had been half as tough as Izzy, maybe that night would have turned out very differently.

Shit. He peered into his empty glass. Been a while since thoughts like that had invaded his conscious.

"Hey," Izzy said, cutting through his morbid trip down memory lane. "You got a funny look on your face. You good?"

"Yeah." He polished off his drink. "You're pretty fucking fierce, you know that, Iz?"

A slow smile curled the blood-red lips he wanted to crush against his own. Looked like she appreciated the compliment. God, she was gorgeous.

"You're not so bad yourself, Jig."

He glanced down suddenly when he realized their hands were still intertwined. The air between them thickened and cracked with high-voltage electricity. The chemistry they shared was enough to burn the place to the ground. Friendship and chemistry—sounded like a recipe for a relationship neither was able to accept.

Orgasms. That's what he needed. A warm, wet place to sink his cock and lose himself. That's all he wanted, and that's all he'd allow himself with her. Time to rip the emotions from this encounter and bring it back to the safety of the physical.

Leaning forward, Jig reached out and hooked a finger into the collar of her sweatshirt. One little tug, and her mouth was millimeters from his. "Not to mention," he said. "You have the sweetest fucking pussy I've ever tasted."

Her eyes went tire-wide, and she sputtered. It wasn't often someone caught her off guard, but it was damn fun. As her mouth flapped opened and closed, Jig's attention was rapt on her lips. Shiny with that bright red gloss, they looked like the perfect place to sink his teeth. He leaned in, ready to do just that

—

"Oh, my god, I am so sorry." Stephanie's voice had Izzy wrenching back and spinning on her stool. Their friend rushed through the door over to the bar. "Were you waiting forever?"

"Ah..." Izzy cleared her throat and stood to accept Steph's enthusiastic hug. "No. Not at all. Felt like two minutes."

Jig snickered and discretely adjusted himself behind the bar. "Want a drink, Steph?"

"No thanks." She waved a hand back and forth. "Mav will be here in ten, and we're going to grab something to eat." Stepping back, Steph looked between him and Izzy with a raised eyebrow.

Izzy's face reddened, and she looked everywhere but at him. Then her body straightened and she said, "Oh, I got what you asked me for." Snatching up the envelope, she handed it to Stephanie.

A mix of disappointment and relief bombarded Jig. The interruption was necessary and jerked his mind out of ridiculous fantasies, but left his body in a state of unfulfilled desire. "All right, ladies. I'm out. Good chatting with you, Iz. See you at the gym tomorrow?"

"Yeah, I'll be there by eight."

"Good deal." Jig accepted a kiss on his unscarred cheek from Stephanie as he made his way to the exit. Within seconds of walking away from the women, he could hear them chattering on and giggling like school girls. It brought a smile to his face. Izzy might not realize it, but her guard was coming down.

Them fucking was inevitable. It was going to happen. They had the type of attraction that couldn't be ignored. And it would be fucking earth-shattering.

But that's all it would be. Fucking and a shaky friendship. Because no way in hell was Jig letting a woman, even a woman as boss as Izzy, melt the thick layers of ice around his heart. He would never survive a devastating loss like he'd suffered with his wife and child's deaths, and his life now was a hundred times more dangerous than it had been years ago. After knowing Jig a short time, Izzy had already been attacked by his enemies.

No matter the conflicting emotions Izzy dredged up in him, she wouldn't ever be more than a friendly fuck buddy. Anything more could destroy them both.

And no amount of chemistry was worth that.

CHAPTER FIFTEEN

Izzy concentrated on slowing her inhalations and filling her lungs. Damn, it felt good. She'd hit three miles easily today and without an ounce of pain. Parts of her were still a little discolored, but the discomfort had all but disappeared. Only a slight amount of a.m. stiffness remained.

Now, it was time to get back the endurance she'd lost over the past week or so and get back to her pre-beatdown ten miles per day. Thankfully, Zach was still willing to keep the gym open an hour or two after closing for her and Jig. Tonight, one of Jig's newer brothers, Screw, had joined them. The guy was hilarious. A total screwball, hence the name.

Wiping a stream of sweat from her cheek, she attempted to clear her mind of the muscle fatigue and focus on something else. All that accomplished was a return to her obsessive thoughts about Jig. He'd been in the forefront of her mind since she'd spilled her guts all over the bar the prior night.

Why the hell had she done that?

Alcohol. It had to be the alcohol, an uncharacteristic feeling of loneliness, and the proximity to the anniversary of her mother's death. In just a few weeks, the thirteenth anniversary would be upon her. That had to be some kind of bad omen, right? Thirteenth anniversary of a horrific death?

A shiver ran down Izzy's spine. Shit, she was getting maudlin. She never thought she'd say it, but obsessing over Jig was far better than ruminating over the dead and buried past.

It seemed they were now friends. He didn't even scowl at her when she came into the gym. Sure, he didn't run over and give her a kiss on the cheek like Zach did, but a non-scowl from Jig was pretty much the equivalent of a bear hug from any of the other guys.

It was what it was. The MC had adopted her, and she'd just have to deal. She had plenty of practice keeping herself from disappointment and hurt. She could do it again and have some fun with her new social circle.

A band of outlaw bikers. The thought made her snort out a laugh which had her sucking a quick breath and coughing. "Shit!" She hacked and tried to breathe as she lowered the treadmill speed to a fast walk. Oh, look at that, four point two miles.

She'd hit the target.

"You know, it's a lot easier to run if you're actually breathing." Jig sauntered over in all his sexy, sweaty glory, and folded his way too muscly arms across the top of the treadmill.

Her breath caught in her lungs at the sight of him glistening with sweat and wearing a royal blue T-shirt that molded to every ridge in his chest and abs.

She swallowed around a suddenly very dry throat and focused on his statement instead of his drool-worthy physique.

Things were progressing quickly. From non-scowl to teasing in one evening. Izzy flashed him a smile. He could mess with her all he wanted. She was queen ballbuster, and he'd be eating those words in a matter of minutes. "Sorry, saw your brother, Screw, doing some squats, and it stole my breath. That man's got one helluvan ass." She winked and lowered the speed even further.

Jig's jaw ticked, and she must have been speaking louder than she realized because Screw yelled, "Damn straight, baby," from across the room. He bent forward a little and slapped his own ass. "Any time you wanna cop a feel, sweet thang, you just say the word."

A laugh bubbled out of Izzy. Even Jig's lips quirked. Screw was ridiculous, but always good for a fun time.

"You're gonna pay for that," Jig practically growled at her. He tapped his knuckles on the top of the treadmill then made his way back to the weight rack he'd been lifting. Izzy was helpless to do anything other than stare at the flex and release of his calves, thighs, and ass as he moved like a powerful animal. When he was halfway to his destination, he peeked over his shoulder and threw her a wink. "Ain't Screw's ass you're drooling over now, is it?"

A normal woman would probably be embarrassed, but, hell, Jig was one sexy man, and he damn well knew it. No point in caring she got busted gawking. Any sane woman would.

Screw hooted out a laugh and clapped his hands. "Jig with the jokes. Who the fuck knew? You just might have to marry him, Iz."

And like a bucket of ice-cold water had been upended on them all, the fire was doused instantly. Jig stiffened so fast she thought he might snap right in half. Then came the first scowl of the day. With a sigh, Izzy jumped her feet to the outer frame of the treadmill and hit the off button. It was just a stupid comment, one she could let roll off her shoulders, but then she'd never been married before. And never planned to marry. A front row seat to the tanking of five marriages throughout her childhood was enough, thank you very much. But Jig had been married, and it had been destroyed by something vicious and out of his control. The pain of that had to be extraordinary, and both her heart and stomach clenched at the thought of his suffering. Something about the thought of him in agony tormented her deep inside.

Bringing herself back into the moment, Izzy hopped off the treadmill and headed straight for a matted area. Sitting with her legs outstretched, she bent forward and wrapped her hands around the soles of her feet. Damn, that felt amazing. She'd give

Jig a few minutes to deal with whatever poison was invading his mind then go over and see if she could coax another one of those almost-smiles out of him.

Just as she was about to move into another stretch, Zach barreled out of his office, cell pressed to his ear. "Motherfucker!" he shouted. "Tell me exactly what the fuck happened."

He quieted for about fifteen seconds, then picked up a spray bottle and hurled it across the room. When it crashed against the wall mirror, the top flew off, exploding cleaning solution all over the mirror. Thankfully, the glass didn't crack.

"Why the fuck are you the one calling me and not Toni? She okay? Yeah, thanks." Zach paced back and forth.

Izzy rose and glanced at Jig then Screw. Both men had abandoned what they were doing the second they heard the distress in Zach's voice. They crowded around their brother, waiting for news.

"Hey, baby," Zach said, rubbing at his bowed forehead. Whoever'd been on the phone must have passed it off to Toni.

Izzy's gut twisted. She hadn't known the other woman long, but the thought of something happening to her was sickening. She was already too attached to this group.

"You okay?" Zach asked into the phone, his voice taking on a softer quality she'd only ever heard him use with Toni. "No, babe, don't worry about the diner. The guys will have it fixed up in no time. I want to know if you are okay. Any motherfuckers lay a hand on you?"

Izzy took a few steps closer but remained out of their personal space. Head still bent forward, Zach massaged the back of his neck. "All right, baby, I'll be there in ten minutes. Some of the other guys might start showing up before me. Don't leave LJ's sight. You hear me?" Then he turned and took two steps away from his brothers and lowered his volume. "Fuckin' scared me, baby. Yeah, okay. Love you too, Toni."

He ended the call and turned back to his brothers. Before he spoke, his gaze flicked to Izzy. "I can go," she said, motioning her thumb toward the exit. She probably should have left already, but curiosity and worry for her friend had gotten the best of her.

"No, it's fine. Stick around." Zach sighed, though it was more of a half growl, half hiss. "Diner was vandalized. Toni swung by to grab something she'd forgotten. Entire front of the place is covered in red spray paint. Says shit like "biker whore" and some threats against her. Godfuckingdamnit." Zach violently kicked a weight bench, upending the thing with a tremendous clatter.

Izzy jumped but remained quiet. His brothers would take care of him. For now, it seemed he needed to rant and get it out.

"She coulda shown up while they were there. You have any idea what would have happened if these assholes walked in on Toni alone in the diner?" He stalked over to the mirror and rested his palms against it, staring at his own murderous expression.

Jig froze, and Izzy held her breath. For a second, you could have heard a pin drop, and she sent a quick prayer out into the universe, hoping Jig would keep his cool. Zach and Toni were in love in a way Izzy had never experienced, but Jig had. Zach's fear for his woman had to be resonating with Jig in a soul-crushing way. She wished there was something she could offer besides moral support. Something bigger. Something that would actually help distract Jig from his memories and ease the worry for his brother.

"Shit. Fuck." Zach ran a hand down his face. "I'm sorry, brother," he said to Jig. "That was a dick thing to say."

"Ain't a thing," Jig replied, but the words sounded forced, as though someone had to reach down and drag them out from inside him.

"I gotta get to her."

"Right behind you, brother," Screw said as he dashed into the locker room. He returned less than five seconds later, cut on and ready to roll.

"Shit," Zach said, running a hand down his face. "I have to close the place up. And I made a fucking mess."

Jig jogged into Zach's office, emerging with Zach's cut. "Forget that, Z. Iz and I got it. Just get to Toni." With one hand, he tossed the cut to Zach.

"You sure?" Zach asked as he snagged the cut out of the air and shrugged into it.

"Yes, totally sure," Izzy piped in. "Go be with Toni."

"Thanks, brother," Zach said, holding a hand out to Jig who ignored it and pulled him into a man-hug. "Want these fuckers' blood, Jig."

"I hear ya," Jig said.

"It's gonna end in war. You know that, right?"

With a nod, Jig shoved Zach toward the door. "Go to your woman. We'll figure it out."

As he passed her, Zach dropped a kiss on Izzy's cheek. "You're the best, Iz." Then he whispered, "This'll fuck his head up. Take care of my boy tonight."

The request went beyond simple friendship. It brought her into the family and firmed her connection to the club. Despite knowing she was setting herself up for disaster, there was only one answer in her head. She nodded. "I'll check in on Toni tomorrow."

Without even an ounce of hesitation, no thought necessary, Zach's brothers did what needed to be done. Rushed right to his side with unconditional support and love. It was a novel thing for Izzy to witness, and something she didn't trust. But it wasn't the first time she'd seen it. They'd done the same when she was injured. That kind of support scared the shit out of her because it was the kind people came to rely on. The kind that drew a person in. And the kind that would leave a person shattered and broken once it disappeared.

Once Zach and Screw were gone, the gym fell into an uncomfortable silence. Jig's expression had hardened and an iciness reflected in his eyes. Posture stiff, he stood staring off into space, probably lost in the horrors of the past. Did he want her ass gone so he could deal with his shit on his own? Probably. But if he was anything like her, and she was starting to think he was, at least in this regard, he needed something else to release the pressure. And the one thing that opened the valve for her was fighting. Learning to read his moods and expressions was frightening on an emotional level, but valuable if she was going to help him.

"Come on," she said, grabbing him by the sleeve as she headed for the boxing ring in the far corner of the gym.

"What the fuck? What are you doing Izzy?" Jig resisted, but she tugged harder, and he relented. When they reached the ring, she climbed in and motioned for him to follow.

"This isn't the time for this, Izzy. We gotta clean and shut the place down for Zach."

Planting her hands on her hips, she gave him her best don't-fuck-with-me look. "Get your ass in the ring, Jigsaw. You need to work this shit out of your head so you can be there for your brothers." Witnessing how they supported each other, she had a feeling that would get to him.

Sure enough...

He bent his head side to side, cracking his neck. "Fuck it," he muttered and climbed into the ring. "What exactly are we doing here?"

Izzy shot him a grin and bounced on the balls of her feet. "Let's see if you can take me on. For real. No boxing, just grappling." It was stupid. He had six inches and sixty pounds of muscle on her, but she wanted, no needed, to go all out.

His hands landed on his hips, and he gave her a glare that would make a lesser woman run screaming. By now, he should know it took a fuckuva lot more than a little eye-murder to scare her.

Biting her lip to hide the evil grin, she charged. Jig was taken completely off guard, probably the only reason she'd been able to take him to the ground so effortlessly. They hit the mat with a thud, and she moved fast, straddling his waist and pinning his arms above his head.

With a raised eyebrow, she laughed. "That was pretty damn easy, Jig. Maybe you need to think about upping your training."

She almost fell off him when he burst out laughing. It was the biggest, most unfiltered response she'd seen from the man yet, and it transformed him from a brooding, sexy, biker to a playful, still-sexy, potential lover.

"You fucking cheat," he said, still chuckling.

"Not hardly. I warned you what was about to happen."

"All right," he said. "Have it your way." Then, with a lightning-fast move, he bucked his hips and sent her flying to her back, reversing their positions.

"All right," Jig said. He was on his knees, hands laced behind his head. "You win. I need this."

"Well, we haven't known each other that long, so I guess I can't expect you to realize I'm always right just yet. It'll come with time."

He rolled his eyes and placed his hands on her knees. "You're such a smartass."

"My special gift to humanity." Izzy snorted out a laugh and kicked into gear. They grappled for about ten minutes, going at it hard and reversing positions again and again until they were both panting and exhausted. Neither was fully trying to get the other to submit, but that didn't mean they held back.

Astride him in the upper-hand position once again, Izzy glanced down at Jig. "Ready to give up?" she asked.

"Never."

Izzy froze to a statue above him as the rumble of his laughter vibrated through her pussy which was intimately pressed against his abdomen. Arousal hit her, hard and fast, drenching her panties and stealing her focus.

Jig bucked his hips, sending her careening forward. On autopilot, her hands splayed on his chest, an action that had happened at least three times since they started grappling. But this time, she wasn't focused on wrestling him, but absorbed the sensation of his hard pecs beneath her fingertips. Those fingertips flexed of their own accord, probing the hard muscles and sending a delicious thrill of need through her.

Jig took advantage of her distracted state and flipped her once again until she landed flat on her back with him between her legs, which were wrapped around his hips, ankles locked across his lower spine. The weight of him pressed into her sensitized sex ripped a low groan from her.

"Shit, did I hurt you?" Almost as if he wasn't aware of his actions, Jig slid his hands over her skin-tight leggings and up her inner thighs. Halfway between her knees and her pussy, he froze, his large hands gripping her legs tight.

Her body reacted, letting both of them know how much she wanted those hands to continue their journey. Her nipples tightened until she could feel both of them beneath her sports bra, and the need to touch them became almost unbearable.

He got with the program then, eyes zeroing in on the twin points popping out on her chest. Against her ass, the hard ridge of his growing erection nudged her. More wetness flooded her pussy at the feel of his desire, and Jig's nostril's flared. Fuck, could he smell her arousal?

The thought was damn hot.

Immobilized in time, they locked gazes and panted as the brewing storm between them grew to hurricane strength.

Without a word, Jig skimmed his hands forward until his thumbs met at the apex of her thighs. He swiped one, then the other, over her mound and her hips jerked as a lightning bolt of sensation shot through her core.

He met her gaze, and she nodded. "I want you, Jig," she said.

He brushed her again and shook his head, withdrawing his hands. "Not tonight, Izzy. I'm no good tonight. My head's too fucked. No way I could be anything close to gentle."

With a huffed laugh, Izzy propped herself on her elbows. "Jig, anything about me give you the impression that I'm down with gentle?"

That earned her a ghost of a smile. "Not what I mean. I'm angry. Fucking pissed. About the diner, about our enemies, about…other things. Can't promise I can control myself."

Little did he know those words only fanned her flames. Her pussy wept for him, and if he kept talking, she just might beg him to fuck her. It'd be easy to flip him in his distracted state, and part of her was tempted to do it. Just a quick twist of her hips and a squeeze of her thighs and he'd be under her. At her mercy. Once he felt the heat of her damp pussy grinding on his dick, he'd never refuse her. Then she could fuck him. Her usual style. Submission wasn't her thing.

But he needed this, and he'd been there for her when she needed help, so she'd give him what she sensed he needed and let him have control. She stayed where she was, determined to get him to let loose of that control. They'd both benefit from it in the most pleasurable of ways.

"I'm game for a little rage-fucking, Jig. Trust me, I can handle you. Whatever you want to dish out." She'd never spoken words like this to a man she wanted sex from, and a small niggle of unease teased the base of her brain. Not having control was a dangerous position to be in. Someone could slip past the defenses she'd set up if she let them control her.

That wouldn't happen tonight, though. Jig wanted no part of emotion, connection, or a relationship. She didn't have to worry that he'd want a date or romance. He'd want to fuck, train, and hang at the occasional party. So she could hand him this very unprecedented gift and let him have the reigns.

"Iz—"

"Shut up, Jig." She laughed at the surprised look on his face. Okay, maybe she'd hold onto one of those reigns. With a little wiggle, she shimmied her tank top over her head, then grasped the band of her sports bra and gave it the same treatment. Both landed in a pile over her head.

Jig sucked in a breath, his pupils widened, and his cock

pressed into the V of her thighs.

Hello, fly, welcome to my web.

While he gawked, she started at her stomach and ran her hands up over her ribs. Finally, she settled them on her tits.

Jig's chest rose and fell, and his hands returned to her thighs, squeezing hard. With a grin she hoped was as sexy as it felt, she pinched her nipples and arched her back, letting a moan out.

"Christ, Iz, you are the sexiest fucking thing."

She winked as she played with her nipples. Each tug and pinch sent shocks straight to her clit. "I hear I'm not your usual type with my dark hair, height, and run-a-way mouth. Your cock seems to like what I've got to offer, though."

His eyes narrowed. Was she crazy for baiting an already pissed-off man? One who had warned her it'd be hard and rough if he gave it to her?

Yeah, crazy, but oh-so good.

"Come on, Jig," she said. "Do your worst." She moaned again and rubbed her heated pussy against his hard-as-stone cock.

He sprung to his feet and rushed to Zach's office. Izzy's heart sank. She'd pushed too far. Just as she was about to reach for her shirt, he reappeared, foil packet in hand.

He stalked over and stood between her spread legs, looming over her. And the look on his face.

Holy shit. The animal had been let loose.

CHAPTER SIXTEEN

Jig stared down at the sensual, willing woman spread out on the mat waiting for him to take her. She still toyed with her nipples, and the attention was working because she writhed against the mat.

As she pleasured herself and stared at him, he toed off his shoes, stripped out of his shirt, then lost his shorts and boxer briefs in one quick yank. Izzy's eyes widened, and her hands fell from her plump tits.

"Jesus, Jig, that's some heavy artillery you're packing there." Pushing up onto her elbows, she licked her lips, and he groaned. With a firm touch, he wrapped a hand around his shaft and stroked, giving a twist over the tip.

She cocked her head. "You gonna share or am I just here for a show?"

"Oh, I'm gonna give it to you. When I'm ready." When a drop of precum beaded at the tip, he swiped it away with his thumb.

"Looks like you're ready to me." Izzy's voice had lowered to a rasping, almost whisper that had his cock leaking even more. She wanted this. Maybe as much as he did.

"Lie back down."

She did.

"Bend your knees. Spread further."

She did.

"Hands over your head."

Jigsaw

That one had her hesitating, but to his surprise, she did it. He kept waiting for her to tell him to fuck off and start barking orders of her own, but it seemed like she was playing this his way. She was right about two things. She was not his typical lay. And if anyone could take what he had to dish out, he had a feeling it was her.

Never had he hurt a woman, but he rage-fucked, to steal her phrase. It was the truth. Rough, raw, intense, punishing. And most women, at least the delicate little flowers he fucked, couldn't handle him and never came back for more. He heard the gossip, how all his brothers assumed he was punishing his dead wife for leaving him. And maybe there was some truth to that, but it also ensured they'd never want more from him. No hearts, flowers, or I love yous.

Nothing but down and dirty fucking.

Kneeling between Izzy's legs, he shoved her knees wider to accommodate his bulk. Then he planted his hands next to her head and hovered inches above her face. "Give me that smart mouth that likes to bust my balls so much."

She flaunted a sassy grin and tilted her chin up. Bracing on one hand, he grabbed her jaw with the other. Just before his mouth descended, he saw a quick flash of uncertainty in her eyes, and he fucking loved it. Call him sick, but it's exactly what he wanted from her. He wanted to take everything she had to give and, even more, wanted her to give it willingly despite her unease. He wanted to conquer her. To get this strong as hell woman to submit to his every desire.

His mouth crushed hers. No soft lead-in, but a hard, bruising clash of lips that claimed her. She gave as good as she got, eating at his mouth and making his cock leak even more. God damn, even when he had her at his mercy, she had control over him. She was just that sexy.

Her tongue explored his mouth with bold, confident strokes, and he swore he could feel each one swiping over his dick. In the very near future, he had to get that tongue on him. It was bound to shoot his head straight off his body. He captured her lower lip between his teeth and tugged, loving the gasp that escaped her.

Still holding her jaw, he turned her face away from him and licked a line from her collarbone to her ear. She shuddered beneath him, and her hips rose, stroking her still clothed pussy over his cock. Time to take it to the next level.

He kissed down her neck, harsh, biting kisses that had her moaning and writhing under him. Surprisingly, she obeyed and kept her arms high above her head. As he continued his journey, he ran his hands up and down her thighs, pausing to squeeze the outsides of her ass with each pass. When his mouth reached her nipple, he latched on with strong suction.

"Jig," she cried out, arching her back until her tit nearly smothered him. He sucked hard, soaking up each whimper of pleasure. Izzy wasn't a shy lover. She openly relished the pleasure he dished out. As he drew away, he caught her nipple between his teeth and tugged. "Fuck, that's good," she said then chuckled. "Not sure how much more of this I can take."

He smiled as he licked his way to her other tit. "You can take it. You really have no choice."

She hmphed, but it quickly turned to a sharp cry when he grabbed her other nipple with his teeth hard enough to pinch. Her pelvis ground against him, wet through the fabric of her yoga pants.

"Shit, Iz, you're soaking me through your clothes." He rose to his knees and looked down at her flushed nipples, wet and swollen from his mouth with a trail of red marks running down her chest.

"I want you," she said. The statement simple, yet powerful.

Sliding his hands under her, he cupped her ass in both hands, hard enough to leave marks and she moaned long and loud. "God, I fucking love this ass," he said. "Lift it for me, babe. Gotta get these pants off so I can fuck you."

She complied, and he peeled the pants down her legs. When he reached her feet, he yanked off her shoes and socks, chucking them somewhere across the room. In no time, she was clad only in a tiny black thong. "Panties stay on," he said.

"Works for me."

He grabbed the condom and rolled it down his length. Izzy watched his every move, eyes hungry. When he was suited up, he knee-walked his way back between her legs, cock in hand. "You ready for this?"

"You have no idea," she said on an exhale.

"I have some idea." As he spoke, he couldn't resist teasing her. He ran the tip of his dick through her saturated folds. Unfortunately, he hadn't planned too well because the heat of her and the way her opening flexed as though trying to suck him in nearly had him filling that condom way too early.

"Christ, Jig. Fuck me already." She sounded pissed off, and he laughed two seconds before he powered into her with a brutal snap of his hips.

"Holy fuck," Izzy cried, her back bowing and arms no longer above her head. Hands landed on his shoulders with a hard slap one second before a set of ten nails scored his skin. "Christ, Jig, you're fucking huge."

A man could hear that phrase a million times and love it every single time. He winked then fucked her exactly like he'd promised. Hard, fast, raw, ruthless. She kept with him, meeting him thrust for thrust, her hands clawing at his back like a wild animal. Every time he slammed into her, Izzy's pussy clenched at his cock, and she let out a soft whimper. Those sounds amped him up almost as much as the feel of her tight heat surrounding him.

At one point, their eyes met, and it was like taking a sucker punch to the gut. The damn woman had a grip on more than just his cock. He had to put an end to it immediately. He pulled out, flipped her over, yanked her to her knees, and shoved back in before he even gave her a chance to catch up. She cried out as he picked the pace right back up.

"Fuck, this is insane," he swore he heard her whisper, but she didn't miss a beat, pushing back on his dick with every fierce thrust.

He fucked her, fucked her, and fucked her until his strong woman's arms gave out and her upper body collapsed on the mat. Then he gripped her hip with one hand and pushed on her lower back with the other. When Izzy arched, her stellar ass rose. The angle tightened her pussy on his dick, and his eyes nearly crossed.

"Oh, my God," she said as the new angle affected her as well.

Jig palmed her ass, grabbing a healthy fistful in one hand as he banded the other arm under her hips. He had about thirty seconds in him before he unloaded and he'd be damned if she didn't explode first. Pinching her clit, he squeezed her ass cheek and used it to bounce her on his dick. Three thrusts later, Izzy's pussy clamped down on him, and she stiffened, screaming through the orgasm.

The feel of her coming all over his cock pushed him past his limit. He powered into her twice more before shooting into the condom. The pleasure was so great, his vision went completely white as he lost all sense of reality. He hadn't come that hard in, well, ever.

Izzy sagged beneath him, utterly spent, and let out a happy little sigh. Bending forward, he licked a line of perspiration off her back then latched on to her neck with his teeth. She moaned, a weak sound full of exhaustion. "You took it all," he whispered in her ear.

Her left cheek was on the mat, eyes closed, a smile on her lips. "Told you," she mumbled. "Also told you that you needed that. We both did."

He nipped her earlobe then rolled onto the mat next to her. He was fatigued, but sated and now able to take on all the problems that awaited him and the club. She was right. He had needed that.

Izzy had figured out exactly what he needed and given it to him without question even though it wasn't her usual way of doing things. That went far beyond the call of duty for a friend, and even further than what'd he'd expect for a fuck buddy. Their chemistry topped the charts, but this was more than chemicals and heat. And he had no idea what to do with that. For now, the plan was to just ignore it. Ignore the growing emotion and connection because he had no use for it and had no fucking clue how to deal with it. Not anymore.

Thankfully, Izzy seemed to be of the same mind.

"We need to get this place cleaned up and get out of here before Zach catches wind," he said, even though he wanted nothing more than to take a nap right where he lay.

Still prone, eyes closed, Izzy said, "How would he ever know?"

"You've got a guard dog waiting outside for you to go home, remember? Half these guys gossip worse than high-school cheerleaders. Guarantee he's already been on the line with Zach, telling him we're still here. Hell, the perv probably peeked in the window and got off watching us fuck."

Izzy's eyes popped open, and her mouth formed a surprised O. Then she burst out laughing. He should have known embarrassment wouldn't be her first reaction. She was a sexual woman and owned it.

"Well, shit," she said. "I forgot all about him. I hope he's not pissed."

Jig rolled to his side and faced her. "You better have forgotten all about every other man in the universe while my dick was inside you. If he's pissed, who gives a shit? And if he watched, I guarantee he's satisfied, not pissed."

With another laugh, Izzy slapped his leg. "You're terrible."

"You were singing a different tune five minutes ago, sweetheart." He stroked a hand down the curve of her spine, smoothing over her ass which was dotted with his fingerprints.

"All right, Casanova, I'll give you that one. You sure can fuck."

A swell of pride rose in him as he stared at the marks he'd left on her body. It looked like she belonged to him. His woman.

A pit formed low in his gut. No woman would be his. Not ever again. But if he were to have one, he'd sure be proud for it to be Izzy.

Shit. Those thoughts needed to go before he did something stupid like ask her on a real date.

"Let's get moving," he said, sitting up and grabbing her clothes for her. As he held them out to her, he didn't miss the flash of disappointment in her eyes.

That was fine. Minor disappointment was a million times better than an obliterated heart any day.

CHAPTER SEVENTEEN

"See ya tomorrow, Rip!" Izzy yelled out as she left work on a rare early day. She'd had her last appointment at noon, and Rip told her to take off when finished, he'd handle the walk-ins for the rest of the day. So at two, she had a free afternoon. And she knew just how to spend it. Hanging the valences over her front windows.

Not exactly a wild adventure, but she'd been too busy to get it done and couldn't wait to see how her favorite part of the house looked all dressed up.

"Bye, babe!" Rip called over the hum of his tattoo machine.

The fifteen-minute drive home passed quickly, and she only spent about seven of those minutes thinking about Jig.

Progress. At least twelve minutes of the drive into work that morning had been devoted to him.

They hadn't spoken in the three days since they'd fucked like crazed maniacs in Zach's gym. Jig clearly needed time and space to process what went down, and to be honest, so did she. The radio silence hadn't actually bothered her.

Too much.

But she was annoyed by the small part of her that was disturbed by the cold shoulder treatment. Because she shouldn't care. And never had in the past. One and done. Get hers and get out. No messiness, no insincere promises, no potential for hurt.

This was exactly why she should be glad they hadn't spoken.

He screwed with her mind as well as her body, and only one of those was acceptable. "You're pathetic," she mumbled as she turned into her long driveway. "What the…?"

As Izzy coasted closer to the house, she leaned forward, and her heart dropped straight out of her chest. "No!" She slammed the car in park and flew out the door, not bothering to shut it. "No, no, no."

Her house, her pride and joy, had been vandalized in the worst way. Tears sprang to her eyes, and she slumped to her knees in the grass. All six of her gorgeous windows had been smashed to smithereens. Sharp shards of glass glittered everywhere she could see, inside the house, on her porch, scattered throughout the bushes and grass.

Her heart stung with an ache similar to what she experienced when her mother died. It was dumb. A house was a house, a *thing*, but it was hers. One hundred percent hers. Something she'd worked and saved for all her adult life. She'd achieved it all on her own. The house was so much more to her than wood, nails, and drywall. It was a symbol of her independence. A validation of her choice to remain single, unattached, and trudging through life without help.

Now, it was a huge fucking mess that would take all weekend to clean up. Not to mention the expense of replacing six large windows. Did homeowner's insurance cover that sort of thing?

Of course, if it did, she'd have to report it to the insurance company. And they'd probably demand a police report. Which would no doubt be a problem for the Handlers. First the diner, now her place. This reeked of Lefty, and her involvement with the MC would come to light if she called the cops.

Shit.

This was a crotch kick to the bank account for sure.

Anger burned in her gut, hot and lethal, chasing away the unshed tears. Who were these pieces of shit to think they could mess with her sanctuary and get away with it? They could do their fucking worst, and she'd bounce back every time. Some broken glass was nothing compared to what she'd battled in her life. With that thought, she tried to ignore the heartache caused by the loss of her beautiful windows.

"Well, fuck them."

First, she'd get some lumber to board up the house, then once she'd simmered enough to have a reasonable conversation, she'd call Copper and ask him what the fuck he planned to do to stop these assholes. Izzy rose just as the rumble of a motorcycle came cruising up her driveway.

Great, her watchdog. How could she have forgotten?

As she stormed back to her car, LJ hopped off his bike, his face a picture of disbelief. He'd backed off on the flirting—she had a sneaking suspicion Jig had said something—but was still very protective and sweet toward her. "What the ever-lovin' fuck? Izzy, you okay? What the hell happened?"

"How the fuck should I know? How about you find Lefty and ask him?" She jammed her hands on her hips. "Actually, that's a great idea. I'd like about five minutes alone with that guy to ask him myself." Shaking her head, she back-walked toward her car.

"Izzy, wait, where are you going?" LJ pulled his phone from his pocket. "I gotta call this in to Copper."

She gave him her back and waved a hand in the air. "Do what you gotta do, buddy. I'm going to the hardware store."

"Iz, wait!" When she didn't stop, he roared, "Goddamnit! Isabella, get that tight ass back here."

She slid in the driver's seat and called out the open door, "Don't you Isabella me, you overgrown babysitter. Call Copper if you need to. I'll be at the hardware store." With that, she slammed the door and peeled out to shouts of "goddamnit!" and "woman!"

In the ten minutes it took her to drive to the hardware store, she hadn't cooled in the slightest. In fact, stewing in her anger had caused it to swell to epic levels. She parked like shit, shoved out of the car, and marched into the store, right past LJ who'd rolled in just behind her.

Once inside, she beelined straight for the lumber. Since she'd recently measured for the valences, the window dimensions were fresh in her mind. She wandered the aisle, trying to determine precisely what she needed when someone called her name.

"Hey, Izzy." Stephanie and Mav walked over hand in hand, smiles on their faces. If LJ had reached Copper, the president hadn't gotten the word out yet.

"Hey, guys." She blew out an unsteady breath and tried to still her shaking hands as she hugged Stephanie and accepted a kiss from Mav.

"You doing some work on your house?" Mav asked.

"Uh…" She swallowed. Lying had never been her strong suit, but she really didn't want to talk about what happened until she had time to process it.

"Mav, what the fuck are you doing over here? Thought you needed a drain snake." Jig rounded the corner and walked into their aisle. "Oh, hey, Iz," he said when his attention landed on her.

"Yeah, I do, but Steph saw Izzy across the store and wanted to say hi."

Jig's phone rang, and he frowned as he pulled it out. "Copper. Let me take it quick," he said, walking back down the aisle.

Well, shit. There went her reprieve.

Jig answered the call then slowly turned around, his gaze piercing her like a burning laser. It seemed every muscle in his very buff body grew more rigid with each tick of the clock. The ever-present scowl morphed into a twisted sneer that had her biting the inside of her cheek. Oh, boy, he was not pleased. He spoke for about thirty seconds then stuffed the phone in his pocket and stormed back over to them.

"Yikes," Stephanie murmured. "That is not a good look. You do something bad, girl?"

Izzy sighed. "You're about to find out."

Mav shot her a curious glance as Jig got right up in her face and stared down at her. "You want to tell me why the fuck my president is calling to tell me your house was fucking vandalized?"

Stephanie gasped. "Oh, my God, Izzy! What happened?" She shoved her way between Jig and Izzy and grabbed Izzy's upper arms. "Were you there? Are you okay?"

Izzy nodded and kept her comments directed to Jig. "I got out of work early and came home to find all six of my front windows completely smashed."

"Fuck," Mav spat out while Stephanie sucked in a sharp breath.

"Wait," Stephanie said, giving Izzy a chastising look. "Why didn't you call Jig? Why are you here?"

"I have to get some plywood to board up my windows."

Stephanie laughed like Izzy's words were hilarious. "No, you don't." She motioned her thumbs toward Mav and Jig. "That's what you have these guys for."

"It's my house," Izzy said, "my responsibility. Why wouldn't I have come here?" Did Stephanie really think she'd pawn the task off on someone else?

"Is that fucking so?" Jig asked, his voice so menacing Izzy flinched.

"Oh, boy," Steph whispered, slinking out from between Izzy and Jig. "Uh, Mav and I are just gonna, uh, go...somewhere else. Come on," she whispered, yanking Mav away by the shirt sleeve. The idiot had the nerve to laugh as his woman led him off.

"Geez, Jig, simmer down. I wasn't hurt. I'm pissed but fine." What was he so furious about?

"Oh, I'm so glad to hear it." His voice was laden with sarcasm as he folded his arms across his chest like he was trying to intimidate her. Fat chance.

"What the hell crawled up your ass?"

"It's just Izzy against the world, isn't it? Didn't even cross your mind to call the man who took you home from the hospital when you'd been beaten by the same assholes who destroyed your house? Didn't think the man who had his cock buried in you up to your throat just a few nights ago might want to be kept in the loop?"

"Jesus, Jig, keep it down, will you?" she said in a harsh whisper, looking up and down the aisle. Any shoppers had scattered the moment Jig raised his voice. "What? You think fucking me three days ago gives you some kind of rights to my life?" She snorted out a laugh. "You haven't even talked to me since then."

Whoops. That wasn't supposed to come out. Now she sounded like a jilted lover.

Which she was not. She was just a pissed-off woman with a stupid biker overreacting to something that wasn't any of his business. Okay, that wasn't entirely true since his club's enemies were the ones who kept coming after her.

"Maybe you missed the memo, Jig, but I take care of myself. I don't need a big man to hold my hand in the hardware store while I pick out lumber."

He threw his hands in the air. "This isn't about fucking lumber," he yelled. "It's about you being too stubborn to ask for help. It's about you thinking you can be a fucking island and do every goddamn thing by yourself."

"What the hell do you think I've been doing for the last thirteen years, Jig? Actually, for my whole life. I've managed just fine this far without any big bad bikers standing between me and the world. I think I'll be good going forward. I don't need anyone else."

"That's the stupidest thing I've ever heard," he shouted. "Everybody needs someone else at some point."

"Why do you give a shit? Because you fucked me?" She was yelling as loud as he was and had now crossed from irate into irrational. Part of her brain was aware of it, but her mouth kept running forward, out of control. "You have no say in anything I do Jig. Get used to it."

Jigsaw

"Um, excuse me," a timid voice cut through their very public screaming match.

Both she and Jig whipped their heads around and stared at a slim man in a blue vest with a name tag that read *Horace*.

"We've had some complaints. I'm going to have to ask you to take this outside. I'd hate to have to call the cops."

Izzy threw up a hand. "Not necessary. I'm leaving." She tromped down the aisle then turned when she was halfway to the end. "Hope it was good for you because you're sure as fuck not getting inside me again."

Boom. Mic drop.

Izzy left a fuming Jig standing in the lumber aisle. She ignored the curious gawks and whispers from the other patrons as she practically ran to her car. Once inside, she cranked the ignition and pulled out of the lot, flipping off LJ as she passed.

Never had a man brought that kind of unfiltered reaction from her. The urge to strangle Jig had her fingers clenching the steering wheel, as she imagined it was his neck. House vandalized, a man making demands of her, her own jumbled feelings about that man, it was too much for one day. Shit, she needed a fight to deal with all this emotional garbage and didn't have anything on the horizon.

Going straight home was out of the question. If she saw the state of her house in the mood she was in, she was bound to lose the last threads of her sanity.

For the next forty-five minutes, Izzy drove the mountain roads of the Great Smokies. With each curve of the winding roads, her anger ebbed and faded until she was well and truly mortified by her behavior in the store.

Jig was right. She was a stubborn fool. Thing of it was, she had no idea how to ask for help. How to lean on people. How was she supposed to know who to trust? What if she put her faith in Jig and his brothers, only to have that ripped from her in a crushing disappointment?

Been there, done that. The T-shirt wasn't worth it.

With the loss of anger and adrenaline came profound fatigue. As she rolled to a stop at a red light, Izzy banged her forehead on the steering wheel. The energy to fix up her house was long gone, and now she wished she'd had someone help her with it. Looked like she'd be crashing in a motel for the night.

A steady rumble pulled up next to her. LJ was crazy for still riding his bike in this cooler—actually, it was downright cold—weather. A bit of guilt topped off her embarrassment. Here she'd been leading the poor guy on a wild goose chase through the mountains when he had to be freezing his ass off. He flipped up his face shield and raised an eyebrow.

She nodded. Yes. She was going home to grab some stuff, then she'd hit a motel.

As she pulled into her driveway for the second time that day, she received the second shock of the day. At least six guys milled about, hammering wood over her windows, sweeping up glass, and tossing trash in the back of a pick-up.

After killing the engine, she swallowed a golf ball-sized lump in her throat. Never had anyone done something like this for her. No one had ever jumped in and taken care of a problem without a word from her. And to do it after she'd been such a bitch?

That just didn't happen.

She owed Jig one hell of an apology.

LJ opened her door and bent to eye level. "You pull your head out of your ass? You ready to give in yet?" he asked.

"Give in to what?" She kept her gaze on the house, scanning for Jig.

"To the fact that you're one of us, woman." He rapped his knuckles on her roof then winked and wandered off to help his brothers.

One of them. A terrifying thought. For the past thirteen years, Izzy had closed herself off to any relationships deeper than acquaintances. Even then, she'd been burned a time or two. At this point, she wasn't sure she possessed the ability to let people below the surface.

Jigsaw

But she had to try, at least a little bit, because the fact was they were here, going out of their way to help her. Anything else would make her an ungrateful shrew. And maybe she could work on letting Jig in a little more, too. Not deep enough to pierce her heart, that would be a suicide mission, but she'd shared some with him the other night and hadn't died from it. Maybe she could do it again.

Her gaze caught him as he emerged from the house. She followed his movement down the three steps of her porch and onto her lawn where he crunched over a layer of glass. He said something to one of his brothers then made his way straight to her.

Izzy climbed out of the car and squared her shoulders. Time to put on her big girl panties and apologize. It was the least he deserved.

His long stride ate up the distance between them, and within seconds, he was mere feet from her. "Jig," she said, looking him straight in the eye. "I owe you an ap—"

"Save it." He wrapped his long fingers around her upper arm and steered her down the driveway then onto the grass. One of his brothers had parked a sizeable black work van on her lawn. The back doors were open, but the van was empty. Must have been used to haul all the wood. Something she hadn't considered on her little solo trip to the hardware store in her Accord.

Jig dragged her behind the van, spun her, and shoved her up against the side. She hit with an oomph. "Jig, what are you doing? I was trying to—"

Once again, he cut her off, this time with his lips on hers. The kiss was harsh, a punishment of sorts if she had to guess, but it fired her blood in an instant. Izzy met his tongue stroke for stroke and gave as much as she took. They devoured each other for long seconds. Jig smelled faintly of sawdust, sweat, and leather. The combination tickled her senses and only made her want him more.

Without breaking the kiss, Jig's hand slithered between them and went to work on the button of her jeans. He had it open almost before she could register what was happening and the zipper down one second later. And then his hand was in there, long fingers shoving their way into her panties, brushing her clit and sinking deep inside her. Izzy sank her teeth into her lower lip to keep from crying out. Half his club brothers were just twenty feet away.

"Fuuck," Jig whispered against her lips. "You just walk around this wet all the time?"

Izzy chuckled, but it turned into a gasp when Jig grazed his teeth over the muscle running the length of her neck. She tilted her neck to the side as she said, "Nope. Only when you have your hands on me."

A grunt rumbled out of him. "Good answer."

He sucked the spot he'd just bitten, keeping up a slow, lazy pace with his finger in her pussy. Enough to feel damn good, but not enough to get her where she needed to be. And that was coming. Coming hard and coming soon.

Jig must have sensed her desperation because he inserted another finger, then one more. Izzy moaned, and he pressed a quick, firm kiss to her lips then drew his head back. His thumb brushed her clit as he fucked her with his fingers, hard and fast.

On a mission now, Izzy rocked against his hand, her clit bumping his thumb with each forward rock. Lefty, her windows, the Handlers, even her own internal bullshit faded to the background as she gave herself over to Jig's skilled fingers.

Izzy's lips curled into a smile, and her eyes fluttered shut as her head bumped against the van. This was gonna be one hell of an orgasm.

"Eyes on me," Jig said on a growl, increasing the pressure of his fingers. Izzy whimpered and opened her eyes to find herself staring into his burning hot gaze. If she didn't know better, she'd swear the man was about to eat her alive.

She kept the eye contact as he worked her to a panting frenzy. When his thumb circled her clit then landed on it with consistent pressure, her knees buckled, and she grabbed the back of his arms for support. A smug grin curved his mouth. He knew the power he had over her at that moment and loved it.

"Shit, Jig, I'm gonna come."

"Do it," he bit out, his fingers moving impossibly faster. His gaze still drilled into hers, daring her to look away. She didn't. She let herself have a moment of vulnerability and kept her gaze locked with his.

"Fuck, fuck, fuck," she whispered as her pussy latched onto his fingers and her stomach clenched and released. Her mouth dropped open, and she breathed through the orgasm, forcing herself not to scream. It was a monumental effort because the pleasure was a harsh attack on her system. Just five minutes ago she'd been devastated, embarrassed, and frazzled, and now she was riding a high that nearly catapulted her over the mountains.

The whole thing started and ended so fast, she was left with a spinning head and turbulent emotions.

Jig's hand stilled, but he kept it inside her as he leaned forward and laid a soft kiss on her lips. "Feel better?" he asked.

Izzy spared a second to take stock of herself. And yes, she did feel better. Relaxed, less embarrassed, not nearly as worried or angry. Maybe psychologists should start getting their patients off. Could be the cure for all kinds of ails.

Sure worked for her.

CHAPTER EIGHTEEN

Jig slowly withdrew his hand from between Izzy's legs. It was soaked, covered in her juices. Her sated eyes flared as she watched him bring each of the three fingers to his mouth and lick them clean. Her sweet flavor exploded on his tongue, and the only thing that kept him from turning her around, yanking down her pants, and burying his rock-hard cock in that wet pussy was the gaggle of club members working at her house.

He'd have to wait until later.

But it would come later. Rather, he would come later.

Looking like she could melt into a pile of goo on the ground, Izzy reached for the button of her jeans. Those damn things were so skin tight, it'd been an effort to get his hand in there. He swatted her fumbling hand away, zipped her up, then returned the button to its intact state.

"Ready to go see what the guys have been up to?" He held his hand out to her. An olive branch. Honestly, he wasn't sure what he was doing or why he was doing it. A relationship wasn't in the cards for him, but there was a connection with Izzy. She was as reluctant to form any deep entanglement as he was, maybe even more so.

The one thing he did know was the sick feeling of rage that overtook him when he received Copper's call. Someone had violated her privacy, messed up her safe haven, and destroyed something she'd worked so hard to achieve on her own. And then he'd realized Copper calling meant Izzy hadn't come to Jig on her own. Either she hadn't trusted him to help her, or he just didn't blip on her radar.

Either option sucked. He just wasn't entirely sure why he cared. So he'd overreacted and screamed at her in the middle of the hardware store. Christ, had he yelled something about his cock and her pussy?

Way to get her to trust him. Somewhere between her fleeing the store and his calling in the cavalry to repair her home, he decided to just go the fuck along with it. He liked her. He enjoyed her company. He loved fucking her.

Enough said.

Once he'd calmed down, he was able to reason it through. Her lack of trust in his friendship wasn't personal. It was born of years of negative experiences and abandonment. Railing at her in the store couldn't have been a worse way to handle it. When she walked out of that car and gazed at her vandalized home, she looked one stiff breeze away from snapping in half. The woman needed to relax.

And he'd gotten that job done gladly.

Izzy slid her palm over his, and he curled his fingers, keeping her captive. As he tugged her forward, she resisted, and he raised an eyebrow. "I'm sorry," she said. "That was not—"

Jig pulled again, this time harder until she fell forward into his chest. He kissed her once, deep and slow, making her melt against him. Her mind might be resistant to him, but her body was fully onboard.

"Not necessary," he said when he ended the kiss. "Don't need that shit. Just let my brothers fix your house. Okay?"

She studied him for a second, probably gauging his sincerity or deciding whether or not to risk it. He almost reassured her there was no way in hell he'd let her down, but he kept his mouth shut. She needed to come to that conclusion on her own. Needed to learn to trust her instincts and read on people. Jig might be an asshole to most, but he didn't welch on those few he gave a shit about.

With a nod, she said, "All right," but her expression read, "You get one chance."

She let him lead her away from the car, and he slung an arm around her shoulders as he guided her toward the house. "The glass is fucking everywhere. We'll get to that next. Wanted to get the windows boarded up first since it's getting cold at night now."

Five of the windows were already covered with slabs of plywood.

"Hey, Iz, you're looking more relaxed than you were a few minutes ago," LJ said as he carried a long board over his head toward one of the uncovered windows. When he strutted past them, Jig just swore LJ flexed his massive biceps a little extra for Izzy's benefit. Then he flashed her that grin one of the Honeys had described as "lube in a smile."

He had to remember to knock a few of LJ's teeth out later. See how many ladies he reeled in leering like a jack-o-lantern.

Izzy rolled her eyes and flipped LJ off, saying, "Bite me, LJ."

A laugh burst out of Jig. So much for her being impressed by the prospect.

"Where should I order the windows from?" Izzy asked. "Any recommendations?"

"It's taken care of already. They'll be here tomorrow."

"What? Seriously? How is that even possible?" Izzy's face lit up. "It's end of day."

"Rocket is a contractor."

Rocket, who was just emerging from the house with a heavy-duty trash bag full of broken glass slung over his shoulder, must have heard his name. "What's up, brother? You need me?" He stopped a few feet from them. "Hey, Iz, sorry about all this shit."

They all called her Iz and freaking loved her and accepted her as one of the crew. It was a slippery slope.

"Thanks, Rocket. It sucks"—she shrugged—"but it is what it is. I appreciate you guys dropping everything to take care of this for me."

"I was just telling her about the windows." Jig tightened his hold across her shoulders and tucked her to his side. She gave him a curious look, and Rocket chuckled. Shit, he was acting like a lovesick moron, trying to hide her from every male in town.

"Oh, yeah." Rocket adjusted the hold of the bag. "Let me throw this heavy fucker away first." He strode toward the dumpster and deposited the load, then jogged back over. "I gave my glass guy a call as soon as I got here and took some measurements. He's gonna be able to get them to me tomorrow. It'll probably be pretty late in the day so we may not get them installed until the next day." He shrugged. "Still pretty good turnover."

"Pretty good? That's amazing. I thought I'd be windowless for weeks." She broke free from Jig's hold and threw her arms around Rocket. "Thank you so much for doing that."

Rocket shot Jig a shit-eating grin that had him itching to rearrange his brother's face. Holding her just a little too tight for a little too long, Rocket said, "Nothing more than a few phone calls, babe."

And that was about enough of that. Jig snagged her by the elbow and pulled her back against his chest, wrapping his arms around her. She stiffened in his hold before letting herself settle against him.

"Give us an hour, and we'll have most of the glass cleaned up, and the guys will get out of our hair," Jig said against her ear. The short hairs on the shaved side of her head tickled his face.

"Our hair?"

"Yeah, I know you're gonna hate the fuck out of this, but I'm not leaving you alone tonight. A boarded-up house is just an invitation for trouble."

She sighed, and he knew she was battling it out internally. Her need for independence, fear of accepting help and friendship, versus an intelligent idea. Izzy wasn't stupid and would know she shouldn't be alone. She might be a kick-ass fighter, but as she'd learned the other night, three men on one woman wasn't ever good odds. "You're right. I do hate it."

He chuckled. Guess that was her way of agreeing without actually having to agree. "How about we order some pizza? You've gotta be starving. Then we can watch a movie and fuck like rabbits. Might take some of the sting out of having an unwanted houseguest."

Izzy's body shook in his arms as she laughed, that pert little ass rubbing all over his cock. He focused on one of his brother's whacking a nail into the plywood over and over, trying to will his cock down.

"You find me a pizza place that delivers all the way out here, and you got yourself a deal, bubba."

Jig gave her a squeeze and rubbed his scarred cheek against the smoothness of her face. She giggled and squirmed as his facial hair tickled her skin. "What the hell do you think prospects are for, woman?"

"You're gonna make LJ go get us pizza?"

Jig snorted. "Damn straight." It was the least that flirting asshole deserved.

"You'll order enough for him, right?" She peered up at him, eyes dancing. "We could invite him to join us. I was a bit of a jerk to him earlier."

Okay, now she was just fucking with him. "Fuck no! He's off shift after he gets us some grub. Another prospect will take his place. LJ can go eat all the pizza he damn well pleases after that."

Four hours, one large pepperoni pizza, and one hundred and sixteen minutes of action-packed superheroes later, the credits rolled across Izzy's large-screen television. After the guys left, she and Jig got along like they'd known each other for years, eating and teasing. He'd regaled her with stories of stupid shit his brothers had done throughout the years and she spoke about the most ridiculous tattoos she'd ever worked on.

It was the most Jig had spoken to a woman in one stretch for years. And he found he liked it.

Izzy reached for the remote and killed the tv, plunging the den into darkness. Without the moonlight streaming through the windows, the place was like a tomb. "Shit," she said as she flicked on a tableside lamp. "Never realized how much light those windows let in. Even at night."

They sprawled on the couch side by side, feet propped on her coffee table. Jig's cut rested on the back of an armchair. The whole scene was very domestic. He'd given up any thoughts of that life years ago, but would be lying through his ass if he said it didn't feel nice. It felt too nice. Intimate in a way that had nothing to do with sex and everything to do with appreciating the person he was with for nothing beyond her company.

Izzy rolled her head in his direction. "Can I ask you something?"

"Shoot." He grabbed his beer and took a good pull. Nothing like beer and pizza to round out a shitty day.

"You're not going to like it."

His gut tightened, and he lowered the bottle, unable to take another sip. "What's your question?"

She reached out and traced a finger over the scar pattern on his face. Feather-light, her finger tracked the puzzle-piece shape that had given him his nickname. Each spot she smoothed over tingled with awareness until he could feel the entire scar on his cheek. Not the burning that came when the shit hit the fan, but a pressure, almost like someone was pushing a template of the pattern onto his face.

Jig froze, couldn't move a single muscle, couldn't speak, could barely draw in a breath. Over six years he'd had that scar, and none of the women he'd been with had touched it. Most of them would never want to, and the two that had tried faced fury they hadn't bargained for.

Anger didn't come this time, just a paralyzing terror for the question about to fall from her lips.

"Will you tell me about this? About how it happened? About

what you went through?"

Not only had his face been untouched, but no one dared ask him about the event. No one was willing to face the consequences. Copper knew the entire story, but he was the only one. Everyone else knew the basics, but never learned the depths to which Jig had sunk after the tragedy.

But Izzy was brave and didn't back away from a fight or let fear control her actions. There was true caring gleaming in her gaze, not morbid curiosity. The intense events of the day had deepened the bond growing between them, and he now realized that, even though neither was prepared, the connection between them was growing into deep affection. So she touched. And she asked. And for the first time since Copper, Jig found himself willing to unload the story. There was a chance she'd run screaming before he was finished, but he still felt compelled to tell her. The gentle way her fingers caressed his face and the uncharacteristic way her body melted against him made him putty in her hands.

He cupped his hand over hers on his face and held her palm against his cheek, then turned his head and pressed his lips to the very center. Izzy straightened on the couch and faced him, folding her legs underneath her.

"About six and a half years ago, I had a wife and a little girl." His voice cracked over "girl." "They're both dead now." For so many years, he'd refused to voice that truth, and while it was painful to say, it wasn't quite as gut-wrenching as he'd imagined. And that was all due to Izzy and the compassion flowing from her. Not pity, just concern and patience.

She didn't feed him bullshit, didn't tell him it was okay, didn't say she understood. It was appreciated. Because nothing about the story was okay, and how could anyone ever understand? But she sat in silent support, listening with focused attention and holding his hand.

"I was—" He huffed out a humorless laugh. "I was very different back then. You probably wouldn't recognize me if you crossed me on the street. Fuck, I wouldn't recognize myself anymore. I was a Ph.D. student in physics. I'd never been in a fight, hardly swore, never held a gun. I was…normal."

Izzy gave him a small smile of encouragement and squeezed his hand.

"My wife was…" He blew out a breath and stared at the ceiling as a host of unresolved feelings washed over him. It was astounding how sorrow could feel so fresh even after six years had passed. "She was the definition of sweet. Small, a tiny little thing, soft-spoken, non-confrontational, a pacifist."

His gaze met Izzy's, and though neither of them spoke the words, they both had to be thinking about the differences between the women. Callie and Izzy couldn't have been farther apart on the spectrum.

"She was just a good, loving, supportive wife. We met when we were fifteen, and I fucking loved her." He snorted. "She'd have hated me saying it like that. Don't think I ever heard a four-letter word come out of her mouth. Everything about her was so damn sugary sweet. I swear, we never even fucked. Just made love. Callie was a hopeless romantic. And my daughter was a carbon copy of her mother. Two peas in a pod."

He rested his head against the back of Izzy's couch and closed his eyes. The sensory memories from that night were so strong he could easily take himself right back to his kitchen. "The night before my graduation, I came home after dark. As soon as I walked into the house, I knew something was wrong. There was an abnormal silence. The power had been cut.

"I remember that silence. It's burned into my mind. It was so quiet I could hear my own heart racing. I remember the fear, too, the certainty something was seriously wrong but, honestly, I never expected what I found."

He stared off into space as he was transported back in time. Then Izzy stroked his cheek again, pulling him from the dark water that threatened to drown him. "I walked into the kitchen to find Callie bleeding out on the floor, but before I could even register what I was looking at, I was grabbed from behind. There were two guys. When I say I had no skills back then, I mean it. As much as I struggled, there wasn't a damn thing I could do to save her, my daughter, or myself.

"And it was all a fucking mistake. The wrong fucking house. They wanted my neighbor. All a sick, twisted, fucking mistake." He continued to gaze at nothing, speaking on autopilot just to get the words out. Now that he'd started, they felt like a poison, eating him from the inside out, and he needed to purge. "They knocked me down, carved the fuck out of my face, and threatened me over something that had nothing to do with me. I couldn't get away. All I could do was take it and pray they'd leave before they realized there was a sleeping child upstairs. They beat the fuck out of me until I passed out on the floor next to my dead wife, having no clue where my baby was."

"Jesus, Jig," she said, her voice heavy with sorrow. "But…" Her voice cracked. "But they found her?"

He nodded, tears burning his eyes. "I never saw my daughter alive again, Izzy. I was late getting home so I didn't get to kiss her goodnight." God, how he missed the soft weight of his daughter in his arms. The way she'd light up and quiver with excitement as she stood by the door waiting for him to come home from work each evening. "She was a fucking baby." Wetness tracked down his cheeks, and his chest tightened until he could barely breathe.

"Shhh," Izzy said, wiping his tears away even as she ignored the ones trailing down her own face. "You can stop. You don't have to tell me more." There was so much genuine caring in her voice and in her touch. He wanted to soak it all up because it was the only thing warming his heart enough to prevent it from turning to a block of ice.

Jig shook his head and clutched her hand like a lifeline. "No. I want to say it. You need to hear it. Hear who I am. After their deaths, I fell into a deep depression. I stopped going to work, cut ties with both our families, I couldn't even get out of bed. Cops had nothing, though I'm pretty sure they were in the pocket of the asshole who killed my family. Then, one day, I was watching the news, and I saw a mugshot of one of the guys who'd been in my house. Who murdered my—" He swallowed, unable to repeat it. "He'd killed someone else in a carjacking gone bad and was on the loose. That story snapped me out of my fog. I was done being a pussy. Done being unable to protect myself or anyone else. Done letting life happen to me. In that moment, I decided I'd be the one controlling what happened in my life from then on out, so I went to the gym and learned how to fight, training ten to twelve hours a day for months. I also went to the range and learned to shoot. Basically, I turned myself into an entirely different man."

"Jigsaw," she whispered.

He nodded. "Yeah. About eight months after their deaths, I went off in search of the two men who'd broken in, their boss, and anyone else in their gang's chain of command." He looked her straight in the eye. "Their boss was a powerful crime lord, and it took me months to track him and formulate a plan to kill him. In that time, I became obsessed with uncovering every aspect of his life. The combination of grief and anger nearly destroyed me. I killed two men one night after following them from a bar. The men who killed my family. I was nothing more than a rabid animal bent on revenge."

Izzy scooted closer then threw a leg over his lap, straddling him. Her hands went to his face then she laced her fingers behind his head, cradling his skull. He opened his eyes and stared into the eyes of a beautiful woman who held no judgment.

"You're shaking." She said the words so low he almost missed it.

He circled her with his arms, hugging her flush against him, and buried his face in the crook of her neck. Her arms immediately tightened, giving him comfort.

"I finally found the shot-caller here in Tennessee, in the

mountains at some rundown bar. My head was so fucked I was going to kill him right there in the parking lot where anyone could have walked out and seen me. And someone did. It was Copper. He said he'd had his eye on me all night because I looked like a volcano ready to erupt, and he suspected I was going to do something stupid."

"What'd Copper do?" She sifted her hands through his hair, almost unconsciously. Each caress of her fingertips stroked along his wounded soul, healing him. It was the first time he'd allowed himself to draw comfort from another person.

A woman.

And, fuck, if it wasn't better than the best drug in the world.

"Copper made sure there weren't eyes on me, then he knocked the guy out cold. We stuffed him in my trunk and drove into the middle of nowhere. He demanded I tell him my story in return for his saving my ass."

"So you told him."

He nodded, her soft skin brushing over his face. "I spilled every last ugly detail."

Still playing with his hair, she lightly ran her nails over his scalp, eliciting a deep shiver from him. "And then? Did Copper talk you out of killing him?"

Jig lifted his head and stared at her. Izzy now knew things about him that no one else knew. Things that could put not only him, but his president, away for the rest of their lives. Yet he trusted her completely. She'd never tell a soul his story. He felt that in his bones and saw it in her compassionate gaze. Most women would run screaming in fear after listening to his story. Who wanted a man that admitted to spending nearly a year of their life on a murderous revenge mission? But Izzy didn't even flinch. She was unique. An independent fighter who understood that violence was sometimes the way.

"Then Copper watched me kill him, helped me bury the body, and I prospected with the club."

CHAPTER NINETEEN

In every life, there are snippets of time so significant their mark brands a person's heart, mind, and soul. Typically, those moments are the extremes of positivity or negativity. Falling in love, achieving a dream, death of a loved one, epic failure.

At some point, almost everyone experiences those very same moments. Books are written, careers spent, and studies are performed to dissect, learn from, and advise people on how to handle their emotions and survive those very powerful times.

Then there are moments so unique, so out of the realm of ordinary experience, that there are no scripts, no playbooks or instruction manuals on how to handle them. Those experiences carve away at a person, exposing raw nerves and a bleeding heart.

Jig's confessions, his pain, and catastrophic heartbreak reached inside Izzy and touched a place she didn't even know existed. Platitudes wouldn't help. When her mother died, everyone she knew hit her with cliché on top of cliché.

I'm so sorry for your loss.

I understand what you're going through.

Time will heal your pain.

Bullshit.

She wasn't going to offer empty phrases to Jig.

Never had Izzy considered herself much of a nurturer. She certainly wasn't the one friends ran to when they needed a shoulder to cry on, but she found herself needing to relieve Jig's suffering. Needing to be the one to bring some light into the all-consuming darkness he'd lived in for years.

As she stared into his tortured eyes, her insides twisted with pain for this man. He'd endured more in one fated night than anyone should in their entire life. If she had the capability, she'd take every single ounce of his pain and suffering away from him. She'd even endure it herself to keep him from the torture.

How did she tell him what he'd done with his life was okay? How did she let him know she could accept who he was and what he'd become after tragedy blasted a hole in his life?

"Thank you for sharing that with me," she said, sliding her hands up and down his arms.

"You're the first besides Copper."

Izzy's eyes widened. "Why? I couldn't have been the first to ask. What made you tell me?" Their voices were hushed, and Izzy was afraid speaking at a higher volume would break the spell of trust and acceptance surrounding them.

His fingers played with the strip of skin at her low back where her shirt ended. She wasn't a tiny, delicate flower of a woman, but he made her feel feminine all the same.

"For the first time, I wanted to know," he said.

"To know what?" Her heart raced as she waited for his answer. Part of her wanted to run because she knew it was going to change things. Force her to take a terrifying leap off a very high cliff.

"To know if someone could accept what I've done. I killed three people in cold blood, Izzy, and never had one second of regret. The mild-mannered physicist with a full life waiting to be lived turned into a murderer who people fear. And you know the craziest part?"

She tilted her head and squeezed his shoulders. "What?"

"I'd do it again for any of my brothers or their women. I could have gone back to my staid life when it was over, but I chose to join the Handlers. Copper would have let me walk. There wasn't any pressure. Once darkness entered my life, I embraced it. And I chose it. Now I live with it in some form every single day. My wife would have hated the man I am today." He shook his head. "Makes me sick sometimes."

Ahh, there it was. The real devil that wouldn't release its grip on Jig's soul. Izzy was swimming in deep water with a raging hurricane rolling in. She didn't have a clue how to free him from the clasp of pain and guilt, but in some ways, she could relate to him feeling lost in his own skin. For years, she longed for love, affection, connection, but forced herself to harden, shove those feelings aside, and mold herself into a woman who needed no one. So she went with her gut. "I think you're wrong," she said, wrapping her arms around his neck.

"Excuse me?" There was a bite to his words that hadn't been there moments ago, but Izzy could handle that. The man was entitled to whatever emotions he wanted after all he'd been through.

Sharp teeth didn't bother Izzy, anyway. She raised an eyebrow. "You told me she was sweet, kind, not judgmental. You told me how much you loved each other. How happy you were." A small pang of something Izzy feared was jealousy pinched her heart. What kind of horrible person did that make her? Jealous over a man's prior love for his dead wife.

"I don't think…" Izzy said, swallowing past thickness in her throat. "I don't think it sounds like there was anything you could have done to make her hate you."

Please let that have been the right thing to say.

Jig stared at her so hard it was as though he could see straight through to her insides. Two broken souls afraid of leaning on others for comfort, but who probably needed it more than most, though the universe didn't seem to care what either wanted. It had its own plan, bringing Izzy and Jig together and forcing both to confront feelings they hadn't before. She swallowed. There was something kind of sweet about having him hold a little piece of her vulnerability and vice versa. Not that she was ready to admit that out loud.

He slid his hand up her spine until he reached the back of her head. Bringing his mouth a breath away from hers, he whispered, "Thank you."

Then he captured her lips in a kiss so deep it stole her breath. Gentler than their last kisses, it was so powerful all she could do was hold onto his arms while he explored her mouth and zapped her brain.

Minutes, or it could have even been hours later, he released her mouth. As they panted for breath, Izzy stared at his lips wet from her mouth. He was so handsome, so dangerous, so potent she almost forgot all of her reasons for keeping her distance.

Almost.

"Why haven't you kicked me out, Izzy? I have nothing to offer you. No future, no happy ending. Just a one-percenter with murders hanging over his head who thinks about fucking you at least a hundred times a day."

Izzy grinned. "You don't scare me, Jig. Neither does the darkness inside you." At least not physically. And she'd have to find a way to keep him from destroying her heart. "I'm no one's moral authority. Do I want you to become some masked vigilante killer? No, but I don't judge you for what you did." She shrugged and gave him a smile. "Not my style." Then she grew serious. "I don't trust anyone, Jig. You get burned too many times, and you learn to only rely on yourself. At this point in my life, I don't think I can learn anything different. So I have nothing to give you either." Izzy ground her hips on the erection that had grown between them after she'd climbed in his lap. "Except this. And maybe some kind of friendship."

This time when he kissed her, it was so hard it was almost savage. She moaned into his mouth as his tongue filled her. A deep shiver racked her entire body. Long minutes later, she broke the kiss. "More of this and a friendship works for me."

He chuckled as he skimmed a path back to her mouth and dove in once again. Something about this man's kisses was different than any other she'd experienced. Deeper, more powerful, and so much sexier. Every time his mouth touched hers, her panties dampened, her pussy ached, and she felt the profound need to have him inside her. They were going to have a problem if she demanded he fuck her every time he kissed her. Could lead to some compromising scenarios.

Jig stood, holding her by her ass. She hooked her legs around him, locking across his lower back. "If I'm not fucking that sopping pussy in the next five minutes, you're gonna see just how savage I can get," he growled against her mouth.

"How are you so sure I'm wet?"

"All I have to do is look at you, and that pussy drips for me." He smirked. "Tell me I'm wrong."

As arrogant as his statement was, she wasn't a liar, so she said, "You're one hundred percent correct. Now, what are you going to do about it, bubba?" The use of the nickname gave her the illusion of keeping her heart at a safe distance.

He squeezed her ass and started for her bedroom. Somehow, he managed to get there without knocking anything over even though they devoured each other as he walked. Izzy had her arms wrapped around his head, hands sliding through his hair. It was the perfect length, long enough to fist and hold, but not at the shaggy stage.

He seemed to like the attention because a low rumble erupted from his chest when her nails scored his scalp. One second, she was trying to climb him like a tree, and the next thing she knew, she was flat on her back with a horny biker hovering over her.

Dark hair, dark eyes, dark leather, scarred face, Jig looked every bit the dangerous man he was. And she was about to experience it firsthand. If it was anything like the other night, she was seconds away from being dominated by this man. And for the first time in her life, she wanted it.

Jig curled his fingers into the sides of her yoga pants then ripped them off her body in one rough swoop. Then he stripped out of his own clothes and grabbed a condom from the nightstand—yes, she'd bought them after they fucked in the gym—and dropped it next to her head.

He leaned forward, kissing just below her navel then inhaled. "Love smelling how much you want me," he said, his breath so close to her mound she trembled with need. "Want to eat this juicy pussy again."

"Do it," she said, lifting her pelvis.

Then the world went crazy as Jig grabbed her ass, flipped the both of them, and settled her astride his hips. "Next time. I'm in the mood for a ride tonight."

Izzy's jaw dropped. He was giving her the top? Not what she'd expected. All that power, all that hard-won control under her. At her mercy. Hers to give and take pleasure from at her discretion.

Fuck yes. Her nipples tightened until they were so sensitive she could barely stand the feel of her shirt brushing against them. She wouldn't have thought it possible, but her sex released even more arousal. It leaked out of her, coating his lower abdomen.

"I see you like the idea," he said, interlacing his fingers under his head.

"I fucking love the idea." Before he had a chance to change his mind and flip her again, she grabbed the condom and tore it open with her teeth.

"Now, that is sexy," he said. "You're going to have to do that again sometime. When I can video it. This way, if I have a hard-on and you're not around, I can just whip it out, and I have the perfect visual to get me off."

Izzy laughed a genuine happy sound. Who was this man? Since confessing his sins to her, he seemed lighter, able to let himself go, even be playful. Hopefully, the frisky Jig would stick around for a while.

His teasing turned to a groan when she rolled the condom down his cock. As she positioned herself over him, their eyes met and held. Izzy rubbed the tip of him through her opening then slid all the way down to the base in one fast motion.

"Fuuuck," he said on a moan. His hands clamped on her hips, holding her in place. "You gonna fuck me hard, baby?" he asked through clenched teeth.

Izzy breathed in and out, trying to ignore the clawing need to move. Jig still retained some of the control and held her firm. "I can go easy on you if you'd like," she said in the sweetest voice she could muster.

"Don't you fucking dare." Jig's fingers bit into the flesh of her hips. She tried to rock her pelvis, but he prevented any movement. "Get that shirt off and give me those tits."

Izzy crossed her arms at her waist and drew the shirt over her head, arching her back a little for dramatic effect. The feeling she got when his eyes flared at the sight of her bare breasts was the ultimate power trip for a woman. She was queen of the world at that moment. At least the little world they'd created in her bedroom.

She cupped one of her breasts then leaned forward, bracing herself on the headboard with her free hand. When she was dangling just an inch from his mouth, she said. "This what you had in mind?"

"Fuck yes," he breathed. His hands left her hips and landed on her tits, pushing them together. With his very talented tongue, he licked back and forth between both nipples before alternating with sucks and bites all over.

Izzy gripped the headboard so hard she worried she'd crack the twenty-year-old wood. It was then that it dawned on her—he wasn't holding her still any longer. She rolled her hips in a circular motion, eliciting a deep moan around her nipple. His head tilted back, and he released her, groaning a second time when she did it again. And again.

She took that as her cue and straightened, leaving her hands on the top of the headboard as she increased the speed of her hips. Jig's hands coasted up and down her sides, occasionally running over her tits and pinching her nipples. With every forward motion, her clit ground into his pelvis, bringing her one second closer to coming.

Fuck, it felt so good.

Jig moved his hips as well, fucking up into her and making her crazy. Even as she had him, the need for more grew and grew until she was riding him so hard she worried her knees would leave bruises on his sides. He didn't notice if the grunts and moans were any indication. Besides, he was back to a punishing grip on her hips, aiding in moving her like a madwoman.

"I need to watch you come," he said as he stroked a thumb over her clit. Izzy jerked at the lightning bolt of sensation. She removed her claws from his chest and rested her hands on his thighs behind her. The change in position altered his angle inside her, and they both cried out. Izzy completely lost herself in the onslaught of pleasure, letting her head drop back between her shoulders as she fucked him with everything she had while he continued to torture her clit.

It didn't take much, three swipes of that callused thumb, and he threw her into an intense orgasm. Her back bowed with the force of her contractions. She screamed out his name and ground hard against him, riding it out for as long as she could. As her body began to calm, she tried to pick the rhythm back up for him, but she was so boneless it didn't quite work.

Jig wrapped his arms around her and flipped them again before hiking her legs over his shoulders. Then he went to town, fucking her so hard her body moved up the bed, and she had to brace herself against the headboard. Within seconds, a second orgasm slammed into her, making her cry out in pleasure. Now, limp and sated, she absorbed his brutal pounding.

Jig's body tensed and his thrusts grew frantic, almost frenzied. Izzy watched him as his dick drilled in and out of her. "God, that's hot," she said. And then all of a sudden, she needed something she'd never wanted. In fact, she'd have throat-punched any man who suggested it.

"Come on me," she said.

Jig froze, buried so deep she squirmed around him. "What?"

She swallowed. Why on earth had she said that? But she wouldn't take it back. She wanted it, wanted to be marked by him, wanted to be his. She'd never actually tell him she wanted to be owned by him. She couldn't put a voice to those thoughts and make them real. It'd leave her too exposed, too vulnerable, and too open to damage. But she could ask for this physical act as a representation of the emotions she couldn't handle. She could own this.

"Come on me," she said, more forceful this time.

His nostrils flared, and his breathing grew more erratic. He withdrew from her and pulled the condom off with a snap, sending it flying to the ground. Two fingers dove between her legs, gathering her cream before he fisted himself and furiously stroked. One arm braced on the headboard, his muscles bulged and bunched. With each passing second, he became more rigid, his grunts lower, more desperate. His neck corded with the strain and his face looked almost in pain.

It was the sexiest thing she'd ever seen, and she needed to do more than just watch. Slapping his hand out of the way, she grasped his cock and stroked as she'd seen him do.

"Fuck, baby, you're going to kill me," he said, then threw his head back and erupted all over her chest and stomach. Hot cum splashed on her, leaving milky white streaks. Izzy ran her fingers through it smearing it around her breasts and abdomen.

Breathing like he'd just run a marathon, Jig stared at her. "That's the sexiest thing I've ever seen. My mark on you like that."

Their eyes met, and the now familiar punch of emotion hit her. She was neither able or willing to admit there was more between them than just friendship and fucking, but she felt it. And she ignored it.

Jig leaned forward and kissed her. Hunger ignited as though she hadn't just come twice. Wrapping her arms and legs around

Jig's back, she gave herself over to it. They needed to shower, to clean off, but somehow this was perfect.

It was raw, it was dirty, it was a little screwed up.

It was them.

CHAPTER TWENTY

Jig booted the door open with his size twelve and exited the john as he hauled his zipper up. In all the years he'd been a Handler, he'd managed to avoid touching the inside of the bathroom door. A trip to the clinic wasn't his choice of a fun day, and that place was crawling with DNA from God knew who. Actually, he probably did know who, and somehow that made it worse.

"C'mere, brother," Zach called out as Jig reentered the main area of the clubhouse. Zach was one game of pool away from losing his shirt, but the guy didn't seem to give a shit. He'd sucked back five beers and had his woman draped all over him, so empty wallet or not, he was pretty fuckin' satisfied.

"What's up, Z? I ain't fronting you a penny. Club's gonna have to send Louie to beat your own ass if you keep losing all our money," he said as he wandered over to Zach and Rocket's game. Copper may have banned parties and Honeys until the dust settled, but prez could sense when his men were reaching their limit, so he'd allowed everyone and their ol' ladies to chill at the clubhouse that night. It wasn't quite a party, no heavy music, no scantily clad Honeys, and no one was allowed to get too trashed, but it was still nice to blow off some steam with his family.

"Sorry I couldn't come out today to help with your girl's house. Had a clogged sink issue in the women's locker room that tripped me up all day. How the fuck the sink got clogged full of

183

blond hair, I'll never know. We have fucking showers. No one should be washing their hair in those sinks."

Your girl.

Zach was the third person to call Izzy his girl that evening. And Jig hadn't corrected a single one. She wasn't really his. No woman would ever be his again, but the thought of it, of calling her his woman, not only made him hard, it thawed something frozen inside his chest. What fucking man wouldn't want to call Izzy his woman? She had a smokin' body, befriended everyone she came across, had a kick-ass job, and was fierce as shit. Plus, she had a bit of a violent streak that made a sick bastard like him want her even more.

"Hey," Toni said, slapping Zach's arm. "We stand at the mirror and brush our hair over the sink." She shrugged. "It falls in. Get over it."

Jig chuckled. He sure as hell remembered that. Callie's blond hair had pretty much taken over the bathroom at times. Shower drain, sink, on the floor— He froze. Holy shit. Second time recently he'd thought of his wife in a casual context. Not something he ever allowed. Just once a year on her birthday did he indulge in the agonizing memories of his younger, happier years. But she kept popping into his head lately, and it was... almost pleasant. Not the usual heart-grinding punch of misery, but a memory that could induce a grin.

He'd never accept Callie's death, never be at peace with the way she was ripped from his life, but could he find some peace within himself? Could he finally accept that he still had a life, one he could live and actually enjoy?

His gaze met Izzy's across the room where she sat at a table with Shell and Beth. Her nose wrinkled in a cute, inquisitive look, so he shook his head. He was fine. With a smile, she winked then went back to braiding Beth's hair.

"Hello? Earth to Jig," Zach said on a laugh. "Look at the poor bastard. He's smitten. Like a love-sick puppy dog. It's disgusting."

Jigsaw

"What?" He tore his attention away from the woman who was taking up way too much real estate in his brain. Damn, he'd zoned the fuck out. "Sorry, no worries. We had enough guys to get the windows installed in a few hours. The house is good as new."

Toni giggled and leaned against her man. "That was the question you missed five minutes ago. I asked if Izzy had any fights coming up. The girls and I were talking, and we're dying to see her in action."

Shrugging, Jig said, "Not sure. It's not too often another woman wants to fight her, so her matches are few and far between." Fine by him. Sure, she'd been a rock star in the ring, but he wasn't in any hurry to watch her take a fist to the face again. Stubborn woman had enough bruises in the past few weeks to last years.

"Well, keep us posted. Jazz and I are dying to go. Steph, too. Haven't talked to Shell about it yet, but I bet she'd be a go as well."

Jig grunted out an agreement and did his best to pretend his full attention was on Toni and Zach while, really, he was replaying the soft smile Izzy had gifted Beth. It wasn't one he'd seen from her yet. Maybe only reserved for children.

Children... Shit, did she want those? That was one thing he'd sure as fuck never be up for again. Losing his daughter broke something inside him he was one hundred percent certain could never be repaired. Being in Beth's presence was barely tolerable, and he often bailed if she was too close. Didn't matter she was one of the cutest kiddos he'd ever seen. Being anywhere near kids twisted his insides so bad he could barely breathe. It was only recently he was able to pretend holding her didn't tear out his insides.

Did he need to make his stance on kids clear to Izzy?

No. Fuck no. He'd never allow a woman in enough to necessitate that conversation. Izzy got that.

"I'll, uh, see what she's got coming down the pipe," he said.

Were they still talking about Izzy fighting?

Zach laughed and turned Toni so she was facing him. "Think we've lost him."

"You might be right. And I think you're done with this game." Her voice was coy as she said, "What should we do instead?"

Zach growled like a lion on the prowl then said, "I can think of a few things." He worked his hands into the back pockets of Toni's tight jeans and gave her ass a squeeze.

She squeaked then giggled right before Zach kissed her. Within seconds, the kiss grew heated. Jig gave them two minutes before they made their way to the room they shared at the clubhouse. It wasn't often they stayed here seeing as how they both had houses, but they'd probably head there now and wouldn't emerge until well past sunrise.

"Jesus," Rocket grumbled. "I'm outta here. Unless you want to go a round?" He held a pool cue out to Jig.

"I'm good, brother. Next time."

With a snort and a mumble about everyone being pussy-whipped, Rocket stowed his pool cue then wandered his way to the bar.

"We're going too, man," Zach said, coming up for air. "'Cept we're going up to bone."

Toni flushed and rolled her eyes. "To bone? Seriously?"

"That's right, baby." Laughing, Zach slapped her ass. "After you, gorgeous. I want to watch this sexy thing as you walk up the stairs."

"Zaaach," she whined. "Really thinking Jig doesn't want to hear that." She was so full of it. Toni loved every second of Zach's attention, and the wink she shot to Jig proved it.

"What?" Zach asked. "He's got his own woman now. He doesn't want to hear it, he can do some boning of his own."

A giggle erupted from Toni just as Jig was about to add his two cents. "Yeah, let's see what the state of his boning instrument looks like after he calls it 'boning' in front of Izzy," she said. "I'm pretty sure she could unman him with her eyes closed."

"All right. Will you two idiots just get the hell out of my face," Jig said, giving Zach a shove.

"Holy shit." Zach slapped a hand over his heart. "That's the second time tonight I've seen you smile and laugh." Then he grew serious. "She's good for you, brother." After another pop to Toni's ass, the two disappeared up the stairs, giggling and groping like teenagers.

Jig swung his attention back to Izzy and Shell just in time to see Beth leap from Izzy's lap and pump her chubby legs as fast as she could in his direction.

"Beth, no," Shell called out, her voice matching the abject horror on Izzy's face. Both women stood and reached out as though they could grab Beth across the twenty-five feet that separated them from the speedy toddler.

Everything around Jig seemed to freeze except for the little bundle of energy hurtling toward him. Time stood still, the busy clubhouse disappeared, even the air calmed. Jig's lungs stopped functioning, and his breath caught in his chest. It wasn't the first time she'd run to him, but it caused a temporary freak-out each time.

One second the red-haired three-year-old was speeding his way, a broad smile on her round face, and the next second, her toe caught, and she was flying toward the ground. Pure instinct kicked in and Jig lunged forward, catching her under the arms milliseconds before that adorable face hit the hardwood floor.

"Weee!" Beth squealed as she was swung into Jig's arms, still smiling as though she hadn't been a heartbeat away from a very different outcome.

"Shit, princess," he said, holding her close, hoping it would calm his runaway heart. "You almost bit it there. Don't run faster than those shrimpy legs can carry you, huh?"

Beth's eyes grew wide, and she grabbed his face with both her hands. "You said shit," she whispered. "Mommy says it's a bad word."

He winced. He'd never had to watch his mouth around his child because he hadn't swore back then. As the image of his beautiful little girl filled his mind, he braced himself for the onslaught of pain.

It never came.

Sure, there was a twinge of sadness and regret, but Beth's scolding grin took up the majority of space in his head at that moment. He could breathe, his gut wasn't churning, hell, he could even smile.

He flicked his gaze to Izzy and Shell who wore twin looks of worry. As though the attention from Beth would send him spiraling. One wink in their direction, and their eyes widened so in tandem that it looked like they'd rehearsed it.

Jig chuckled and gave Beth a squeeze. Holding the slight weight of a wiggling child in his arms was having the complete opposite effect that he'd always feared. It felt nice, electrifying… right. "You're right, squirt. I shouldn't have said that. Guess you hear a lot of bad words around here, huh?"

Her nod was so solemn he couldn't help but laugh again. "Mommy says Copper has a potty in his mouth and that's why he says bad words the mostest."

A potty in his mouth? Shit, he'd laughed more in the past thirty seconds than he had in years. The kid was a trip. "I'll try to be more careful."

"Good. Mommy will put you in the timeout chair if you say the bad words. Timeout is no fun. What's a squirt?" As she spoke, she laid her head on his shoulder and closed her eyes. He'd overheard something about her missing her nap and Shell expecting a meltdown at any point. Maybe she'd just pass out on his shoulder. If it'd spare Shell some grief, he'd take one for the team. Had nothing to do with the fact that he was falling in love with a kid he'd been terrified of from the moment he met her.

"A squirt is a super cute little girl that everyone loves."

"I always thinked you was scary, but mommy said you was just sad. Are you sad right now?"

He glanced at Izzy again. She and Shell had sat back down and were chatting again, but Izzy's eyes kept flicking in his direction and she had a bit of a goofy grin on her face. Jig had a feeling his own smile matched hers.

"No, squirt, I'm not sad at all right now."

"HOLY SHIT," SHELL whispered in awe. "This is only the second time I've ever seen him hold her, and last time he looked like he wanted to die. Usually, he finds every excuse in the book not to be near her."

"You're kidding?" Izzy found herself just as fascinated by the big man holding the little bit of a child.

"Nope. But it's not surprising if the rumors are true about his own daughter."

It wasn't Izzy's place to confirm what Shell thought she knew, so she just hummed.

"Gets you, doesn't it?" Shell asked with a knowing smirk.

"Huh?" Izzy tore her attention away from the sight of Jig holding a drowsy Beth. His expression had started as one of terror, then uncertainty, and now he had a dreamy look people got when snuggling a sleeping child.

"Right here"—Shell patted her stomach—"in the ovaries."

Izzy leaned back in her chair and crossed her arms over her chest. Stupidly, she'd worn a sleeveless dress and could have used a sweater or maybe a Snuggie right about now. "What the hell are you running on about?"

Laughing, Shell pulled her oversize black cardigan snug around herself as though Izzy's chill was trying to reach out to her. "Don't even try to pretend you don't feel it. There is nothing that makes a woman's ovaries stand up and dance like the sight of a hot as hell man holding a sleeping child. Especially one that's usually all growls and scowls."

Izzy rolled her eyes. Ridiculous. "My ovaries aren't doing anything. I don't even want kids. That is having absolutely no effect on me."

Liar. Well, not about the not wanting kids part. She'd never really imagined herself having children with such poor models of parenting in her life. But Shell was right about one thing. Seeing Jig holding Beth was making her insides all kinds of soft and squishy.

Those insides just needed to harden back up because no way, no how, was she going to get all swoony over a man. No matter how he looked holding a child. She was not that woman. Izzy took a giant mouthful of her favorite bourbon. Case in point, she wasn't willing to give up this any time soon, if ever.

Still, an image of a dark-haired little boy with Jig's navy-blue eyes and her fiery personality flashed through her mind.

Shit. She was losing it. Big time.

"Mmhm," Shell said then clucked her tongue. "If you think that is sexy, which you do no matter how much you deny it..." She tapped her fingers on the table top. "I wish we knew someone with a new baby. Put one of those in Jig's arms, and you'll be flat on your back, legs spread in no time."

Izzy sucked in a breath, and liquid sailed down her windpipe. She coughed until her lungs almost flew out of her mouth. "Jesus, Shell, you trying to kill me?"

"Sorry." Shell winced. "I was just trying to say no woman can resist a man with a baby."

"I can't resist him enough already. We do not need any help in that department," Izzy said, this time taking a tiny, cautious sip.

One of Shell's blond eyebrows rose. "Do tell."

"Uh, no."

"Oh, come on." Her glossy lips popped out into a pitiful pout. "I work two jobs, I have a three-year-old, and mean-as-hell bikers babysit my house every night. When do you think the last time I had sex was? I need to live vicariously through all my well-laid friends."

It was at that moment that Copper emerged from his office and headed straight for their table, looking just as intimidating as usual with narrowed eyes, compressed lips, and clenched fists. Hell, he didn't even need all that to be intimidating. His six-foot-five-inch bulky frame and president's patch took care of that all on its own.

"Don't think your schedule and your kid are what's killing your sex life," Izzy mumbled as Copper neared.

Shell followed Izzy's gaze and looked over her shoulder. When her focus landed on Copper, she tensed. "Shit," she muttered.

"Why the fuck didn't you tell me your refrigerator wasn't working, Shell?" Copper ground out, hovering above them.

Izzy wasn't one to be intimidated by a man, yet angry Copper had her feeling a tad uncomfortable.

Shell either didn't notice or didn't care because she waved away Copper's concern. "Because it's my refrigerator and my problem, Cop. Has nothing to do with you or the club." As she spoke, she straightened her shoulders and looked him right in the eye. Sure, even standing, she was more than a foot shorter than him, but Izzy had to hand it to her, she did not let him mow her over.

"Woman," he said on an exasperated sigh, "we could have had a new refrigerator out to you in less than a day. Why do you insist on being so damn stubborn?"

"Because it's my life, Copper. I can handle it myself."

"How are you supposed to take care of your child if you can't even keep her food cold?"

Uh oh.

Shell's face reddened, and she seemed to grow an inch or two. Her fingers curled into small fists that landed on her hips. "Are you trying to say I'm a bad mother?" she asked through teeth clenched so tight Izzy swore she could hear them grinding.

"What?" Copper ran a hand down his face and tugged at his beard. "That's not what I'm saying. A fridge will be delivered tomorrow."

Izzy could practically smell and see smoke coming out of Shell's ears and nose. She couldn't blame the woman. Accepting help from a man she was in love with who didn't return the sentiment would be absolute hell. Copper didn't seem to understand that. He probably thought he was helping, taking care of her in his own way, when all he was doing was crushing her more each day.

And that was why Izzy steered clear of love and relationships. Too fucking painful.

"Don't waste your time or money. I won't accept the delivery." Shell was practically screeching now.

Out of the corner of her eye, Izzy saw Jig start to head their way with an out cold Beth draped over his chest.

"Then I'll have it fucking installed while you're at work," Copper yelled, just as loud.

"You wouldn't dare!"

Jig cleared his throat. "Hey, Shell," he said in a low, very calm tone. "Want me to put the squirt somewhere for you?" He winked at Izzy, and she relaxed. Perfect timing as she hadn't had a clue how to de-escalate the verbal smackdown ramping up in front of her.

Shell's shoulders lost their tension, and she dragged a hand through her curls. "Thanks, Jig. I should just go and get her home to bed." She held out her arms. "I'll carry her to my car."

Gently, Copper nudged Shell aside. "I got her. You were just saying the other day how heavy she's getting, and I'm sure you have to grab her stuff from upstairs." With a skill Izzy never would have guessed he possessed, he shifted Beth from Jig's arms to his without so much as a peep from the sleeping child.

Shell visibly relaxed and softened toward Copper the moment her child was in his arms. Huh, maybe there was something to her theory because two minutes ago, Izzy would have sworn Shell was about to strangle him. Now she looked ready to hop on and ride him into the sunset.

"Thanks, Copper. I'll be right out." Shell turned to Izzy. "Bye, girl." They hugged, and Shell whispered, "Grab it while you can because nothing sucks more than wanting what you can never have." Then she gave Izzy a sad smile and went off to fetch Beth's things.

Izzy turned to Jig. He snagged her by the waist and drew her flush against him. Immediately, her focus went to the small spot of drool running down Jig's cut. "She slimed you," Izzy said with a smile.

There was an odd look on his face, one Izzy hadn't seen before. Shouldn't be surprising. It had to be unnerving being around children, especially one who was close in age to his own child who died. "You all right?"

He nodded. "Yeah, I'm actually pretty damn good." Then he kissed her, and anything else she might have said fell straight out of her head.

The man kissed better than any other man had ever fucked her.

"Upstairs," she said, breathless when they broke apart.

"Yeah," he said then smirked. "Wanna bone?"

Izzy pulled back and narrowed her eyes. "Excuse me? What did you just ask me?"

CHAPTER TWENTY-ONE

Izzy was on him the moment the door slammed behind them. He grunted as she none-too-gently shoved him against the closed door until his back hit the wood.

"My show," she said as though daring him to disagree.

He bit off his laugh. Sure, her show...for now.

"All right," he said. "Your show. Can I make two requests?"

Her lower lip tucked between her teeth as she considered his question. "Let's hear it. Then I'll decide if I want to grant it." One black eyebrow arched. Izzy was like a queen lording over her subject.

"I want to see you strip."

Her eyes darkened. She liked that idea. "I think that can be arranged."

"And I want your hair down."

That made her hesitate. Each time he'd been around her, except the one day in the diner, she'd had her hair in that same tight Dutch braid, or whatever she called it. It was hot as fuck. With the buzzed sides, she looked like some sort of warrior from a dystopian movie. But that one time it'd been down, when he caught her off guard at the diner? She'd been stunning. Feminine, vulnerable, softer.

Probably all the reasons she never let it down.

"O-okay," she said, a small hitch in her usually confident voice.

"Just for me," he said.

A smile curved her gloss covered lips. "Just for you," she whispered.

He got comfortable, resting against the door with his arms crossed over his chest. "Get to it, sweetheart."

Something happened to her every time he called her "sweetheart." Some of her sharp edges dulled, and she wasn't quite so prickly.

Izzy shot him the sexiest, most teasing, smile he'd ever seen as she took two steps back. Far enough away, he couldn't reach out and haul her in if he got tired of being hands off.

"No touching the merchandise," she said wagging a finger at him that moved in time with the seductive sway of her toned hips. This might have been a stupid idea. He was already hard as a stone, and now he had to restrain himself as he watched her peel out of that skin-tight thing she called a dress.

One at a time, she lowered the straps off her shoulders and slid her arms out. The black dress was so tight it didn't puddle at her feet, but stayed in place, giving him the same glimpse of cleavage that had been driving him wild all night.

Her gaze darkened as she hooked her thumbs in the top of the dress and did a little shimmy. Way too slowly for his comfort, she wiggled and tugged the dress down her body, over her hips, and then let it pool on the floor.

"Fuck," he hissed as he took in the sight before him. Black strapless bra, black satin covering her bare mound, thin black ribbons tied in tiny bows on each side of her hips, and sky-high black booties any ol' lady would high-five her for wearing.

Jig's blood heated and his breathing grew shallow just from the sight of her. He pressed the heel of his hand over his denim-trapped cock in a failed attempt to ease the ache. Izzy took a step toward him. "Bra and panties off," he said. "Leave the fucking shoes."

"You like my shoes?" she asked as her hands went around her back. With one quick motion, she had the bra undone and tumbling to the ground. Two full, perky tits with pebbled nipples stared at him, just waiting for his mouth.

He licked his lips, already feeling them on his tongue, and Izzy's breath hitched. "Like what they do to your legs and ass. Those panties wet? Get them off and hold them up so I can see."

One hand went to each of her hips, and she slowly pulled the strings at the same time, loosening the bows. By the time she held them up and Jig saw the glistening proof of her arousal, he was nearly salivating for a taste of her. But he could control himself. He'd let her play at being in charge a while longer, then take what he needed.

After tossing the soaked panties to the side, she threaded the tail of her long braid over her left shoulder and yanked off the blue rubber band securing it together. Jig's cock twitched as he watched her work her skilled fingers through the tightly woven hair. After a few seconds, long, wavy locks of black silk flowed down her back and over her shoulder.

Her eyes held a hint of vulnerability. She could no longer hide behind the badass, controlled look she preferred. All her sharp edges had been smoothed over, exposing the conqueror's feminine underbelly.

His warrior was also a queen.

Still fierce, still powerful, still formidable, yet all woman.

Now, wearing only the sexiest fucking ankle boots in history, she walked toward him like a model working the runway. Each step had the hair draped over her tits swaying and brushing across her hardened nipples. He could tell by the way her breath quickened, it was getting to her. Good. He wanted her as fucking out of her mind as she was making him.

When she was just an inch away, she grabbed the hem of his shirt and drew his shirt over his head. He let her and returned his hands to his sides when she went to work on his jeans. After a minor struggle, she had his boots, jeans, and boxer briefs lying in a pile on the floor.

From a squat at his feet, she rose to her full height, only a few inches shorter than him with those boots and whispered, "Let me do this. All the way. Do not stop me."

Then her mouth landed on his, and he hissed out a, "yes."

Wasn't the plan, but who could refuse her?

She gifted him a triumphant smile and returned to his skin, licking and sucking a slow trail of brutal kisses down his torso. Each time her warm, wet mouth latched onto him, his cock twitched and wept with need. After she reached his navel, she sank to her knees then stared up at him from the floor.

Shit, he wasn't going to last ten seconds in her hot mouth.

Izzy must have sensed his thoughts because she winked. "Don't worry, Jig, I'll be gentle."

He snorted. "Don't you dare."

Her gaze grew needy, and she slid a hand between her legs, rubbing her clit. "I want you just as bad," she said with a low moan.

Then her free hand wrapped around the base of his dick, and he saw stars. Precum leaked from the tip. Izzy swiped her tongue over his slit, capturing the fluid right before she sucked the head into her mouth.

"Fuck," Jig barked out as his head slammed against the door.

"Good?" Izzy asked around his cock one second before she removed her hand and sucked him deep.

"So fucking good," he managed to say even though his brain was going haywire.

Bobbing on his dick, she drew him farther into her mouth with each pass, until, by the fifth go around, he hit the back of her throat. Given that she was out of practice, she gagged slightly, her throat muscles squeezing him and making him cry out. "Shit," he said. "I almost came right there."

With her mouth stuffed full of him, she giggled, and he groaned. There was a good chance he'd die right here buried halfway down her throat. She fingered herself as she sucked him in, again and again, her fingers increasing speed in time with her mouth.

At his sides, Jig opened and closed his fists until he could no longer resist the need to dive his fingers into all that thick hair. Sweeping it away from her face, he gathered it into a ponytail high on her head, giving him a better view of both her mouth on him and her hand between her legs.

He held her hair firm, taking some of Izzy's control as he guided her mouth along his cock, but she didn't seem to mind. In fact, she groaned at his rough hold and rocked her hips on her hand. Jig watched every move she made. The visual, the heat of her mouth, the strong suction, and her moans of pleasure had him racing toward orgasm faster than ever before.

"Fuck, Iz," he said as she swallowed and squeezed the head of his cock just the right way. He widened his stance as his gut tightened and his balls drew up tight. "I'm about to come, baby. You want to bail, now's the time." He tugged her hair, letting her know what he meant.

She shook her head and grabbed his hips, sinking him all the way to the back of her throat. Then she swallowed again and sucked the cum straight out of him.

Jig's hand tightened in her hair. Hell, he was probably pulling too hard, but as the orgasm hit, he lost the ability to control his muscles. He bent at the waist, riding out the spasms and holding himself deep in her mouth as she rocked his world.

It seemed to last longer than ever before, but eventually, he stilled and began to soften in her mouth. Izzy pulled back, a look of triumph strong on her face. Licking her lips, she rose to her feet.

Jig didn't give her a chance to say anything. He kissed her, not caring he could taste himself on her tongue. Then, before she could react, he lifted her, carried her to the bed and tossed her in the center. The moment her back hit the mattress, he spun her and shoved her face down on the bed. She huffed out a startled laugh as she landed.

"You come yet?"

"What?" she asked peering over her shoulder. Her dark eyes

tracked him as he climbed up behind her.

The picture she made was the most beautiful thing he'd ever seen. All that dark hair spilled over the tanned skin of her toned back. The generous, firm swell of her ass leading into long, shapely legs. She was worlds better than any centerfold he'd ever seen.

"Did. You. Come. Yet?" he asked in a harsh voice. Playtime was over. He was back at the wheel, and she was going to take everything he gave her.

"No. Not yet."

"Good. I don't want you coming until I'm inside you." He ran his hand down the center of her spine, enjoying the little shiver that coursed through her.

Izzy chuckled. "You just came like the world was ending there, bubba. Guess I'm going to be waiting a long time for my turn, huh?"

Jig's lips twitched. Little smartass. Easily dealt with. He cracked his palm across her ass, eliciting a sharp yelp and that narrowed-eyed look that stirred his blood. "Don't even think ab —"

He did it again, and her breathing increased like it did in a fight. She was trying to control herself. Resisting the urge to give in to the desire. He reached between her legs. Completely drenched. She may not want to like it, but she fucking loved it. "Done with the sass?"

One terse nod was the only answer she gave before she turned her gaze forward. Not acceptable. For this to work, she had to admit she could give up control and enjoy it. He'd given up control for her a few moments ago...mostly.

Jig wrapped her hair around his fist and tugged her head back. She moaned and tried to pull away, but he held her firm. "You're still a badass, Izzy," he whispered against her ear. "What we do in here can never take away from that. I will never think anything less of you. But you don't have to be tough and hard with me all the time. You can give in to this other part of you, and no one will ever know. Just you and me, sweetheart."

He loosened his grip enough that she turned her head and met his gaze. Relief, uncertainty, lust, and compliance were what he read from her.

Pushing back to his knees, he palmed her ass and squeezed, hard. Even with just his hands on her, he was in heaven. "Why do you think I had you lay on your stomach? I'll be hard again in two minutes looking at that ass." Halfway there already, he couldn't tear his eyes from the round globes. He leaned down and bit into the flesh of her ass.

"Jig," Izzy cried out then moaned.

He did it again, then again until she was squirming beneath him and grinding her pelvis into the bed.

Searching for the relief only he could give her.

"Jesus," she said, panting as her head dropped down to the bed. "I've never let—what the hell are you doing to me?"

"I'm letting you be you. No walls. No masks. Just you. Just me."

She swallowed audibly and in a soft voice said, "Please, Jig."

Goddamn did he love the sound of her begging. He was sporting a raging erection once again, as though it'd been ages since he'd last come, not five minutes.

"Please what?" he asked. Sure, he was pushing her. She'd probably never asked for it in her life and would have knocked any other man six ways to Sunday. But he wasn't any other man. He was the one who wanted to peel back her layers and reveal the core of what made her who she was.

In her presence, he was raw and exposed and would accept nothing less in return for however long it lasted.

"Please fuck me," she said, voice rife with need.

Shit, he needed to see her. As though she was nothing more than pint-sized, he flipped her to her back. "Hands up," he ordered.

She hesitated, but just for a fraction of a second before placing her hands above her head, giving him her trust, giving up her control.

"Keep them there." Jig grabbed one of the pillows next to her head and shoved it under her ass. Next, he fished a condom out of the nightstand and rolled it down his cock, gritting his teeth against the pleasure his own hand brought. Then he fisted his cock, stroked twice, and ran it through her folds, making sure to tap against her clit.

She cried out and begged again. "Please, Jig. Now."

"You sure you're ready for this? You sure you can handle me, Iz?"

She lifted her head and looked him straight in the eye. "I can handle every single part of you, Jig."

They both knew she was referring to more than his need to fuck hard. She was accepting his past, his pain, his fucked-up head, the dangerous present they were living in and maybe, just maybe, the future.

The need to possess her raged within him, and he slammed home in one powerful thrust.

"Yes," Izzy cried as he gave her what she'd been begging for.

Jig completely lost himself in the woman who took him at face value and cast no judgment. The woman whose walls he was knocking down. The woman who was crawling so deep inside him he could feel her flowing through his veins. Never before had he felt so connected to another woman on such a raw, primal level.

Not even his wife.

And what the fuck was he supposed to do about that?

CHAPTER TWENTY-TWO

"Did you make the call?" Stephanie asked, her voice giddy with excitement.

Izzy smiled and spoke above the noise of her tattoo machine. "I did. I told Mav I locked myself out of the shop and couldn't get a hold of Jig or Rip. He'll be here in fifteen minutes, and I've got about ten left on your tat. You holding up okay?"

"Yeah, I'm good. I mean, it's not like getting a massage, but it's not as bad as I feared either." She was face down on the table while Izzy inked the phrase *Through every dark night, there is a brighter day* onto her shoulder. The quote obviously held significance for Stephanie and Maverick. On top of that, the ink looked terrific on Steph's tan skin. Instead of writing it straight across her friend's shoulder, Izzy started the words at the outer edge, where her shoulder met her arm and followed the natural curve of Stephanie's body in one long line.

Gorgeous.

Below the quote was a date. A few months ago. A large part of Izzy was dying to know what made that date so significant, but her personal policy was to never ask. Not all clients wanted to share the personal nature of their choice, and she'd never want to make them uncomfortable. Even if they were friends.

"Mav's gonna lose his shit," Steph said of her heavily tattooed boyfriend. The man would have to grow some extra limbs if he wanted any more ink. "I'm so freaking excited. We met under rather intense circumstances, both taken prisoner by the Gray Dragons on the date there." She sighed. "Got pretty dicey for a while. Both of us were injured, Mav far worse than I was. But we wouldn't have 'us' if it wasn't for that experience. Today is definitely a brighter day even with Lefty's shadow looming over the club."

Wow. That was more than Izzy could have imagined. If the rambling was any indication, Steph was nervous about Maverick's reaction to the tattoo. Izzy just grunted her agreement but was too much in the zone to carry on more of a conversation. She worked for another five minutes, then wiped the area she'd just completed. "All finished."

"Yay!" Stephanie practically bounced off the table. "Can I look now? It's been so hard to not be able to see it while you were working. Can I look?"

"You bet." Izzy pointed toward the floor length mirror. "Have at it. I can take a picture for you too if you want to see it closer."

"Oooh, yes, would you?" She stood in the middle of the store holding her shirt over her bare chest. Rip wasn't due in for another hour, and no walk-ins had shown up that morning, so it was just Izzy and Steph.

"Yeah, where's your phone?"

"In my bag. You can grab it," Steph said as she twisted her head around trying to get a better view.

"Here." Izzy handed the phone to Steph who used her thumb to unlock it. "Turn around and hold still a second."

A laugh bubbled out of Stephanie. "I'm so excited I'm buzzing with energy. Not sure I can be still."

"You're good." Izzy snapped a few pics then returned the phone to Stephanie.

"Oh, man, Izzy. This is absolutely perfect. You are seriously amazing." Stephanie squealed like a kid on Christmas morning.

"Thanks. I actually love doing quotes. Some fonts can look so beautiful."

Still holding the shirt across her front, Steph tilted her head and gave Izzy a sly smile. "So, I've been here for two hours. Think I've held out long enough. What the hell is going on with you and Jig?"

What was going on with her and Jig? That was the question on her mind constantly. They ate together, they watched television together, they fixed her broken faucet together, they slept together, and they fucked in every corner of her house. They also had this intense connection that allowed her to let her guard down and show Jig parts of herself she hadn't known existed. Then there was him spilling his guts about his past, a past not even his brothers fully knew.

She didn't allow herself to delve too deeply into it. For now, what they shared was enough, but Izzy felt a tugging on her heart the more time they spent together. And that was unacceptable and would have to be dealt with sooner rather than later.

"We're...friends," she said and then winced because it sounded like a crock of shit, even to her.

Stephanie burst out laughing. She laughed until her eyes watered and she could barely breathe.

"It's not that funny," Izzy grumbled as she began to clean up.

"Oh, but it is. You two can't keep your hands or lips off each other, but it's fine. You can keep your little secrets for now. Just know that with this group, nothing stays buried for long." She flashed a toothy grin.

"It's not my fault he's so damn sexy."

"No," Steph said as she walked closer. "It's not. But it is your fault the man is smiling for the first time since I've met him. And it's your fault he's laughing, hanging out more, and seems to be actually enjoying his life. I'd say that's completely your fault."

Tears filled Izzy's eyes. Shit. She blinked and stared at her equipment. She didn't fucking cry, and hearing that Jig was doing so well wouldn't be the thing that made her do it for the first time since her mother died.

She cleared her throat. "Thanks." It was all she could manage.

Jigsaw

Stephanie winked and nodded. Then the jangle of bells announced Mav's arrival.

"Busy Izzy, what's going on? I thought you were lock—babe?" He stopped a few feet in the door and whipped his head back and forth between Steph and Izzy. "What are you doing here? And without your shirt on." Then he staggered back with a hand over his heart as though he'd been shot. "Holy shit, is that dream I had the other night about to come true? I told you about it. The one where you and Izzy were naked and you—"

"Maverick!" Stephanie held up her hand in a stop motion while Izzy cracked up. Maverick never failed to say something ridiculous and borderline inappropriate.

Okay, over-the-line inappropriate, but hilarious nonetheless.

"Your little fantasy did not and is not going to happen," Steph said, shaking her head at Maverick's dramatic pout. "Sorry to disappoint you."

"Well, if you're not going to get naked and eat strawberries off each other, what are you doing here?"

Izzy snorted and mouthed, "Strawberries?"

With a roll of her eyes, Steph said, "It's better not to ask. You learn to just smile and nod." Which she did in a very staged fashion.

"You two are too much." Izzy walked her dirty equipment over to the autoclave.

"All right," Mav said. "Enough bullshit. What's really going on?"

Steph bit her lower lip and spun on one heel. "What do you think?" The woman had handled the needle like a pro without an ounce of trepidation, but now her voice shook. Mav's opinion meant everything to her.

Behind her back, Izzy crossed her fingers and held her breath.

"Holy shit," Mav said on a harsh exhale. He rushed across the room and straight to Stephanie. When he reached her, he traced a finger across her skin below the fresh tattoo. "Jesus, baby." He visibly swallowed, his voice choked with emotion.

"Do you like it?"

"I fucking love it. You—" He rested his head between her shoulder blades, took a deep breath, then whispered something in her ear. A glowing smile appeared on Stephanie's face just before she spun and threw her arms around his neck.

"I love you so damn much, Maverick," she said.

"Love you too, babe." Then they were kissing in a not-fit-for-public make-out session. Izzy averted her eyes. Not because of the show, nah, she was down with a little visual porn, but the depth of feeling and love between the two was more than she could bear.

She hadn't had much experience with successful couples, and it was clear these two were one of the ones that would make it.

They loved each other.

Not infatuation, or lust, though they had that in spades, but a deep love and connection the world could see. They needed each other to survive.

And it fucked with Izzy's mind too much for her to keep watching.

After a few minutes of pretending she wasn't seconds away from a live sex show, she rolled her eyes. "Okay, you two crazy kids, let me get that tattoo dressed and go over the after-care before you start rolling around on my floor naked. Then I'll be forced to clean up all the vomit that will come from my mouth because, Mav, no one wants to see you naked."

Stephanie laughed, and it killed their make-out session. Mav didn't have an ounce of fat on him. Nor did he have the muscular bulk of his brothers. Not to say he was a slouch. No, he was definitely as hot as the rest of them, and she'd heard he was scrappy as hell. But it was always fun to kid the kidder.

"Do your thing, Iz, so I can take my woman home and fuck her." He scratched his chin as though deep in thought. "Though I might not be able to wait that long. Izzy, you mind if we go fuck around the side of your building?"

"Jesus, Mav," Stephanie said with a shake of her head, but

Jigsaw

Izzy didn't miss the flash of interest in her gaze.

"Fine by me as long as I can't see or hear anything. And as long as you don't have her back against the wall. I get a little cranky if you mess up my work five minutes after it's done." Just as she finished speaking, the sky opened up and rain pelted down.

With a shrug, Mav snapped his fingers. "Oh, darn. Guess that's out of the question. My woman's a screamer anyway." He winked at Stephanie who was now bright pink and trying to hide her face.

Izzy laughed as she dressed the tattoo. Spending the morning with Steph had been more fun than she'd expected. By the time the ink was covered, she'd reviewed the after-care and was ready to send her friends on their horny way. She and Steph hugged, kissed cheeks, and promised to have a girl's day soon. Well, a girl's day plus their respective biker shadows.

After they left, Izzy finished cleaning up, then the bell jangled and the prospect watching her popped his head in. It wasn't someone she'd seen before, a newer guy whose name she was embarrassed to admit she couldn't recall. "Hey, Izzy, I'm fucking starving. Mind if I run out to grab some food? I'll be twenty minutes tops."

Jig wouldn't like it, but Rip was due any moment so she shouldn't be alone for more than thirty seconds. "Nah, go ahead. It's fine."

"You want something?" what's-his-name asked.

"No, I'm good. Thanks, though."

He disappeared, and she got back to her cleaning only to have the bell ring out again.

"Hey," she called over her shoulder, "Welcome to—oh Rip, hey. Right on time." At least she wouldn't have to tell Jig she'd been alone in the shop.

He shuffled his way into the shop and straight to her station. "Yeah, I know. Wanted to talk to you about something for a few minutes."

A wave of discomfort washed over Izzy. That phrase was never a good way to start a conversation. Pretty much always meant some kind of bad news.

God, was he about to fire her?

She'd never had a customer complain about her, she worked whatever hours he requested, and she never caused drama.

Rip chuckled and sat on a rolling stool. "Get that terrified expression off your face, kid. It's nothing bad."

"Well, maybe you shoulda started with that, old man," Izzy said as she plopped on the empty stool. She'd never admit how relieved his reassurances made her.

"I'm moving to Montana in a month," he said.

Izzy blinked. "I'm sorry, what?" How was that not bad news?

His eyes sparkled. "You heard me, Iz. I'm moving."

"But, but why? Are you buying a new shop?"

"Nah," he said. "I'm retiring."

"You're fifty-two."

Rip chuckled. "I'm well aware of my age." He shrugged. "I've got money saved from an old inheritance. I, uh…" His round face turned an adorable shade of red. "I met someone who lives out there, at a convention last year. We've kept in touch ever since, and I want to be closer to her."

What the hell was with everyone pairing off? "Rip?" she asked in a sing-song voice. "Are you in love?"

He snorted and flipped her off. "Shut up, kid. Let me get to my point here."

She wasn't sure she could take much more. One more person leaving her life. Someone she'd thought would be in her life for years to come. Add it to the tally. Swallowing, Izzy steeled her face and tried not to show the ache of disappointment. "Moving wasn't your point?"

"No. God, have you always been this sassy?" He stared at the ceiling and threw up his hands.

"Yes." Izzy laughed. "Sorry, old man. Get to it."

"I want to sell you the business. Can't think of anyone I'd

rather leave the place to."

For the second time that day, Izzy's eyes welled. "Shit, Rip, you know I'd love nothing more than to carry on your legacy, but I'm in no position to buy a shop."

He held up his hand and scowled, but it was all for show. Deep down the man was as soft as a melted marshmallow. "Can you stop running your mouth and let me finish?"

"Yeah." She was truly going to miss her gruff mentor.

"I'd like to sell you the place for one dollar."

"Rip—" Was he out of his mind?

"I say it was your turn to speak yet?" His brusque voice was full of affection. People didn't do things like this. Didn't just hand over a store to someone not even a blood relative. What was it with this town? First, the bikers had jumped in to help her on more than on occasion, now Rip practically was handing her his shop on a silver platter. Of course, he was still leaving her, but somehow his wanting to make sure she was well set up eased some of that sting.

Izzy rolled her lips inward to keep from giggling. "Nope."

Was the other shoe about to drop? Because people didn't just help and give; they took and neglected.

He grunted. "I told you I got money. Don't need to sell this place for more of it. Thought of it closing is the only thing that makes me sad about leaving. So, you take it. Keep 'er open for me. Give good ink."

Arguing was pointless. Rip's mind was made up. The determination to get his way was evident in his narrowed eyes and the set of his jaw.

"Am I allowed to talk now?" she asked after enduring a few seconds of the stare-down.

"Long as you don't say some stupid shit about not deservin' it or not feelin' right takin' it from me."

"I won't."

"'Kay." He rested his elbow on the tattoo chair to his side.

"Thank you," she said with a crack in her voice. "I-I'm

honored, and I'll take excellent care of your baby."

He stood and patted her shoulder. "Know you will, kid. Wouldn't have given 'er to you otherwise." With that, he disappeared into his office. That was about as touchy-feely as Rip got. For anyone else, it was the equivalent of a bear hug and vomiting feelings all over the room.

Her shop. She glanced around the very simple and understated room.

Her shop.

Already, ideas for growth, expansion, and remodeling were pinging around in her head. Izzy smiled just as the bells jangled once again. "Hey, welcome to Inked. What can I do for you?"

The potential client looked about five minutes out of puberty with a scraggly smattering of light brown peach fuzz on his chin, a few zits, and about a gallon of goop in his sand-colored hair.

Izzy's bullshit meter started to rise.

"Want some ink," he said, puffing out his chest like that would somehow make her believe he was of age.

Folding her arms across her chest, Izzy leaned her hip against the reception counter. "Hmm," she said. "You got any ID on you proving you're eighteen?"

"What?" He froze for a second then said, "Oh, yeah. I, uh, got it right here." After a few moments of hunting in his baggy pockets, he dug out a card and handed it to her. She took one look at the Tennessee license and burst out laughing. The guy in the photo had ten years and fifty pounds on this kid. Only thing they had in common was the inability to grow a full beard.

With as gentle a smile as she could muster when she wanted to boot him out the door for wasting her time, she said, "Sorry, kid, but there is no way this is you." She held out the ID. "Come on back when you turn eighteen. Unless you want to bring your parents. I can ink you if I have their consent."

He snatched the license back and got right up in her face. Too bad he was two inches shorter than she was in her heels. And she could probably snap his twiggy neck with ease. "Listen, bitch—"

"Hey!" Rip emerged from his office and made his way to the counter. "We got a problem here?"

Izzy resisted the urge to roll her eyes. It was still Rip's shop so she wouldn't give him hell for jumping in front of her and handling her hiccups.

"Yeah, we got a problem, old man." Dumb kid probably thought Rip would be in on his boys' club mentality and take his side. "This bitch won't give me my tat."

Rip raised an eyebrow at Izzy. "Never known her to refuse a customer. Must be a good reason, buddy. Even better than you calling her a bitch. I've seen her hand better men than you their asses for less."

Izzy coughed to cover her laugh. "There is. He showed me the shittiest fake ID I've ever seen. Told him to come back with mommy and daddy, and I'd be happy to ink him. Otherwise, he's gotta wait until he's eighteen like everybody else."

Rip's lips quirked, but he didn't smile. Much more even keel than Izzy, he said. "Sorry, bud. Don't be a dick to her. I'm the one who makes the rules. See you in a few years."

"Fuck this," the teenager said. As he pushed through the door, his phone rang and he cursed again.

"You good?" Rip asked.

Izzy smiled. Sure, his overprotective attitude toward a little boy Izzy could swat easier than a fly was on the annoying side, but it was also endearing in a fatherly kind of way. "I'm good, Rip. Thanks for the backup."

With a nod and a wave of his hand, he headed back to his office. "You're done for the day, right?"

"Yeah, I'm free now. Have a good one, Rip."

"See ya tomorrow."

She grabbed her bag, popped on her sunglasses, and headed out to the parking lot. An ominous gray sky greeted her, ready to dump buckets of rain. "Guess I don't need these," she said as she removed the dark glasses. Digging through her purse for her sunglass case, she heard some muffled chatter and looked around, but appeared to be alone.

"Lefty needs my help? Fuck yeah, I'm in."

Hand in her bag, Izzy froze.

Confident the sound came from around the side of the shop, Izzy tiptoed as close as she dared to get a better listen.

Lefty.

The kid was one of Lefty's guys? She strained her ears, trying to pick up any and every word that was spoken. The wind kicked up and made it harder to hear, forcing her to sneak closer.

"Bring food to the guys guarding the barn? Yeah, man, I can do that. What the fuck's the barn? What are they guarding?"

Izzy held her breath. Whoever was on the other end was reaming him out so loudly she could hear muffled scolding through the phone.

"No, sorry man. Yeah, I know. Don't ask questions, just follow orders. Got it." He fell silent for a few moments. Izzy could practically feel the waves of excitement flowing from him. He was obviously low level if he was even in the gang at all yet. An eager puppy who had far more ambition than brains, as evident by the fact he was having this conversation outside.

"Four guys. Yeah, okay, I'll pick up a few pizzas and bring 'em right there. You gonna text me directions?"

The barn. Guarding someone.

Izzy's gut went haywire. And she'd learned to trust it after taking care of herself for years. Something was up here. Something big. A barn with guards sounded like the perfect place to stash a bunch of kidnapped girls being sold to the highest bidder.

Her heart raced, and her fingers and toes tingled. This was it. She could feel it in her bones. This was what the Handlers needed to get Lefty off their backs.

Not to mention the potential to rescue the women—girls—Lefty had kidnapped.

The idea of being caught snooping wasn't one she relished, so the moment it sounded like the kid was winding up his call, Izzy hoofed it to her car as silently as possible. After slipping into the driver's seat, she kept her eyes on the kid but acted as though she was searching for something in her bag. Adrenaline coursed through her system, similar to the feeling she had right before stepping into the ring. Used to it, it was typically easy to channel the anxious anticipation into something productive, but today her usual methods failed her. There was far too much at stake.

The sky opened up, dumping buckets of rain in seconds. Maybe the pelting rain would create some distraction and keep him from realizing she intended to tail him.

The kid pulled out of the parking lot, and Izzy forced herself to count to ten before driving after him. This was her first time following someone with stealth in mind, so she just did what she'd seen on TV. No headlights despite the rain, stayed a reasonable distance behind him, avoided turn signals. After about ten minutes, he pulled into the parking lot of an Italian restaurant. Izzy drove past, flipped a U-ey, then pulled off to the side of the road within eyesight of the kid's car.

When he disappeared into the restaurant, she dug out her phone. Time to call in the steel cavalry.

CHAPTER TWENTY-THREE

"Of course, it's fucking pouring," Jig grumbled as he sprinted from the clubhouse to Zach's idling truck. Cold rain, sharp as shards of ice, bounced off his leather jacket and bombarded his face in a shower of stabbing pricks.

When he reached the truck, he yanked the door handle, only to find it locked.

What the...?

With a scowl, he peered through the dripping truck window into the cab of the truck and at Zach's shit-eating grin.

Asshole.

Pounding his fist on the window, he yelled, "Open it the fuck up, shithead. It's colder than a witch's tit out here, and I'm fucking soaked."

Zach glanced over his shoulder to the back seat where Rocket was laughing like a loon. His brothers were a bunch of sadistic cockwaffles.

"What?" Zach lifted his hands and shook his head. "I can't hear you," he mouthed.

"Open. The. Fucking. Door." Jig gripped the handle and pulled with all his strength as though he could just rip the damn thing off the hinge. But what'd he'd apparently missed was Zach unlocking the door, which now flew open, sending Jig stumbling back, nearly to his ass.

Both Zach and Rocket were so hysterical they could barely

speak.

"Can we go please?" Jig reached out and cranked Zach's heat. The other two could sweat their nuts off for all he cared.

"Oooh," Zach said as he tried to calm his hilarity. "That was fucking good. Hey! Don't drip all over my new leather interior. If I gotta ride in a cage, I want it to at least be in good condition."

Jig finally smiled. "Should have thought of that shit before you locked me out in the rain, asshole. Let's get moving. Copper will skin us alive if we don't follow up on this lead." Rocket had gotten some intel on where Lefty was hiding out. Today's mission was to scout it out, see if there was a chance the info was good. Possibly a long-shot, but worth the trouble if it got them what they needed.

As Zach pulled out onto the road, Rocket leaned forward over the center console. "You know," he said, facing Jig. "Two months ago, we couldn't have pulled that shit on you."

Jig's eyebrows drew down. "What do you mean?"

"You were such a grumpy motherfucker that it wouldn't have been any fun. You'd have just walked away or some shit. You're actually not a dipshit now. What the fuck's going on with you?"

With a laugh, Zach steered onto the highway. "Pussy, brother. Our man Jig is getting it from all angles from his sexy fighter girl. You should try it."

"Huh." Rocket sat back against the seat. "Guess that explains it."

With a roll of his eyes, Jig said, "I've always had pussy. This is no different." Even as the words left his mouth, they felt dirty. And his balls shriveled a bit at the thought of what Izzy would do to him if she'd heard that.

"Ha," Zach said, slapping the steering wheel. "No different, my ass. That's the biggest crock of shit I've ever heard."

Jig was beyond over this conversation but, apparently, he was to endure the idiocy of his brothers a little longer.

"Quality pussy, my man. There's a difference, and you fucking know it," Zach said like he was some authority on women.

That statement caused Jig to grunt. Yeah, he knew precisely what Zach was referring to. Everything about Izzy was quality. Maybe he should just man-up and admit it. Just as he was about to open his mouth, his phone rang.

"Speak of the she-devil," Zach said with a smirk.

"You're like a giant five-year-old," Jig said as he checked the screen. Sure enough, Izzy. "Hey, babe," he said.

Izzy didn't bother with a greeting but launched into a panicked rant he could barely understand. Cold fear washed over him. Nothing scared Izzy. Nothing riled her so much she couldn't be understood. What the fuck had happened?

"Shit, babe, slow down. I can't catch what the fuck you're saying." Unease tightened his gut. "You in trouble?"

"No. Sorry, I'm a little freaked out right now. Okay, this guy, a kid really, came into the shop for a tat. I refused him because he was about sixteen and had the worst fake ID I'd ever seen. Rip backed me because he was obviously—"

"Babe, the point?" Jig cut in because he sensed she'd have gone on for a while before getting to the meat of it.

"Oh, God, sorry. Shit, I need to calm down." Her deep inhalation and slow release were audible through the phone. "Damnit, there he is. Okay, I'm putting you on speaker so I can follow him again."

Red flags were flying all over the place, and Jig's fuse was lit. "Isabella, what the fuck is going on? And why the fuck are you following someone? Swear to Christ, if you don't tell me now…"

"Shit, it's raining hard. Okay, the kid got a call and took it outside, but I overheard it as I was leaving. Whoever was on the line asked him to do an errand. For Lefty. Wanted him to pick up some food for guys out at some barn who were guarding something."

"God fucking damnit!" Jig slammed his clenched fist against the dash.

Zach swerved off the road and hit the brakes. "What's going on, brother?" Once again, Rocket leaned between the front seats, any traces of playfulness vanished.

"Jig?" Izzy asked.

"Babe, I'm putting you on speaker. Repeat what you just said."

Rocket and Zach's reactions were just as violent as Jig's, but they couldn't possibly have been feeling the same rattled turmoil as he was. His woman was out there following some punk to a barn where they housed trafficked woman.

Fuck.

"Fuck!" he screamed again.

Maintaining his cool, Zach put a hand on Jig's shoulder. "Iz, where are you now?" he asked.

"Heading west on Lamar Alexander Parkway. He just pulled out of that Italian place."

Zach caught Rocket's eye in the mirror and nodded. Rocket pulled out his phone and started a low conversation. Jig shook his head then rolled his shoulders and focused on what Izzy was saying. He needed to get his shit together so he could be useful to her and his club.

And an unknown number of abused teenage girls.

His body zinged with an electricity he'd felt a few times before. Bloodlust. Some motherfuckers were going to pay very soon.

"Good, Iz, that's good," Zach said. "We're actually only five minutes away from where you are. Stay far enough behind him that he doesn't spot you, though it doesn't sound like he's smart enough to pick up a tail. Still, be cautious. Stay on the line and navigate for us when he gets off the parkway. Okay? We should be pulling up behind you in a few minutes."

Zach stomped on the accelerator, and his pickup shot forward, way faster than the speed limit and way faster than was smart given the near-freezing rain, but fuck it. They had to catch up to Izzy and fast.

"Will do," Izzy said. Then she fell quiet, probably concentrating on the road and her mark.

"Babe, we're in Zach's black F-150. He'll flash his lights when we're behind you. You immediately pull over and head back home."

A soft snort came through the phone. "Fuck that. You're not getting rid of me that easy, bubba."

Jig clenched the dashboard as hard as he could, trying to rid some of the rage-fueled tension building. "Where the fuck is your prospect?"

Izzy cleared her throat. "I, uh, kinda told him he could go get something to eat while I was working. In my rush to follow this guy, I forgot all about him."

Jig looked at Zach. "He's fucking dead. I want his cut. He'll never patch."

"Simmer down, brother," Zach said. "We'll worry about that later."

Simmer down? Simmer down? "Would you be telling yourself to simmer down if Toni's protection took off to stuff his fucking face?"

Tension filled the car as Zach clutched the steering wheel and shook his head.

"Uh, guys, still here, and turning left about a mile after that rundown silo. Shit, there's no street sign. It's a dirt road," Izzy said.

"Know it, babe, you're doing great," Zach said.

All three men strained toward the phone. With the dull roar of the rain and the phone being on speaker, hearing her was a challenge.

"Okay, turning right three-tenths of a mile down. Another dirt road. It's easy to see, first turn off."

Zach smiled. The asshole was probably loving every second of this. "Your woman's a rock star," he mouthed to Jig.

Pride warmed Jig's insides. Even though he hated her being anywhere near this shit, Zach had a point. Izzy was brave, courageous, loyal, smart, and for however long it lasted, she was his. Fuck, after this, Copper would probably patch her in as the first female member of the club.

"Iz, we'll be coming up on you any second now," Zach said.

"I've stopped," she replied. "I can see a structure about a hundred yards or so ahead. Looks like an actual barn, so I don't want to get closer and be discovered."

When he spotted her crappy car, Jig's stomach finally unknotted. Even though he'd known she was fine, having eyes on her confirmed her safety. "We're pulling up behind you," Jig said. "Get out of your car and into Zach's truck."

"Coming." She disconnected the call, and darted from her car to Zach's truck. She was so fucking brave, Jig wasn't sure whether he wanted to praise her for her actions, hold her until he was one hundred percent certain she was all right, or spank the shit out of her for her recklessness.

"Shit, that rain is freezing," she said, breathing hard as she slammed the door. She rubbed her hands together. "So, what's the plan?"

Seriously? What's the plan? Jig laughed a sound of disbelief. "What's the plan? The plan is that you're going to get that sweet ass back in your piece of shit car and drive straight to the clubhouse while we check this out."

The sound that came from Izzy would have been hilarious if it wasn't such a shitty situation. Part snort, part choke, and part laugh, she clapped her hands together one time then leaned forward until she was right in his face.

"Now, baby," she said in a syrupy-sweet voice so un-Izzy, "you know how much I appreciate your love of my sweet ass, but you're out of your fucking mind if you think I'm going to scurry home and bake you a fuckin' pie like the little woman." There wasn't any sweetness to her tone anymore. Just the narrowed-eyed oh-hell-no look that usually got him hard. Not today.

Bake a pie? What the fuck was she talking about? Women's minds where such a mess of twisted fuckery, he didn't even try to decipher it.

"This is club business, Izzy. It's not your place, and I'm not risking you getting involved in this deeper." He couldn't, wouldn't lose another woman to violence. Why couldn't she just give in?

"Guys, this is not the tim—"

"Shut up, Rocket," Izzy snapped before turning back to Jig. "Not my place? You're not risking me? I'm sorry? Is your brain getting clogged with residual old-world Southern gentlemen bullshit? Because here, in the year twenty eighteen, we actually let women make their own decisions."

"You need a little reminder of what happens when you mouth off to me?" Jig practically growled at her.

The car fell deadly silent, and the look of betrayal on Izzy's face was so profound Jig instantly knew he'd made a fatal mistake. "Fuck!" He slammed out of the car and into the freezing rain, not giving one single shit if he died of fucking hypothermia.

He needed her to be safe. Why couldn't she understand that? If anything happened to her, it would destroy him. God damned woman was so infuriating.

Still, he'd fucked up royally. Just a few nights ago he'd promised her whatever went on between them was private. That whatever secret parts of herself she let only him have, he'd keep them secret.

Izzy didn't trust for shit, yet she'd given some to him.

And he just threw it right back in her face.

She'd never trust him again. He knew it without a doubt.

SLACK-JAWED, IZZY stared after the man who stormed from the truck with her pride dragging behind him in tatters. How could he? She'd gone so out of character by letting him spank her, actually trusting him with a piece of herself she hadn't given to another man ever. And he tossed that trust away as though it was nothing more than trash.

And ordering her to leave a fight? It was like he didn't know her at all.

How many times did she need to learn the same lesson before it stuck? How many people were destined to disappoint and abandon her before she got a clue and stopped forming attachments? Because she was attached, very attached, despite her staunch resolve to remain distant.

It wasn't the time to delve into it, but she feared she might even be in love with him. Her heart squeezed so painfully tears tickled the corners of her eyes. No, it couldn't be love. She wouldn't allow it.

"Izzy, with his past, Jig's just overprotect—"

She looked Zach in the eye. "You think I can't handle this?"

He gave her the respect of a straight answer. "I think you can handle any damn thing thrown your way. This isn't about that. This is about Jig and his fear of—"

"No. It's not. It's about teenage girls who have been kidnapped. It has nothing to do with Jig or his fucked-up view of how women should act. What's the plan? You going to bust in there and get these traumatized girls to come with you? You think they're just gonna hop in the back of your truck and ride off with you? You're all huge, intimidating bikers, and these girls have been abused and raped, probably repeatedly. They're going to be fucking terrified and need a woman present."

Zach's sigh was heavy with frustration. "LJ's on his way with a van. Rocket's got a contact a few hours out of town. Chick who runs a shelter. She can take the girls. Get them sorted. Find the families of the ones who have them. Help the others get the support they need."

"They're not going to leave with a bunch of menacing men." Was she the only rational one here?

"Can you shoot a gun?" Rocket asked from next to her.

"I was a single woman living alone in New Orleans, working alone at night sometimes with occasionally rough clientele. Yes, I can shoot a fucking gun. And I have one in my car."

Zach and Rocket exchanged a look while she seethed in her

seat. Really, she didn't need their permission for any of this, but the boys club she'd fallen in with had her outnumbered, so she was at their mercy.

"All right." Zach ran a hand over his face. He turned in his seat and speared her with a look she hadn't seen from him. This was enforcer Zach, all serious business and don't-fuck-with-me attitude. Izzy squirmed in her seat. "You"—he pointed to her—"are not on point here. You're here for the girls. To keep them calm, to help get them out, and to prevent freak-outs. You hear me? No GI Jane shit."

Izzy frowned and opened her mouth, but Zach held up a hand. "Not because you can't hack it, but because that man"—he jerked his thumb over his shoulder—"will lose his shit if something happens to you. If you can't agree, I'll tie your ass to the steering wheel. Yes?"

Izzy swallowed all the retorts bubbling up in her mouth and nodded. She stared out the windshield at the back of Jig seated in her car. Maybe she'd been too hard on him. Since he'd lost his wife in the most horrifying of ways, the man was bound to be a little overprotective as a result. And he'd probably spoken without thinking, pushed to his limit by her.

Not that it mattered because this had been an eye-opening afternoon. A reminder she couldn't put herself in a position to be disappointed and abandoned once again. It was time to end things with Jig.

The rain had slowed to a thick mist, and within minutes a large panel van pulled up behind Zach's car. Rocket, Zach, and Jig left the vehicles and met LJ at the van. Izzy followed, careful to avoid Jig's gaze. Weapons were distributed, plans were made, then Zach and LJ spent a few minutes hiding the vehicles down the road.

They jogged back just as the rain picked up again. Soaked to the bone, Izzy shivered and caught Jig's gaze. His eyes were cold, shuttered, and flat. Much as they'd been the first few times she'd met him.

Jigsaw

"Okay," Zach said. "Us four"—he indicted himself, Rocket, Jig, and LJ—"are going to do reconnaissance. We'll take out who we can and text when it's safe for you to enter, Iz. You're on lookout. Anyone comes down this road, we need a text ASAP. Your kid said there were four guys here, plus him makes five. No idea on the number of girls. Everyone good?"

They all nodded. Izzy risked another glance at Jig then immediately wished she hadn't. He wouldn't even look at her. It hurt like hell in her stomach, her head, her heart, but she had to shove it aside because it was nothing compared to how the girls in that barn would be hurting.

"All right," Rocket said, "it's go time."

Then all four men disappeared into the woods, weaving toward the barn while Izzy settled herself against the van.

To wait.

CHAPTER TWENTY-FOUR

Rocket and Maverick had access to all sorts of spy-level gadgets, but seeing as how they hadn't anticipated a takedown today, they didn't have comms or any other high-tech equipment. Just four cellphones, three handguns, five rifles, some C-4 Jig would never ask Rocket about, and four men committed to ruining the fuck out of Lefty's trafficking business.

As they crept their way through the woods toward the barn, Jig's anxious fury only grew. The past and present were mixing in his head, causing a host of fucked-up feelings he couldn't handle. These weren't the men who hurt his family, but they were attached to the gang that injured Izzy. And they destroyed the lives of an unknown number of innocent girls. Jig was so hungry to take these fuckers out, he was practically salivating at the thought of making them bleed.

When the barn was easily visible through the foliage, Jig anchored his back against a large oak tree. His brothers were spread out and hidden in much the same way. Both being prior military, this scene was Zach and Rocket's comfort zone. Jig could hold his own, but both of those men were skilled at leading and planning operations. He kept his eyes trained on Zach and waited for instructions.

Wouldn't be long. A few minutes at most. Anticipation flowed through him. If only Lefty were there as well, so they could end his sorry-assed life, but part of him loved the fact that Lefty would be forced to watch his empire crash and burn. To know the Handlers had fulfilled their promise to tear his house apart brick by brick.

Then, when he was at his lowest, they'd kill the motherfucker.

Zach pointed to the barn and held up five fingers. Five men outside. Then he held up one finger and dropped his hand about hip level. One little one. Probably the errand boy who'd come to Izzy's shop. They'd gotten damn lucky, following the kid when he was bringing food to the guards. Most likely, all four of them had abandoned their posts in favor of eating, and the Handlers could catch them off their game.

When Zach held up his fist, Jig readied his weapon. Rocket and Zach would emerge first with Jig and LJ as back up. Zach lowered his fist, and he and Rocket ran toward the barn, rifles secured against their shoulders.

"Hands up! Oh the ground! Now!" Zach screamed, charging forward.

Standing around, shooting the shit and eating pizza, the men were taken completely off guard. "Oh, fuck!" The teen was the first to lift his hands to ear level, letting the half-full box of pizza tumble to the ground.

Two of the others abandoned their meal and dropped to their knees as well, hands above their heads. The remaining two were cockier sonsabitches. One folded his arms across his chest two seconds before Rocket surged forward, ramming the butt of his rifle dead center on the guys forehead.

He screamed like a little girl and crumbled to his knees. "Shoulda fucking listened the first time," Rocket growled out as he circled the bastard, planted his boot between his shoulder blades and shoved him face-first into the dirt."

Clearly missing something between his ears, the remaining guard smirked then took a large bite of his pizza. "Fucking bikers," he said with his mouth full.

He was a big fucker, but then Jig was bigger. His scowl was mean, but then Jig's was meaner.

"Gotta keep my strength up," he said, still chewing. Then he swallowed, took another bite, and winked. "Need energy to give these girls what they're begging for."

It was the last straw. Already hopped up from his fight with Izzy and the fucked-up thoughts in his head, Jig tossed his gun to the ground and lunged forward, catching the pig with a right hook to the side of his head.

A half-chewed gob of pizza flew out of his mouth as his head whipped to the side under the force of Jig's punch. He never had a chance to defend himself. Jig hit him again and the guy crashed to the ground. Following him down, Jig connected his fist with the piece of shit's face again and again until everything cleared from his mind but the satisfying ricocheting from his knuckles to his shoulder each time he smashed the guy's face.

Over and over, Jig pummeled him, the stress leaving his body one crack at a time.

He had no idea how many minutes passed. Could have been one, could have been twenty, but eventually a strong arm crossed his chest and yanked him back. With a grunt, Jig landed on his ass in the dirt.

"Think you made your point, brother," Zach said with a smile. "Don't need to be hauling a dead body back to the clubhouse with us."

Jig blinked and stared at the mess he'd made. The guy's face was pulverized. An unrecognizable mix of blood, snot, and bruising. His nose looked like it had been run through a meat grinder. Jig smiled.

Damn, that felt good.

Blinking, he looked at the other men, now on their knees with their hands zip-tied behind their backs. The kid gawked at the man Jig almost killed. His face had a green hue, and he looked like he was seconds away from vomiting. If Jig wasn't mistaken, there was a faint aroma of urine in the air. The kid wasn't cut out to be a gang banger if a little beat down had him pissing himself.

"Anyone go in to look for the girls?" Jig asked.

Jigsaw

All signs of teasing left Zach's face. "Yeah, while you were kicking that guy's trash, Rocket slipped inside. He heard some terrified shrieks behind a closed door. Didn't want to be the first one in there looking like this. We'll let Izzy go first."

Jig nodded. He could admit when he was wrong, even though he despised it. Having Izzy there would be a lifesaver when it came to the girls. He knew she could handle this with one hand behind her back. He just didn't want her to.

He didn't want her near the ugliness that sometimes invaded his life.

But for a moment back there, in the truck, he'd forgotten who she was. No, he hadn't lumped her in with his wife who'd have run screaming from the scene, but he did let his experience with her cloud his mind. Izzy didn't run from a fight. Izzy didn't quake and hide when confronted with horrors.

Izzy accepted who he was, violent past and present included. She was a woman who could take care of herself. She didn't need or want Jig fighting her battles for her, but for a while, she'd been willing to let him stand by her side and tackle them *with* her. Now he'd fucked that up.

She emerged from the woods, pistol in hand, strutting toward the barn in those damned heeled boots like some kind of mercenary-inspired porn star. If she stopped halfway to them and stripped, Jig would know he'd been cast in a low budget adult film.

But she didn't. She strode right up to him and Zach before she saw the pile of beaten man on the ground. Her eyes widened before her gaze collided with Jigs. He hadn't moved from his spot on the ground, but rose now and held the eye contact.

So much passed between them in that brief moment. Sorrow, guilt, desire, sadness, even understanding and acceptance. The connection only lasted a few seconds then Izzy turned all business. "Girls?" she asked.

He wanted to reach out and grab her. Haul her to him and kiss the fuck out of her, but she'd probably take that heel and stab a hole right through his foot.

"Follow me inside," Rocket said.

She nodded, and without so much as a word for Jig, tromped off after Rocket.

"Hold up," she said when she was in front of the kid who came into her shop.

"It's you," he spat out. "What the fuck are you doing here?"

She grinned down at him. "That's right, it's me. Guess next time you better watch who you're calling a bitch. Might come back to bite ya." With a wink, she stepped to her right, in front of the guard kneeling beside the kid. "Got a message for you to pass along to Lefty." Without warning, she cocked her arm and rammed her closed fist into his face. "That's for my fucking windows," she said, then spat at his feet. "I'll let these guys dish out punishment for the girls."

Then, as though she truly was the warrior queen she resembled, she marched into that barn behind Rocket, leaving the rest of their group outside laughing at the scene.

"Shit, Jig," Zach said when he could talk again. He held his hand in front of his eyes. "Think about your grandma or something. No one wants to see that shit."

Jig glanced down and, sure enough, there was a sizable tent in his jeans. What could he say? Her unique combination of warrior and woman got him every time.

IZZY FOLLOWED ROCKET through the open barn door and straight to the back where a room-sized storage closet waited. The entire place had a lingering smell of horse shit so Izzy breathed through her mouth until she got used to it.

"Have you seen them yet?" she asked Rocket as they walked.

"No. Could hear them crying, yelling. They sound fucking terrified. Zach and I didn't want to go in first and scare them. I'll let you go, and you can assess the situation. When you come out, we'll all have ski masks on. Don't want the girls getting a look at us. You want one, too?"

"Um..." She gave it a moment of thought. It probably would be wise to keep her face covered in case these girls gave her description to the cops. On the flip side, they might lose their shit if a masked person barged into their room. She'd take her chances on convincing them to leave her out of it. "Nah, I'm okay."

"All right," he said with a nod. "Figured you'd say that. That's why I asked in here instead of around Jig. He won't feel the same."

It didn't matter. He'd be out of her life soon enough. Sadness washed over her, but she pushed it away. No time for a pity party right now.

"Here we go." Rocket indicated a door where she could hear sniffling and light crying behind. "It's unlocked. I'll be right here. Holler if you need anything."

Izzy nodded. "I'll be fine. Be ready with the van for the girls."

She gripped the doorknob and stepped into a room she couldn't have imagined in her most fucked-up nightmares. Rotting hay was strewn all over the floor, leftover from the building's farm days. The smell she'd mistaken for horse maneuver reached foul levels in the room. It became clear the odor was human waste. Three buckets lined the wall to her right with rats and bugs crawling all around them.

Her stomach lurched, and she swallowed down the bile before turning her head to the left.

Huddled in the corner with their arms around each other were six young women, girls really, trembling, crying, and so filthy she couldn't even tell the color of their skin.

A few had visible wounds, split lips, a black eye, cigarette burns to their arms. Izzy's heart, which she kept safely boarded up, cracked in two and bled all over the filthy room.

The tallest, and she assumed oldest, took a step forward, all false bravado and pretend toughness. Izzy didn't even know the girl, but at that moment, she felt so proud of the feisty teen who was trying to protect the rest of the girls.

"Who are you? What do you want?" the girl said, standing at her full height of no more than five feet three inches.

Despite the disgusting floor, Izzy sank down until she was sitting cross-legged. Looming over a bunch of terrified kids wouldn't help the situation. "My name is Izzy. I'm here with a group of men who want to help you."

All six of the girls shrank back at the mention of men, and Izzy's stomach rolled. She couldn't begin to imagine what these children had been through.

"Help us how?" the lead girl asked.

"Take you away from here. Back to your families if that's what you want. Somewhere else safe if you don't want that." At the mention of family, two of the girls broke down in harsh, choking sobs. Izzy wanted to gather them all up in her arms and promise no one would lay a hand on any of these girls again, but she had no idea how they'd react if she came too close.

"Why should we trust you? Who are these men?" the bravest asked.

What should she say? How did she reassure these traumatized children that no further harm would come to them? Izzy spent her life proclaiming her independence, telling everyone she met she didn't need anyone else. She was a pillar of strength and a self-sufficient woman. Now, the first time that strength was truly tested by life's ugliest acts, all she wanted to do was weep and pass the challenge of soothing these girls on to someone else. Someone stronger. Someone more capable.

What she wanted was Jig. Wanted him by her side, holding her hand and bleeding some of his power into her. But it wasn't going to happen. If she begged him to stand with her, she might plead with him to stay forever. Then someday down the road when it ended, she might not survive the heartache. This responsibility fell to her, and she'd buck up and do it alone. It was how she'd set up her life, so now she had to practice what she preached.

"They're good men, who would never lay a hand on you.

They are enemies of the men who kidnapped you, and they have all those men tied up outside. None of them can hurt you ever again. I can take you all out of here right now. The men with me will all have masks covering their faces"—two of the girls gasped—"just to protect their identity. I will lead you out to a van, and then I will ride in the back with you away from here. To a shelter where there are only women, no men. And those women will get you anything and everything you need to help you be okay."

The oldest snorted. "Okay?" she asked. "Don't think any of us will ever be okay again." She spoke with a surety that had Izzy's eyes filling. There was no way in hell she'd allow herself to cry in front of these girls. If anyone ever needed her to be strong, it was these girls. "How old are all of you? What are your names?"

The leader stared at Izzy for a moment before saying, "I'm Jenny. I'm seventeen. Youngest is twelve."

Good thing she was sitting because that would have knocked the starch right out of Izzy's knees. Instead of tearing the place down board by board like she wanted, she just nodded. "Will you come with me?"

She was studied again while Jenny seemed to consider their options, which were none. If they stayed, they were prime targets for more abuse and horrors. Not that the Handlers would ever leave them there. Plan B was to drag them out kicking and screaming, but Izzy hoped to avoid any further trauma. Jenny was a smart kid and must have come to the same conclusion. She spoke for the group when she said, "We'll come. I don't want any of the men to touch any of us. Not at all."

"I promise," Izzy said. "No one will touch you."

"Okay. Then we'll come."

Izzy rose and stuck her head out the door where Rocket still waited. "They're ready. It's not good. But there's one girl who seems to be in charge. She's asked that none of you touch any of them in any way. Not even to help them in the van or anything. Okay?"

Rocket nodded, face solemn. "You have my word."

"Okay, I'll lead them out." She started back into the room then popped her head out again. "Oh, I'm going to ride with them… wherever you're taking them."

With a small smile, Rocket said, "You're a damn good woman, Iz. Jig's a lucky fucker."

Ouch. Straight shot to the ticker. She filed it under *To Be Dealt With Later* and returned to the frightened girls. As she led them out of the barn, Rocket stayed a safe distance away, arms crossed over his chest so the girls had a good view of him. Yet each one stared at the masked biker with wide, fearful eyes as though he might lunge forward and attack at any moment.

Despite the thick cloud cover, all the girls flinched at the brightness the moment they stepped outside. "This way," Izzy said, pointing to the open van. One of the girls shook her head and stopped walking, her entire small body trembling.

Shit. She'd probably been tossed in the back of a similar van only to emerge in a nightmare of epic proportions. "It's all right," Izzy told the quaking girl. She kept her hands fisted so she wouldn't reach out and wrap her arms around the poor child. She was smaller than the others. Probably the twelve-year-old. "No one will hurt you anymore. I swear it on my life."

She pointed to where Jig and Zach waited, well off to the side, masks on. "Those men are the good guys, honey. They only want to help and get you far away from what hurt you. They won't be in the van. One guy will drive, but I will be the only one with you in the back of the van. Just me. Okay?"

Lower lip quivering, the girl finally nodded and followed her new family borne of tragedy into the van. Each girl walked with a stiff posture as though sore. Some hobbled along with a hitch in their step Izzy refused to think about too deeply. Her heart ached with each step they took, and when the last girl was in the van, she turned to Rocket. "Give me a minute?"

"Sure," he said, assessing her closely. Too closely.

Izzy stepped around the side of the van, out of sight of all the men and leaned her forearms against the cold metal, dropping her head to her chin. A beachball-sized lump lodged in the center of her throat and tears puddled in the corners of her eyes. The sensation of a thick rubber band wrapping around her chest kept her from drawing air, and she sucked in short, shallow breaths.

How could anyone...?

She shook her head. This wasn't a situation she was equipped to deal with. Not something she knew how to process. This was the greatest depth of human depravity. How did one move on smiling day after day with firsthand knowledge of these acts?

Strong arms closed around her waist, and an immediate feeling of safety surrounded her. After the argument in the car, Jig was the last person she expected to attempt to support her. She wanted to sink into his embrace and let him erase the past hour of her life.

But it would only draw her closer to being dependent on him and thus make the eventual crash and burn that much more devastating.

Straightening, Izzy sniffed, wiped any errant moisture from her eyes and stepped out of his embrace. The moment she was free of him, she felt the weight of loneliness collapsing down on her.

Proof of why she had to do this. Now, she could control the situation. Choose to be alone and on her own. Later? If he left, after she dared let herself love him, she'd never survive that fall. "Hey," she said, squaring her shoulders and turning to face him.

Eyes grim, scar prominent, mouth flat, hair mussed from the mask that he'd removed, he looked about as wrecked as she felt. "You did a good thing for those girls, sweetheart. You were right, they never would have come with us."

Not the "sweethearts." It was hard enough to stay strong without the endearment.

She nodded. "Thanks. I'm, uh, going to ride to the shelter with Rocket." Sticking her hands in her back pockets, she tried to act like her insides weren't crumbling to dust.

"I heard. Want me to tag along?" He stepped closer, and she took one back. If he touched her again, she might crack and lose herself in his arms.

"Nah, I promised them none of you would come along. We'll be good."

One of his eyes twitched, and she had the distinct impression he was biting off what he really wanted to say. "Okay. I'll wait for you at the clubhouse."

She could do this. Just had to spit it out. "Look, Jig…"

He sighed and dropped his head as though he'd been expecting it.

"Don't do it, Izzy," he said, stepping forward and sliding his palms up her arms until he cupped the balls of her shoulders. "I'm sorry for my reaction in the truck earlier. I was a real asshole. Please don't let it ruin this."

"This?" she asked once again, stepping away. Every time he put his hands on her, her body reacted, wanting more. She'd never have the guts to get the words out if he kept touching her. "Come on, Jig. Neither of us is cut out for *this*. We agreed on that from the start. Better to end it now, make a clean break. No messiness."

No chance for you to crush my heart. Except with every word that fell from her lying mouth, she carved a little chunk out of her own heart.

"Iz, you're upset about today. Rightfully so. Anyone would be. Let me help you through this."

Her arms hung limply at her sides, feeling like thousand-pound weights. Suddenly, exhaustion claimed her. "You don't get it, Jig. I don't need you to help me through this or anything else. I take care of myself. Always have, always will." For the first time in her life, those words left a sour taste in her mouth. Despite all her protests, she'd come to rely on him at her side.

"Don't push me away because you're upset." He stepped toward her again, but this time she held a hand up to ward him off. "Sweetheart…" he started.

"No," she whispered because that beach ball in her throat wouldn't allow anything louder. Shit, she was going to cry. Ugly cry. "Please," she said as the first tear fell. She pressed one hand against her stomach, checking to make sure her insides weren't truly pouring out. "Please just let me get in that van and go."

Jig didn't respond for a long moment, then he lifted his hands in surrender. "Okay, sweetheart. But this isn't over. Get through today, and we'll talk."

She nodded. It was the fastest way to get him to walk away and leave her with some of her dignity still intact.

As she watched him go, tears streaming down her face, Izzy knew it was already too late. She'd broken her most strict, firmest rule.

She'd fallen in love with him.

CHAPTER TWENTY-FIVE

Six hours later, Jig sat alone at the bar in the clubhouse, well into a bottle of Scotch. Hadn't done a damn thing to numb the gnawing pain in his gut.

Rocket strode through the door alone, and Jig's shoulders sagged. Izzy hadn't even come to talk to him. That pretty much put the last nail in his coffin, didn't it? "She okay?" he asked as Rocket wandered up and swiped the bottle.

After a long drink, Rocket wiped his mouth with the back of his fist and said. "No. She's pretty damn fucked up right now. Not sure what went down between you two behind the van, but she's been puffy-eyed and silent all afternoon. This business with the girls has her spiraling, too."

"Can you blame her?"

"No." He took another drink. "Didn't say I did. Just giving you the facts. You gonna go see her?"

Jig considered that. Would he go see her? "Not today. She wouldn't want anyone to see her freak out. Especially not me. I asked Shell to swing by later. Check on her."

Rocket nodded and stared into the empty clubhouse. He wasn't one to offer unsolicited advice. Jig appreciated that. He didn't need one of his brothers telling him how to handle the woman he loved.

That's right.

Fucking loved.

As he'd brooded and drank for the past few hours, he realized the sick feeling he'd had since walking away from Izzy was love. The feisty, independent, fierce, gorgeous woman had blown past all his defenses, and he was in love with her.

He'd bucked against the notion for so many years, convinced he couldn't take the risk of losing someone in such a vicious and unexpected manner again. Convinced no woman deserved a man with a violent history, who freely admitted that violence was still a living, breathing thing inside him. And he found loving Izzy was just as terrifying as he'd anticipated, but for entirely different reasons. Izzy wasn't the type of woman to stand behind him. She'd march that firm ass right around and stand by his side no matter what battles came their way. And as an MMA fighter, on some level, she even understood his need for violence.

And she accepted his past, his dangerous present, and even his uncertain future.

Taking the bottle from a pensive Rocket, he said, "You know, we're at the bar. Get your own fucking liquor."

Rocket grunted, but did just that, coming back with an unopened bottle of tequila.

"What happened with the girls?"

With a sigh, Rocket sat back down and opened the bottle. "Well, they'll probably all be screwed up for life thanks to Lefty, but they got off okay. Seems they all took to the woman who runs the shelter. She'll do right by them."

"Guess that's the best we can ask for right now." Jig let the burn of the Scotch chase away some of the shit swirling around in his head. Or at least tried to. Didn't work too well.

"You guys torch the place?" Rocket asked. They sat side by side, drinking and watching the empty clubhouse.

"Mm-hmm," Jig responded, mouth full of Scotch. After swallowing, he said, "Used the C4 to blow it the fuck up. Word is Lefty caught wind of it and went into hiding."

"Fucking pussy."

"Pretty much. You expect anything else?"

Rocket grunted.

"Hey, Jig," Zach said as he walked into the clubhouse. "Oh, hey, Rock. When'd you get back?"

"About five minutes ago."

Zach held his hand out for the tequila, which Rocket readily handed over. The skin around Zach's knuckles was purple, cracked, and bloodied. Evidence of what he'd been up to for the past few hours.

"Jig, Cop wants you in The Box for a minute. Feel free to tag along, Rocket." He took a drink then turned and strode back out.

With a raised eyebrow, Rocket looked to Jig. "What's that about?"

Jig shrugged. "Don't know. They have the guys from the barn in there. Let's go."

Leaving their bottles on the bar, they made their way outside and into the woods where the entrance to the box was. It was a trap door deal they kept covered with leaves and twigs most of the time. Needless to say, they didn't want anyone stumbling upon it.

Zach held the door open as Jig and Rocket descended the long staircase, then he followed behind.

Though they'd taken the five men from the barn, only one remained. And he looked like he'd seen better days. Information extraction and a little punishment hadn't treated him well.

"Where are the others?" Rocket asked.

Copper folded his arms across his massive chest. "Let the boy go after we scared the piss outta him. Literally. Pretty sure he'll be steering clear of the gang from now on. Especially since we told him we'd be keeping an eye on his mom and sister."

All bullshit. Copper would never hurt an innocent woman, but the dumb kid wouldn't know that.

"Others are gone," Copper said with a smirk.

Gone. Probably dead. Copper didn't have much tolerance for mistreatment of women. Kidnapping teenage girls and selling them off as sex slaves pretty much topped the list as far as mistreatment went. It would come as no surprise to anyone in the club that Copper had them eliminated.

But why one still remained...

"So what's with Cyclops here?" Jig asked. Their prisoner was a big guy, not quite as big as Copper, but larger than Jig. And one of his eyes was so swollen it looked like a bubble blown from some chewing gum.

"He's yours," Copper said, holding out a gun.

Jig swung his gaze in his president's direction. He wasn't usually called in for this type of shit. Zach was enforcer, and Copper liked to have a hand in everything that went down.

"Why me?" Jig took the pistol, hefting its weight in his hand. It felt good, too good.

"Cyclops here is one of the guys who busted out your woman's windows," Copper said, smacking the guy on the back of his head. He'd been through the ringer if the bruising on his torso was any indication, and his head flopped forward with the force of Copper's whack.

Jig rolled his shoulders as tension crawled through his body. Sure, that earned the guy a beat-down, but death was a bit extreme. There was more to the story. Jig looked to Copper.

"He was also in charge of the girls at the barn. Worked directly with Lefty on snatching the girls and choosing who they'd be handed over to."

That'd do it. Jig would gladly feed this guy lead for his last meal.

"And he was one of the guys who held Izzy down and helped beat her." When Copper dropped the last bomb, Jig's entire body locked up. The rage started low in his gut and spread like wildfire through his veins.

He'd been ready and willing to kill this asshole for the traumatized girls, but now it was personal. He'd had his hands on Jig's woman. Hurt her, took away her control. And while Izzy clearly didn't need him to fight her battles for her, he was all over this one.

For a moment, he stared down at the gun in his hand. Others wouldn't understand it. The ability to kill another human being, to end a life. Maybe it only came to a person after they knew the horror of having their life ripped away in the most ferocious of ways. Maybe then, someone could understand the deep-seated need to protect others and keep scum like this from ever hurting someone again.

Because he would. If Copper were to let him go, he wouldn't stop. He'd seek his own revenge and continue destroying the lives of innocent girls.

Jig lifted the gun and aimed it at his target.

The guy's one functional eye widened. "Wh-what are you doing? I t-told you everything."

Jig laughed. "So the fuck what?" Men like this didn't care who they hurt. Didn't think twice about ruining women and children. Just like the men who'd murdered his family, this bastard would continue to destroy lives as long as he lived.

Jig killed, but it wasn't the same. This was an execution. Justice.

The law might not agree. Hell, most of society might not agree, but as Jig tucked his finger securely against the trigger, he didn't feel an ounce of guilt, shame, or hesitation. He used violence when necessary and had a woman who didn't judge him for it. It was time to embrace who he was and escape the shadow of the past still looming over him.

"N-no, d-don't!" Their captive struggled against the bindings. "I won't go back to Lefty! Please, you can't do this to me."

The pleas for his life didn't so much as blip on Jig's guilt-meter. He relaxed his arm, took a breath, and fired on the exhale. The bullet flew through the air and embedded itself in Cyclops's gut one second later. The man screamed and doubled over as best he could while being tied up. He freaked out, begging and pleading for someone to save him.

He wouldn't find any angels in here.

Jigsaw

Copper turned a surprised look on Jig.

"Head would have been too fucking fast," Jig said.

Scratching his beard, Copper nodded. Then all four Handlers folded their arms across their chests, leaned against the walls of The Box, and watched the life drain from a piece of scum.

When it was over, Jig took a deep breath. He'd sleep like a fucking baby knowing girls were safer in his part of the world tonight.

And tomorrow? Well, tomorrow he'd work on getting his woman back.

CHAPTER TWENTY-SIX

Izzy inhaled, letting the pungent odor of sweat, triumph, and adrenaline flood her system.

God, she'd needed this.

The only thing that would make the night better was if she was actually fighting. But her instinct had been right on, just attending the underground fight was already quieting the demons that had been attacking her soul the past two weeks.

That's right, two weeks.

Two weeks since she pushed Jig away.

Two weeks since she'd admitted to herself she was in love with him.

Two weeks of bone deep loneliness she'd never experienced before.

And two weeks of ignoring daily calls, texts, even a few door-knocks from Jig, his brothers, and the girls.

Why?

Who the fuck even knew anymore?

She was turning out to be a shitty friend and an even shitter solo companion. Izzy was so sick of herself and her moping she'd called and begged the man who ran the fights to find an opponent willing to go against her. Unfortunately, there weren't any women up for a match that night. She'd even offered to fight a dude. Mac flat-out refused.

Pussy.

As she wove her way through the rowdy crowd, Izzy couldn't help but wish Jig was with her. It'd been that way the last fourteen days, and she'd come to the surprising conclusion she was nothing more than a coward when it came to love.

A coward was the last thing she'd ever considered herself.

But the cold, hard evidence was right in front of her face. She'd shoved him away and run like a scared little mouse, terrified of the prospect of admitting out loud she loved him, only to have him reject her. Or worse yet, getting back together only to end up alone again five years from now.

As though her current heartbreak was somehow better than the other options. She didn't think it was actually possible to feel worse than she had over the past two weeks.

"Ugh," she mumbled. These thoughts needed to jump out of her head. The obsessive thinking was why she'd driven almost two hours away to watch fights she wasn't even invested in.

As she drew closer to the ring, someone slammed her from behind. "What the fuck?" she said, spinning around in time to catch a glimpse of the jerk who'd jarred her walking away. Dressed in boxing shorts and no top, he was clearly fighting tonight.

Her breath stilled in her lungs. She might not have a full-on view, but she'd recognize that cocky attitude and smug face anywhere.

He was the piece of shit who delivered the *message* to her at Zach's gym. The message that had left her bruised and out of commission for a week. A smile curled her lips. This guy was fighting tonight, all right. He just had no idea who his opponent was going to be.

Shoving her way back through the crowd, Izzy rose on her tip toes and searched for the man who ran the whole damn show. Mac, a smarmy dude who loved the power these events bestowed on him.

"Hey, Mac," she said when she reached him.

He was in a crowd with his bookie, collecting money and bets out the wazoo.

"Izzy," he said with a roll of his eyes. Dressed in an expensive, custom-tailored suit, he stood out among the rough and unruly crowd. "I told you about ten times I don't have another bitch for you to fight tonight. Move along." He waved his hands as though shooing a child before turning away from her.

She clenched her teeth and swallowed the urge to punch him in the face for both the dismissal and calling her a bitch. "I don't want to fight a *bitch*," she managed to grind out. "I want to fight that lean guy with the muddy hair, neon blue shorts, and dragon tat on his back."

"Slick?" Mac asked with a laugh. "You bitches are all crazy. Told you, you weren't fighting any men, bitch." He tried to turn away, but Izzy grabbed his arm.

"I can beat him. Swear on my fucking life. You can keep my winnings. I don't want the money." She just wanted to show that fucker he wasn't man enough to take her down without his two goons holding her back.

"Stop wasting my time, Izzy. Ain't gonna happen."

Her mind raced. What could she offer him to change his mind? "You can keep any of my future winnings, too." None of this had ever been about the money for her. It was her therapy.

"What's it going to take to get you to leave me alone? We don't get many bitches wanting to fight. You're once a year winnings won't be worth it." The men he'd been powwowing with started to take notice of her, snickering like she was a little girl who had no business at the grown-ups table.

The chance was slipping away, and Izzy had no idea how to sway this asshole in her direction. "Okay," she said. "What would it take?"

A greasy grin made him look like the perfect image from the sexual predator database. "Hmm…" He reached out and stroked a finger from her elbow to her shoulder. "I'm sure we can think of something."

Revulsion rolled through her. She'd rather fuck a skunk than let this guy anywhere near the goods. Only thing that kept her from snapping his finger in two was the crowd of onlookers who wouldn't take kindly to her breaking their boss.

"Got a bunch of guys here with me tonight. Each and every one will put money down on her. She'll be the underdog. Anyone who bets on her will make a killing. We'll hand over every cent we win if you give her the fight," said a voice she'd know anywhere from behind her.

Jig.

Izzy couldn't move, couldn't breathe. He was here. Supporting her, at her back. He'd been trying to contact her for two weeks. Despite her fears, despite how hard she pushed him away, he hadn't given up.

Hadn't abandoned her.

He was there. Warmth spread through her and, for a second, she almost abandoned the whole plan in favor of throwing herself into Jig's arms. But she needed to see this through. Needed to show the world no one fucked with her and got away with it anymore. And if they tried, she and her sexy biker would be coming for them.

Mac peered over her shoulder at Jig. "You Handlers ain't gonna come after me if she loses, right?"

"She won't lose," Jig said, his voice full of complete confidence and faith in her. "Put your hand on her again, and you'll be going to the ER with your dick in a bag full of ice."

Mac's eyes narrowed, but he wasn't stupid enough to cross the Handlers. "Fine," he finally relented. "But you gotta pay the guy Slick was supposed to fight. I ain't losing a fucking penny over this."

"That's fine," Izzy said, bouncing on the balls of her feet. Yes! She'd been dreaming of getting revenge on that guy for weeks. Never thought she'd get the chance, but here she was.

"You got about half an hour. This fight is almost done, and there's one more before you." He looked at Jig. "Every one of your guys here better bet on her." His gaze shifted to her. "And you better fuckin' win."

"Okay, great. One more thing," she said.

"Jesus, what now?" Mac was quickly losing his patience with her.

"Don't tell him about the change."

"No, that's not happening." He peered over Izzy's shoulder again and paled. Whatever expression Jig wore must have been pretty damn scary. Mac sighed. "You really got a hard-on for this guy, huh?"

Well, she wouldn't describe it quite that way, but... She nodded.

"Okay. We're done here. Get the fuck out of my face."

God, she couldn't wait to see the look on the asshole's face when he realized who his opponent was. It'd be a moment she'd cherish forever.

She chuckled to herself. Maybe she needed some real therapy.

After Mac and his posse walked away, Izzy turned and faced the man she'd missed more than a starving woman would miss food. "Jig," she said, voice breathless just at the sight of him. He looked so damn good. Black jeans, dark gray tee, Handlers cut. The scar growing out of his beard giving him that badass vibe he wore so well. Just one look, and she was almost ready to forgo the fight in favor of a quick fuck in the car.

He gave her a half smile that had her knees softening and her pussy clenching.

Damn him.

"Who is he? Saw him slam into you, but I'm guessing it's more than that." He didn't move toward her, and her heart sank a little. She wasn't sure what she'd expected. Maybe that he'd grab her, kiss her, throw her over his shoulder cave-man style and ravage her in the parking lot.

Not this polite, slightly cold reunion.

"Lefty's guy who beat me up. The one who needed two other men to hold me down while he did it. Tonight, he's going to find out how lucky he was to have those guys." Already, the thrill of an impending fight zinged through her veins.

She kept note of Jig's reaction to the news. Darkening eyes, clenched fists, tight jaw. But he didn't say anything. Didn't try to talk her out of it. Didn't jump in and tell her he'd take care of Slick himself.

"You're okay with this? With me fighting him?" Never would she have asked another man that question, but it mattered. Jig mattered, and what he thought of her choices was important.

He let out a gruff laugh. "That little twig? Bet you snap him by the end of the first round."

"You wish it was you getting to hand him his ass?"

With a shrug, he smirked. "Can't say I'd turn down the opportunity to shove his balls up his ass, but you've earned this, baby."

Baby. Was there still a chance...?

Joy surged in Izzy's heart. He was curbing his own alpha protectiveness in favor of allowing her to be her independent self and run her life. But he had her back. No, he stood at her side. Not once had he or his family of brothers abandoned her. They kept showing up, even when she'd tried to push them away. They showed her she could rely on others. She could have a family that wouldn't desert her and would protect her heart.

Jig took a long step closer. She had the feeling of being caught in a trap, about to be devoured by a hungry predator. "Two weeks," he said when he was so close his breath tickled her ear.

She shivered, and her eyes fluttered close. She wanted his lips on her, his hands, anything to renew the connection and ease the ache being without him caused.

"I know," she whispered. "I—I was just—"

"Freaking the fuck out and running like the coward you are not?" One hand wrapped around the back of her neck, squeezing until she opened her eyes and met his gaze.

"Yes." She swallowed. "Exactly." She'd spent her entire adult life fleeing from relationships, just as her mother had. Sure, she had never let it get to marriage and never had thrown away relationships after they started, but she was just as bad because she never allowed them to begin in the first place. She protected her heart to her own detriment. Just as her mother had.

The realization was jarring, and thankfully she had a man to help her realize the self-destructive tendency before she completely destroyed any chance at happiness and love.

"You done with that shit?" His mouth hovered just above hers, and she nearly wept with the need to feel it against hers.

"Yes."

"You ready to be my woman? My ol' lady? You and me. Nothing coming between us." As he spoke, his beard tickled her chin.

"Yes."

"You ready for me to tell you I love you?"

Oh, my God. Oh, my *God*. He loved her? "Y-yes." She trembled in his embrace. Those were words she'd never expected to hear from a man. Tears filled her eyes and emotion clogged her throat until she couldn't swallow. Her heart was full in a way she'd never imagined possible.

"Good," he said, his eyes growing lust-filled. "You ready to beat this fucker's ass so I can drag you back to that locker room and eat your pussy 'till you're screaming?"

Fuck yes! "Yes!" This time she couldn't keep the elated grin off her face.

Jig kissed her hard, thoroughly, until her knees jellied and need curled her belly tight. "Then let's do this because I've gone two weeks without watching you come, and I'm at my fucking limit."

"You coming in the ring with me?"

"I'd like to see you try to keep me out."

Izzy smiled. This just might be the best night of her life, and she hadn't even dished out the payback yet.

CHAPTER TWENTY-SEVEN

Jig rubbed his woman's shoulders as she waited to be called into the ring. Her hood was up, game face on, and she bounced like there were springs in her heels. "Chill, babe. You could take his guy out with one of those sexy black dresses you own and five-inch heels."

Izzy laughed, and the shoulders under his hands softened. "Cute, Jig. Very cute."

The emcee climbed into the center of the ring and announced the fight, calling Slick into the ring first. He bopped around, looking all smug and conceited. Jig couldn't keep the smirk off his face.

Sure, he fucking hated the idea of Izzy getting in the ring with this guy. But it was necessary to her. And she could take him. There was a chance she'd get banged up, and it would tear at Jig's insides, but he was man enough to deal.

"In the next corner, we have Izzy The Empress."

Jig gave Izzy's shoulders one final squeeze, slapped her ass, and kissed her hard before sending her off.

Half the crowd fell silent, looks of confusion crossing their face. Not Jig's brothers. They went fucking wild, screaming, stomping their boots and chanting "Jig's ol' lady."

He chuckled. She'd hate the fuck outta that.

Even the women had come, dying to see her after weeks of radio silence, and their wild, high-pitched cries were the loudest of all.

Izzy glanced back at him, tears in her eyes. It was about time his woman realized she had a family now. A family that would be all up in her shit all the time, and wouldn't desert her even if their lives were on the line.

"Go get him, baby," Jig called out, clapping his hands together fiercely.

As Izzy slipped through the ropes and jogged into the center of the ring, Jig took the position in her corner.

Slick paid her no attention, screaming like a madman at the announcer, no doubt shocked by the turn of events. Finally, after the announcer told him to shut the fuck up, Slick turned his furious gaze on Izzy. Slowly, like she was unveiling a fantastic surprise, she lowered her hood.

God damn, Jig wished he'd had his phone out at that moment. Slick's mouth flapped like a fish out of the fucking water. His eyes bugged, and his arms hung limply at his side.

"Hey, fucker," Izzy said. "Remember me?"

Slick's eyes narrowed at that, and his mouth finally closed, curling up in a grin. "I sure do, sweet tits. I remember how I left you bruised and crying on the floor."

Jig snorted. He knew for a damn fact Izzy did not cry. And the "sweet tits" comment would earn Slick a private visit from Jig soon. Right about the time he healed from the beating Izzy was about to dish out. Only he might walk away from that meeting with one less appendage.

Izzy smiled right back at Slick. "Took three of you douchcanoes to get the job done, though. Let's see how you do with a little one on one."

"Bring it, bitch."

Izzy ignored the comment, tossed her hoodie to Jig, and went straight into the zone. He could tell because her eyes narrowed, her lips pressed into a firm line, and she held herself ready to attack at full force.

The announcer reviewed the very few rules, and the fight

began. Slick came at her, balls out in a lightning-quick attack. Jig's breath stilled as the man exploded forward and caught his woman with a jab to the face.

Izzy's head snapped back, and when it bounced forward again, there was a trickle of blood running from her nose, but a huge fucking grin on her face. She was a skilled and smart fighter. Slick hadn't caught her off guard; he'd played right into her hands. She took another shot, this time to the ribs, making Jig wince.

It'd been a few weeks since she was injured, but that couldn't have felt good. Slick said something Jig couldn't hear, but it had Izzy's eyes narrowing more. It was then Jig caught on to her game. Reel him in, throw him off guard, and—

Slick got cocky, gave Izzy his back while the crowd cheered for him. It was only for a split second, but enough for his girl to spring into action.

She took him the fuck down.

The surprise on Slick's face as his feet left the mat and his body crashed down was another Kodak moment Jig wished he could have captured. Before Slick had time to realize what happened, Izzy mounted him and went to town with a good old-fashion ground and pound. Fists flying, she hit his face, chest, sides in a rapid pattern of misery for ol' Slick.

Eventually, she let up and leaned over a weakly struggling Slick. "Give up?" she asked.

"Fuck you, bitch," he said.

"I was hoping you'd say something like that." As Slick failed in attempt after attempt to get up, Izzy moved quick as a fox, flipped Slick around and got behind him in a lethal choke hold.

Stubborn enough to resist tapping out, Slick twitched and clawed at Izzy's arm for about twenty seconds before the lack of oxygen took him out. The moment he slumped, the match was called, and Izzy released him. He came to within seconds, red-faced and spitting like a wet cat.

Jig's brothers and their women went nuts once again,

screaming for her and losing their shit. Izzy rose, exhaustion clear on her face, and Jig had a feeling it was as much emotional as physical. Pride surged in him as he looked at her happy face. He was damn proud of her and damn proud to have a woman like her at his side.

He ran to the center of the ring, grabbed her by her ass, and hoisted her into his arms. "Feel good, baby?"

"Sooo good. You have no idea," she said, wrapping her legs around his waist.

"Ready to feel better? Think I made you a promise I'm dying to keep."

"Hell, yes!" Izzy said right before she kissed him. Her tongue slid into his mouth, and she gripped him tight as she subtly ground against him.

"Shit, Iz, got a little post-fight horniness going on?" His dick was about two seconds away from throwing a revolution and busting straight through his zipper. Neither of them seemed to realize they were still standing in the middle of the ring.

"A little bit. Mostly I'm wet because the man I love told me he was gonna eat me out if I kicked this guy's ass." She winked and rubbed her spandex covered pussy over his crotch. Shit, it would be pretty fucking embarrassing if he busted a nut in the middle of a boxing ring with a hundred people around.

"Let's get the fuck out of here," he said, releasing her. They jumped from the ring, ignoring the catcalls from his brothers and made their way to the "locker room," which was really just an area sectioned off by plywood. "Get the fuck out," Jig called to the two people changing.

Both glanced at him and paled when they saw his cut. Being feared had its perks. The moment they were gone, Jig backed Izzy against the wall, boxing her in with a forearm on either side of her head.

Perspiration gave her a glow, and her flushed face spoke to how much she'd exerted herself in the ring. Of course, that damn braid was perfect as ever, not a stray hair in sight. He reached behind her head and somehow managed to unwind the tail of the braid. Then he ripped off the rubber band and dove his fingers into her hair, working the tight strands out until thick waves tumbled down, sticking to her sweat-dampened skin.

The entire time he messed up her hair, he'd had his thigh pressed up in the junction between her legs. By the time the braid was undone, Izzy was moaning and riding his thigh like a mechanical bull.

"I need it, Jig," she said. "Don't make me wait."

"You love me?"

Her hips stopped rocking, leaving that hot pussy pressed firmly against his leg, her juices soaking through both her shorts and his jeans. He moved his hands from her hair to her ass, gripping the taut globes hard and grinding her harder on his leg.

She let out a little moan and nodded. "I love you, Jig."

"You know I'm fucked up, right? That I've got this…thing in me. This beast that claws its way out sometimes. You know it's why I fight."

Izzy pressed two fingers over his mouth, pushing the words back in. "I see you, Jigsaw. I see you, and I see Lincoln, and I see how what happened shaped you into the man you are today. The man I love. I love you, Jig. I love the man standing in front of me, every fucked-up piece of you. And for the record, that beast can come out and rage-fuck me any time he'd like." The smile she bestowed on him wasn't one he'd seen from her yet. It was sweet, intimate, loving, and made him believe every word out of her mouth.

"You know I'm fucked up too, right?" she whispered as he rested his forehead against hers, still holding her ass.

"Yeah, I know it."

She chuckled.

"Looks like I see you too, Isabella. And I love you. Never thought that'd happen to me again. Never thought I wanted it. Now? Well now I want it so bad I'll even let my woman get in the ring and fight some punk-ass moron."

Tears glistened in her eyes, making Jig's chest tighten. There was no way in hell he deserved this fierce, warrior-queen, but he'd take her, run with it, and never look back.

Izzy cleared her throat. "Think you're ready to give me my winnings?" Her smile was sly, teasing. "Because I'm ready to collect my prize."

"Is that so?"

She bit her lower lip and nodded. Shit, that lip had his dick growing even harder, which shouldn't be physically possible. He lowered his zipper just to relieve some of the pressure and prevent serious injury.

"You okay there, bubba?" Izzy asked with a girlish laugh.

"No, I'm not fucking okay. Shouldn't have offered to eat you out. Shoulda told you I was gonna fuck you instead."

"Well," she said, tilting her head and grasping his cock through his boxer briefs. "I'm open to a change in plans."

"Nope," he said, dropping to his knees and ripping her shorts down her legs, making her squeal in shock. "I'm a man of my word. I'll deal."

"Jesus, Jig," she whispered as she stared down at him.

He wrapped his hands around her thighs, just above her knees, then slid all the way up her legs. Eyes on her, he inhaled the sharp scent of her arousal then took a long lick through the dripping folds of her pussy.

"Holy shit," she breathed.

Keeping his eyes on hers, Jig glided his thumbs inward until they met just over the hood of her clit. He lifted the hood, fully exposing the swollen nub, then blew on it. Izzy's entire body jerked, and she gasped. The moment the breath left her lungs, he latched on to her clit and sucked with enough force to have her screaming his name.

Always greedy for more, Izzy gasped and shoved her fingers into his hair, holding him against her. Jig struggled to keep his lips wrapped around her clit when they were trying so hard to smile.

Jigsaw

His warrior-queen had him at her mercy, and he loved every fucking second of it.

Maybe one day, a decade from now, he'd tell her how he viewed her.

For now, it was his own private Izzy-fueled fantasy. And it was perfect.

EPILOGUE

"How did this happen? Shell, I just don't understand it. How on earth did this happen?" Izzy banged her head against the table and made a fake crying noise. Mostly, she did it to hide the actual sob that clogged her throat.

Shell chuckled and rubbed a hand up and down Izzy's back. "I'm pretty sure you know exactly how this happened, hon."

Izzy lifted her head and glared at her friend. "No. I do not get it. Please explain it to me."

"Okay, I'll do my best. Let the seventh-grade health lesson commence." She straightened and lifted both her hands. With her left, she formed her thumb and forefinger into a circle. With her right, she held up her pointer.

"You see," she said, smirking. "This is you." Biting her upper lip, Shell wiggled the circle. "And this is him." She wagged the pointer finger. "Boys have a pee-pee and girls have a hooha. If you like a boy, sometimes you let him stick his pee-pee into your hooha." She demonstrated with her hands. "With me so far?"

Izzy raised an eyebrow. "Yes," she said in a droll tone.

"It feels good," Shell continued, wiggling her finger in the circle. "Then it feels really good, and the man explodes, sending out lots of sperm into you. Those sperm—"

"Shell!" Izzy cried, laughing despite herself. "That is not what I meant, and you know it."

"Oh, well, then the answer is easy. How many times have you

done it without a condom?" She gave Izzy a look she often reserved for Beth in times of misbehavior.

"Uh, since we both got tested…" Izzy's face heated. "Maybe… four," she whispered.

Shell threw back her head and laughed until she saw Izzy's glower, then she sobered. "Okay, I'm sorry, honey, but I'm going to say something you're not going to like. If you weren't willing to risk getting pregnant, why did you guys have sex without a condom."

"Oh, you say it like it's so easy now, but you weren't there. That man makes me crazy. Melts my brain."

"He is rather delicious," Shell said with a sigh.

What the hell was she going to do? Izzy's stomach rolled at the thought of bringing this up to Jig. She wanted to vomit, and that was saying something since there couldn't possibly be a single thing left in her body to vomit after the hour spent riding the porcelain bus that morning.

"Jig does not want kids, Shell. You know. It's only been a few months that he's even been able to be in the presence of Beth without getting hives. And I didn't want them either."

Shell cocked her head and sipped her drink.

Oh, sweet bourbon, how I'll miss you. For nine freakin' months.

"You didn't want them? As in you do now?"

"Well, no, yes, I don't know. I'm all confused ever since I found out I'm pregnant."

"I'm gonna make this easy for you," Shell said as she stood and grabbed Izzy's hand. Pulling her to her feet, Shell dragged Izzy to Jig's closed office door. "You're going in there and you're going to tell him right now."

An icy fear washed over her, and she shook her head, taking a step back. "No, Shell, I can't. Now isn't the time. It's Copper's birthday party for fuck's sake."

"Nuh uh." Shell stopped Izzy's backward progression with a tug to her hand. "Izzy Monroe is not a coward, so get your ass in there. Get it over with so you don't have to sit here all night freaking out. Besides, someone is going to ask why you aren't drinking."

Shit. Shit.

Shell was right. She fought in the ring. She was a tattoo artist. A badass bitch.

"I need a bucket. I'm gonna be sick."

"No, you're not. You're just a baby. Who's carrying a baby." Shell laughed at her own joke, and Izzy made a mental note to put pepper in her drink later on. "All right, good luck!" Shell knocked on Jig's door, kissed Izzy's cheek, then darted away with a cheerful wave.

"No, Shell, wait, I— Hey, Jig," she said as he pulled open the door.

He frowned and stepped aside so she would walk in. "What's going on? You're wearing the fakest smile I've ever seen. You lose a bet or something?"

Izzy swallowed. It was now or never. There was a good chance this would be it. She loved Jig more than she'd ever thought it was possible to love another human being. And she believed he loved her. Yet, a teeny tiny part of her was still fearful he would one day abandon her.

And now, when he was facing the one thing he feared the most, it might just be that time. But she had to tell him. There was no other option.

"I'm pregnant," she blurted, then slapped a hand over her mouth and burst into tears.

She didn't have to tell him like that.

JIG BLINKED.

Then blinked again.

What? First off, Izzy was crying. Izzy didn't cry. Ever.

And did she say…?

Holy shit. Izzy was pregnant.

It took a few more seconds before his brain kicked in enough to realize he was being a bag of dicks and letting his pregnant ol' lady cry in his office while he stood there gaping.

"Holy shit, Izzy," he said, wrapping his arms around her and pulling her against him.

As he rubbed her back and let her hormones go apeshit, he waited for the feeling. The chest-constricting panic. The mental block that hadn't let him so much as be in the same room as Beth for so long. The repetitive what-ifs tapping at his brain like a woodpecker.

None of it came.

Instead, he saw a little girl with ink-black hair, bright blue eyes, and a kick-ass attitude running around, giving him and Izzy hell.

He saw Izzy, panting through contractions and cursing up a blue streak, calling him every name in the book and threatening to withhold her pussy for the rest of their lives.

He saw a boy, kneeling beside him, watching him work on his bike with rapt attention.

He saw his woman, waddling around with a rounded belly, wearing leather maternity pants and attempting to stuff her swollen feet into those damn heels she loved so much.

He saw them. As a family.

With children.

"Izzy," he crooned, rubbing circles on her back. "Baby, it's okay."

She sniffed and lifted her head. Black tracks ran down her face, and he tried to wipe them away, but just made them worse, giving her a true raccoon look.

Still the most beautiful woman around.

"You didn't want this. You told me straight out you couldn't, *wouldn't*, ever have another child."

He had, and that was a shame he'd feel for a long time. "Well, then I shouldn't have fucked you all those times without a condom."

Izzy tried to laugh, but it mostly came out as a hiccup. "That's what Shell said."

"She's pretty wise. She's a mother, too, you know."

"I didn't think you'd react like this. I thought—" She shook her head and rested her cheek on the soaked T-shirt covering his chest.

"You thought I'd freak the fuck out and ditch you. Really, Iz? After everything? You still think I'm gonna cut and run the second shit gets dicey?"

She swallowed and shook her head. "No. I know you won't. I just had a momentary lapse and panicked."

It was rare, but every once in a while, her eyes shone with a vulnerability that broke his heart. Izzy's childhood was shit and had shaped her into the distrustful woman she was. They'd made so much progress over the past few months, but he couldn't begrudge her a few demons sneaking in every now and again.

"I love you, Isabella, and I will love this child just as much."

She swallowed, tears filling her eyes once again. "God, Jig, I love you, too. So much. I can't even remember what my life was like before you, and I never want to think about it without you."

"You'll never have to, baby. You're stuck with me for good. Guess this means you're going to have to marry me."

"What?" She gasped. "Jig, no, you don't have to do that. I know you never want—"

He covered her mouth with his palm. "I didn't want. But then I met you. And I want you. I want you every day of my life. And I want every motherfucker out there to know it. So, Isabella Monroe, will you and our baby have me and my crazy MC family for the rest of your lives?" He'd planned to ask her sometime down the road. But why should he wait? He wasn't going anywhere and never planned to let her get away from him. It was time to lock it down.

"God, Jig. Yes, yes I'll marry you." The tears spilled out, and she rubbed them away with angry strokes. "Fucking hormones."

Jig chuckled. "Guess I'm going to have to get used to a weepy Izzy for the next few months, huh?"

Izzy snorted. "That might be enough to make any man run away." Then she smiled. "But you know..." Snaking her arms around his neck, she rose on her tiptoes and spoke against his lips. "There are a few perks to these hormones."

"Oh, yeah?"

"Oh, yeah." Izzy pressed her mouth to his and Jig's heart soared.

He'd been given a second chance with this warrior-queen, and there was no woman he'd rather have kicking ass right by his side.

Thank you so much for reading **Jigsaw**. If you enjoyed it, please consider leaving a review on Amazon or Goodreads.

Other books by Lilly Atlas

No Prisoners MC Sereis
Hook: A No Prisoners Novella
Striker
Jester
Acer
Lucky
Snake

Trident Ink
Escapades

Hell's Handlers MC
Zach
Maverick
Jigsaw
Copper (Coming Early 2019)

Join Lilly's mailing list for a **FREE** No

Jigsaw

Prisoners short story.
www.lillyatlas.com

Join my Facebook group, **Lilly's Ladies** for book previews, early cover reveals, contests and more!

About the Author

Lilly Atlas is an award-winning contemporary romance author. She's a proud Navy wife and mother of three spunky girls. Every time Lilly downloads a new eBook she expects her Kindle App to tell her it's exhausted and overworked, and to beg for some rest. Thankfully that hasn't happened yet so she can often be found absorbed in a good book.

Made in the USA
Middletown, DE
28 May 2021